"Don't trust anyone, Miss Winter.

"Even you?"

"Especially me."

Jake glanced away from the curiosity in her shrewd gaze. While he admired the wholesome honesty in her striking blue eyes, this was no place for a tenderfoot.

"Why warn me away if I can't trust you? Isn't that a bit contradictory?"

"If you stay in this town, you're in danger. You were hired to keep those children safe. If something were to happen to them, could you live with yourself?"

She blinked rapidly. "No."

"Then, trust your gut, Lily Winter."

"Trust my gut, but not you."

He let out a gusty sigh. She had the kind of pure innocence about her that made a man think about a different way of life. The unexpected thought shook him to the core, and he forced the weakness aside. Strong feelings were a distraction. He was a man who gave 100 percent to the job, and there wasn't anything left over for anyone else. That sort of man was no good for raising a family.

"I'm not the man for you, Miss Lily. Never forget that."

Sherri Shackelford is an award-winning author of inspirational books featuring ordinary people discovering extraordinary love. A reformed pessimist, Sherri has a passion for storytelling. Her books are fast-paced and heartfelt with a generous dose of humor. She loves to hear from readers at sherri@sherrishackelford.com. Visit her website at sherrishackelford.com.

Books by Sherri Shackelford

Love Inspired Historical

Prairie Courtships

The Engagement Bargain
The Rancher's Christmas Proposal
A Family for the Holidays

Cowboy Creek

Special Delivery Baby

Visit the Author Profile page at Harlequin.com for more titles.

SHERRI SHACKELFORD

A Family for the Holidays

⟨H⟩ HARLEQUIN® LOVE INSPIRED® HISTORICAL

Recycling programs
for this product may
not exist in your area.

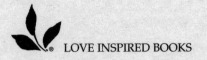

LOVE INSPIRED BOOKS

ISBN-13: 978-0-373-28380-4

A Family for the Holidays

Copyright © 2016 by Sherri Shackelford

And ye shall know the truth,
and the truth shall make you free.
—*John* 8:32

To Barb. I miss you.

Chapter One

Frozen Oaks, Nebraska, 1885

Lily Winter's gaze flicked over the gunfighter and rapidly skittered away. Her brief glimpse of his unyielding profile sent a chill snaking down her spine.

The afternoon stagecoach had long since banked the horizon, dissolving into a bleak winter haze. Fat snowflakes drifted from the sky and swirled around her feet. Chafing her hands together, she blew a puff of warm air over her aching fingers. Her two young charges, Sam and Peter, huddled against her on the wooden bench outside the livery. The rest of the stagecoach passengers had either remained on the stage after the speedy change of horses or hastily escaped the biting wind. Only the three of them remained unclaimed.

The sharp air brought tears to her eyes, blurring her vision, and she blinked rapidly. Obviously there'd been a misunderstanding about their arrival. No need for panic.

Her vantage point allowed an unimpeded view of Main Street, and hearty shoppers darted in and out of storefronts. Their progress offered tantalizing glimpses of light and the promise of warmth. The shelter of the hotel restaurant and a cozy drink beckoned—save for one slight impediment.

The gunfighter had taken up residence on the boardwalk before the restaurant.

As though deliberately taunting her, he'd kicked back in a sturdy wooden chair, his legs outstretched, one heel propped on the upper railing, his ankles loosely crossed. His hat sat low on his forehead, shading his eyes.

Peter tilted his head and caught a snowflake on his eyelashes. "Can we have a snowball fight later?"

"We'll see," Lily replied, her attention distracted. "Maybe later."

"Hmph." Peter crossed his arms. "*Maybe* always means *no*."

"*Maybe* means *maybe*."

She pressed one hand against her roiling stomach. The noisy inn where they'd stayed the previous evening had not been conducive to sleep, and the constant pitch of the stagecoach had sent her breakfast churning. Since she was a child, moving conveyances had made her nauseous.

"Are you warm enough?" she asked Peter, adjusting his wool cap over his ears.

"My nose is chilly."

Offering what little shelter she could against the cold, she wrapped her arm around the boy and hugged him closer.

Sam's shoulders slumped. "Has something bad happened to our grandpa?"

"He's late," Lily said. "There's nothing unusual about being late."

At eleven years old, Sam had already experienced too much tragedy for such a youngster. While on a missionary trip to Africa, the siblings had lost their parents to a cholera epidemic. Upon their return to St. Joseph, Missouri, a judge was assigned as their temporary guardian. Their lone remaining relative, a paternal grandfather, was eventually discovered living in Frozen Oaks, Nebraska.

Fortunately for the pair, their parents had been wealthy. Children without ways and means were left to their own devices. A grim fate. Money didn't make the grieving any easier, but the alternative was far worse.

Sam leaned into her warmth. "I'm glad you stayed. The lady who chaperoned us on the ship left us as soon as we docked."

Lily started. "That's unconscionable! I'm not leaving until I know for certain the two of you are safe and warm and curled up by the fire at your grandfather's house."

Though her role as chaperone was fleeting, Lily took her provisional responsibility seriously.

She'd answered an advertisement seeking a spinster to accompany the children on the last leg of their journey. At twenty-two, she figured she qualified. The judge had been skeptical, but she'd eventually persuaded him of her suitability. The salary for the trip was generous, and that money was the key to her future. She'd already put half the down payment on the boardinghouse that she wanted to purchase, and she desperately needed money for the other half.

Her chest tightened. Time was running short. If she didn't apply the rest of the money soon, Mrs. Hollingsworth was liable to rescind her offer.

Peter gazed up at her with his enormous brown eyes. "Maybe that outlaw over there robbed grandpa's stagecoach and left him for dead."

Lily bolted upright. "He's not an outlaw."

At eight years old, Peter possessed a vivid imagination that was both enduring and worrisome. She'd reined in his grisly storytelling more than once during their lengthy travels from St. Joseph.

"There's no reason to be scared," she asserted, despite having reached a similar conclusion. "I'm sure a lot of men carry guns in this part of Nebraska."

Sam snorted. "He's an outlaw, all right. There's a sign on the edge of town ordering everyone to check their guns with the sheriff. No exceptions. But he's sitting there as bold as brass with a couple of six-shooters strapped to his hips. This whole town is probably filled with gunfighters. The outrider told me that folks in these parts don't believe in law and order."

Lily's heartbeat picked up rhythm. There'd been a deep crease between the judge's eyes when he'd reluctantly agreed to hire her as chaperone. With a sad shake of his head, he'd muttered something about fortune favoring the foolish.

"The outrider was trying to scare you." She cleared her throat. "What sort of outlaw lives in a town called Frozen Oaks? Gunfighters live in places called Tombstone or Funeral Mountain. Only a milksop would settle in a place with such a ridiculous name."

The gunfighter lifted his head and met her gaze. Her pulse thrummed.

"Perhaps he has special permission to carry a weapon. Maybe he's been deputized or something." She lowered her voice. "We shouldn't gossip." Just in case he had exceptional hearing. Better safe than murdered.

"Do you think he'll shoot us?" Peter raised his voice in a hopeful lilt. "This place is more exciting than Africa. And colder, too."

"He's not going to shoot us."

Gracious, that boy had a vivid imagination. A movement at the far edge of town caught her attention, and she spotted a wagon.

"That's probably your grandfather now."

The buckboard turned away, shredding the last ragged vestiges of her hope. Lily shifted in her seat, searching for a more comfortable position. They'd been forced to abandon the luxury of the train in Steele City some ten miles away. Ten miles on the stagecoach might as well have been a hundred. The boys had thought the bumpy ride great fun, but she was tumbled and aching from the journey.

In deference to her bruised backside, she stood and held out her hand. "Come along. There's no use waiting in the cold."

"You heard Miss Lily." Sam rose and yanked on Peter's collar. "Don't just sit there. Let's go."

"Be nice to your brother," Lily admonished gently. "You two are blessed to have each other."

The siblings didn't realize how fortunate they were. When she was barely fifteen she'd lost her mother and her older brother, Benjamin, to rheumatic fever. Her father, a man who normally relished life, had sunk into a deep melancholy from which he'd never fully recovered. The loss had crushed him. He and Benjamin had been two of a kind. Her brother had always been up for an adventure, just like his father before him.

It only seemed natural that her mother would dote on Benjamin, as well. They were all so alike—full of enthusiasm and always seeking another challenge, and yet so different from her. Once she'd even asked her parents if she was adopted. Her mother had only laughed.

"You two have each other," Lily stressed. "Trust me, being all alone is far worse."

As part of her father's never-ending quest to escape his memories, they'd moved into the St. Joseph boardinghouse. She'd thought his grief had abated until he'd volunteered for the railroad munitions crew. He accepted the most dangerous assignments, and it soon became apparent that he desperately wanted to be reunited with his wife—and with Benjamin. Eventually he'd gotten his way. A reckless mistake had buried him beneath a mound of rubble.

Following his death, her need to own the boardinghouse had become an obsession. Until she had the deed in hand, Mrs. Hollingsworth, the current owner, could toss her out on a whim. Ownership of property was permanent and lasting. A safe and sensible investment in her future.

"I miss my parents," Sam said. "But I'm glad you're here, Miss Lily."

"So am I." Her gaze misted over. "The two of you have been extremely brave these past few months. Your parents would be very proud of you."

"Do you really think so?" Sam hopped from foot to foot beside her. "Peter and I are supposed to grow up and follow in their footsteps. That's what our mother always told us. We are meant to serve others in this life."

"And so you shall. But I'm quite certain your parents meant for you to be children first. They're at peace now, and they'd want the same for you."

Her father was at peace, as well. Lily took comfort in knowing he'd been reunited with her mother and brother. She'd always sensed she was a poor substitute for the people he'd lost.

"Miss Lily," Peter began. "Do you have a husband?"

"'Course she doesn't." Sam huffed. "Otherwise she'd be a missus."

"I don't have a husband or a beau," Lily said lightly.

Over the years she'd occasionally engaged in light flirtations with gentlemen passing through the boardinghouse, but she'd never been tempted by anything more. She neither felt nor inspired fervent love, nor was she particularly interested in the experience. She simply wanted a safe place to call home each night. Nothing more, nothing less.

Her father had chosen an early grave rather than life without his wife and son. Even in death Benjamin had inspired more devotion than Lily. She'd survived the pain, but her heart had turned brittle and fragile. From that moment on, she'd protected her embattled emotions with militant fervor. She'd erected a stronghold around her heart and sealed the entrances.

There was no love without loss, there was no joy without sorrow, and there was no reward without sacrifice. She'd simply chosen to forgo the nonsense. Happy endings only existed in fairy tales, and hoping for something different was a sure path to misery.

She was a practical person who sought practical solutions. She'd certainly never known love to be the practical solution.

Taking a fortifying breath, she inhaled the chill air into her lungs. "We're obviously not going to find your grandfather sitting out here in the cold."

She tightened her grip on Peter's mitten-clad fingers, and they marched across the street. Sam trailed behind them. They skirted past a wagon hitched with two enormous draft horses snorting vapor into the glacial air.

"Aw, shucks," Peter said. "I was hoping we'd see a showdown." His shoulders sagged, then perked up when he realized their path led them directly before the suspected gunfighter. He tugged her down to his eye level and spoke in her ear. "How many men do you think he's killed?"

"I don't know, and I don't care. He's not my concern. You are." Lily was made of sterner stuff than this cowardly hesitation. She wasn't letting some ruffian force her to sit in the cold. "Your grandfather probably lost track of time. Maybe he's even waiting for us in the restaurant."

Living in St. Joseph had made her soft. She was being ridiculous. Not even the most villainous outlaw threatened women and children in broad daylight.

Despite that bracing thought, her step faltered on the second riser leading to the raised boardwalk. She sucked in another restorative breath and squared her shoulders. Just to be safe, she tucked Peter behind her as she halted before the gun-toting man.

He didn't rouse.

Lily cleared her throat. "Excuse me, sir. I need to p-pass."

Hesitating, she opened and closed her mouth a few times like a voiceless marionette. With his head tipped forward, the gunfighter's hat shaded his eyes. Had he fallen asleep? What if she startled him and he drew his gun on her?

The outlaw stirred.

She scrambled back and bumped into Peter.

With chilling deliberation one boot lowered. Her heart clattered against her ribs. The outlaw's heel thumped against the boardwalk. As the second boot dropped, Lily muffled a yelp. She couldn't see his eyes or gauge his intent. When the front two legs of the chair hit the ground, a hollow thud sounded.

Her temporary bravado deserted her. Leaning slightly to one side, she searched the street for a sign indicating the sheriff's office. Why hadn't she thought of that earlier? The sheriff's office was a much more practical place to start.

The outlaw unfolded from his chair and rose to his full, dizzying height. Holding her ground, Lily swallowed hard. She tipped back her head and glimpsed his face. Her breath caught in her throat. There was nothing forgiving about this man.

"Wow!" Peter exclaimed. "You're tall."

"Shush," Lily ordered. "It's not polite to comment on someone's appearance."

Even if the observation was accurate. *Especially* if the observation was accurate.

The man crossed his arms over his chest and squinted down at her.

She held her ground. "Isn't it a bit inhospitable for sitting outside?"

"I like the view."

She glanced in the direction he'd been facing and noted the shuttered windows and chipped paint facade of a barbershop.

"Lovely."

He brought to mind the outlaw from the dime novel she'd borrowed from Peter the previous evening when she couldn't sleep. Except this gentleman was taller and more broadly built than the cowboy on the book cover. He was unshaven, with a shaggy mop of whiskers covering his chin. The coffee-colored hair hanging beneath his hat touched his shoulders. His eyes were dark, as well. Dilated against the overcast sky, his pupils nearly blotted out the rich, bronzed hue. Though his general build was pleasing, tall and lean, he had the look of a fur trapper who'd been too long without company in the wilderness.

Despite his unshorn appearance, his dark wool coat and canvas trousers were clean and well-kept. He certainly didn't smell like the fur trapper who'd stayed overnight at the boardinghouse. She'd spent two days scrubbing the rank odor from the bedding. This gentleman had a crisp, masculine scent that hinted of leather, wool and something else. She inhaled deeply and caught the pungent snap of gunpowder.

The realization brought her up short. This wasn't an ordinary chap.

"Well, um." She searched for an innocuous comment. His implacable stance sent a frosty draft through her that had nothing to do with the winter wind. "Your town is quite pleasant."

"It's not my town."

His expression was strangely taut, as though he was sizing her up. *For a coffin.* She quickly squashed the thought. Her imagination was running away with her. After three days of nonstop travel, two by train and one by stage, an aching fatigue gripped her. All of the dime novels and newspaper serials she'd read along with the siblings' ghoulish yarns had infected her thoughts.

Peter snuck a peek around her hip and she urged him back once more. The gunfighter raised his eyebrows. His continued silence left her unnerved.

Peter muttered something. Lily gave his hand a warning squeeze. The boy twisted from her restraint.

"Are you an outlaw, mister?" he demanded. "Is your face on one of them wanted posters?"

"Peter!" Lily splayed her arms. The slice of toast she'd managed to choke down that morning lurched in her stomach. "Children have such vivid imaginations."

The outlaw squinted. "What's your business here, miss?"

"My b-business?"

What was wrong with her? Her lips weren't working properly in the cold.

"Why are you in Frozen Oaks?"

The horizon wavered, and stars twinkled around the edges of her vision. She swayed on her feet. The gunfighter took her elbow and she recoiled from his touch. Something flickered in his expression. A hint of regret that gave her pause.

Sam tugged on her sleeve. "You don't look so good, Miss Lily."

"He's right," Peter solemnly agreed. "You're as white as chalk."

The gunfighter's face swam before her, and her ears buzzed.

"I'm fine," Lily managed weakly. Her eyelids were leaded and she struggled to keep them open. "Let's go inside."

She urged the children ahead of her and reached for the door. If she could just make it inside the warmth of the restaurant, everything would be all right.

Her hand collided with the outlaw's chest instead of the handle.

He caught her fingers in his warm grasp. Tipping back her head, she studied his face. His eyes reflected concern and a tinge of compassion. In an instant she softened toward him. He didn't appear frightening at all. He seemed just like any other mortal man. Albeit a taller-than-average mortal man. The hazy afternoon threw his austere features into sharp relief, and an indefinable emotion tugged at her chest.

The next instant her thoughts scattered. Her heartbeat grew sluggish and each step tugged at her feet as though she was wading in molasses. Why hadn't she eaten more breakfast that morning?

"I don't feel very well."

She mustn't leave the children. As panic chased her into the darkness, the outlaw's strong arms reached for her.

"No, no, no," the outlaw muttered. "Please don't faint on me, lady."

Blackness descended and she dissolved into paralyzing ether.

That judge had been wrong. Fortune did not favor the foolish.

In an instant the woman's eyes tipped back and she crumpled. Surging forward, Jake Elder caught her slight frame against his chest. The brim of her stiff bonnet caught on his shoulder and flipped off. The strings snagged around her collar. He adjusted her in his arms and tucked her head into the crook of his neck. The scent of lilacs teased his nostrils.

The two boys stared up at him with similar wide brown eyes that marked them as brothers. Since they were bundled head to toe in woolens, he had difficulty gauging their ages. Judging by their conflicting expressions, the taller one was old enough to be terrified by the sudden turn of events, and his little brother was young enough to be enthralled.

Thankful the hostile weather had kept most folks inside, Jake frantically searched the deserted street. He'd rather be rounding up murderous outlaws than this bunch. Killers were predictable. They didn't faint at the least provocation.

Was he really that menacing?

The younger boy blinked. "I'm Peter and this is Sam. What's wrong with Miss Lily?"

"Miss Lily fainted." Her name rolled off Jake's tongue. The floral moniker suited her. As he adjusted her in his arms, his chin brushed against her silky blond hair. "Sometimes ladies faint."

"It's true." Sam nodded sagely. "In St. Joseph, our mom had a whole couch just for fainting. She kept it in the parlor."

Which was probably a better explanation than anything an adult might concoct.

"Exactly."

"You never answered Peter's question," the older boy spoke. "Are you an outlaw?"

"That depends on what you consider an outlaw."

Peter cupped his hand over his brother's ear and whispered loudly, "I think that means he's an outlaw."

Jake rolled his eyes.

He'd done his job well. Everyone in town thought he was a gun for hire, and he'd never corrected the assumption. Gazing into the troubled faces of these two young boys, he loathed his deception.

Except this was not the time to dwell on the subject. "Let's get Miss Lily out of the cold."

The boys were wary, but with no other choice, they reluctantly agreed.

Avoiding the restaurant entrance, Jake made his way toward the hotel lobby. The fewer people who saw them together the better. The desk clerk rarely left the back room unless she was summoned by the bell.

Anonymity was key in his profession.

As a marshal for the United States government, he'd traced a shipment of faulty guns sold to the Cherokee back to Frozen Oaks. He had a hunch, but no proof.

The man he suspected, Vic Skaar, never sullied his own hands. Vic hired others, rarely using the same outlaw twice, which made his illegal activities difficult to track. For the past eight weeks Jake had cultivated his reputation as a hired gun.

Holding an unconscious woman while being trailed by two youngsters was bad for his false reputation.

He carried Lily across the foyer and into a small parlor. As he rested her on a mustard-colored damask settee, her eyelids fluttered.

The two boys hovered over her, and a band of guilt tightened around his chest. Admitting his true identity risked all their lives, which meant there was little he could say to put them at ease. In order to be a good guy, he had to play a bad guy.

"Is Miss Lily your sister?" Jake asked the older boy.

"She's our chaperone. Miss Lily Winter."

"I see."

He should have realized immediately she wasn't related. She was too young to be their mother and her coloring was far lighter than the brothers' dark hair and eyes.

"She traveled with us from St. Joseph," Peter said. "To keep us safe."

They should have sent a fourth person along to keep Lily safe. Jake brushed a wisp of blond hair from her pale forehead. The wool collar of her coat had bunched beneath her chin and he released the top button. The thread was darker, indicating a recent mending. The new porcelain button with its painted yellow daisy was a dash of color and extravagance that didn't match her drab wool coat.

Much like the whimsical fastening, Lily didn't belong among these plain surroundings either.

To begin with, she was tiny. The older boy, Sam, nearly topped her. Her clothing was simple and purposeful, which might have dulled another woman. On Lily, the unadorned style perfectly showcased her elegant features. Her heart-shaped face held enormous blue eyes and a mouth in the shape of a bow. Her flaxen hair was shot through with lighter and darker strands, creating a cascade of molten color. In a town where the men outnumbered the women five to one, Lily stood out like the first flower of spring.

His gut twisted. Lilies tended to get trampled underfoot around here.

Peter sniffled, yanking Jake back to his current dilemma.

Jake placed a comforting hand on the child's shoulder. "Has Miss Lily been ill?"

Surely he hadn't felled her with his threatening stance alone.

"Maybe. I don't know." The boy shrugged. "We've been traveling for days and days. I don't think she slept very well last night. She read my book and lost my page." A guilty flush spread across the boy's cheeks. "Not that I minded or anything. She's actually really nice and she let me buy a penny candy at all the train stops." He snapped his fingers. "I think trains and stagecoaches make her sick. She holds her stomach and turns green. But when we're not moving, she's fine. This morning she gave most of her breakfast to Sam and she only ate the toast. But that might have been because Sam is always hungry."

Sam chucked his brother on the shoulder. "She told me I could have it."

The telling sacrifice brought back memories of his own mother, and Jake fought against the tide of the past. In a blink the years slipped away. He'd been little older than Sam when she'd been murdered by outlaws. In what began as an uneventful day, she'd dragged him along on her errands, and her last stop had been the bank. Bored, he'd leaned against the counter and passed the time spinning a penny on its narrow edge. His mother had promised a visit to the general store when they finished.

In a flash there'd been gunshots and shouting. His mother had shoved him behind her, but she hadn't dropped to the ground like the other bank patrons. Her hesitation had cost her her life. The rest of that day was a blur. In an instant his future had been rewritten.

From that moment on, his path had been set. When outlaws roamed free, innocent bystanders were hurt. He couldn't bring his mother back, but he could prevent other tragedies.

"It's not your fault, Sam," Jake said. "I had a brother who took sick every time he traveled by train."

Lily groaned and he reached for her hand. Her pulse kicked robustly beneath his fingertips.

"She'll feel better after she rests and has a good meal."

Judging by the brothers' explanations, Lily was cold, tired and hungry. Not to mention she'd encountered a gun-toting outlaw in her path. No wonder she'd fainted. Jake sat back on his heels and rested his hand on his gun belt.

Some days the deception weighed on him heavier than others. "What brings you three to Frozen Oaks?"

Sam and Peter exchanged a glance.

"Our grandpa Emil," Sam said.

"Emil Tyler?"

"Yep. Our parents died in Africa. We've come to live with our grandpa."

Jake's misgivings increased tenfold. Emil was an irascible old man who ran a barbershop out of the front of his store, and a high-stakes poker game out of the back. A rumor had been floating around Frozen Oaks that Vic Skaar had recently lost deep to Emil. If Vic had lost money, there was one surefire way to erase his debt that didn't bode well for the boys. While Jake didn't peg Vic as a murderer, he wasn't above hiring someone else.

"Yeah," Peter said. "Except Grandpa didn't meet us at the livery like he was supposed to."

A sharp sense of unease pricked Jake. Emil was missing and Miss Winter was fluttering about like a helpless dove in a nest of grackles. "How far have you traveled?"

"From St. Joseph. Two days by train. The trip was only supposed to take one day, but there was a problem with the engine. Maybe that's why Grandpa Emil isn't here."

"Maybe," Jake said.

He had a bad feeling Emil had been detained by something far more ominous than a change in the train schedule.

Chapter Two

Jake carefully considered his options. He hadn't paid much heed to Emil's recent desertion from Frozen Oaks. Given the current circumstances, the time had come to rectify his oversight.

As he calculated his odds of escaping the room unseen, Lily stirred. Her eyes drifted open. Her forehead creased and she glanced around the room. Her gaze landed on his face and he noted the exact moment when she recognized him.

She surged upright and reached for Sam and Peter. "What happened?"

"You fainted," Peter said. "Like this."

He rolled his eyes toward the ceiling, let his jaw go slack and flapped his arms weakly.

"All right, that's enough." A wash of color suffused her pale cheeks. Lily grasped Sam's and Peter's face in turn, then patted them up and down. "Are you both okay?"

Jake backed toward the door. "You shouldn't stand up just yet."

Her wary gaze swept over him. "Thank you for assisting me. I've never fainted before. I don't know what came over me. You mustn't put yourself out any longer on my account."

As her words tumbled over each other, she discretely reached for her reticule and squeezed the bag. No doubt checking to see if he'd pickpocketed her traveling money.

Jake pinched the bridge of his nose and silently willed his forbearance. In that moment he missed being a plain old US marshal. He missed the time when ladies had looked upon him with admiration instead of wariness and distrust.

He shook the unexpected thought from his head. What did he need of ladies' attention? He'd long ago forsworn having his own family. The world was too dangerous for raising children. Especially out West. He did this job for a greater good than his own. In the beginning he'd felt the occasional twinges of loneliness. Given time, the hollow ache in his chest had eased. He was the rare man who accepted his fate. Some payments went beyond money.

Lily touched a hand to her forehead. "Perhaps you're right. I need a few more minutes. The room is spinning a bit."

"Try taking some deep breaths." His fingers itched to ease the lock of hair from her forehead once more. The feel of the silky texture lingered on his memory. "That should help."

He retrieved his gloves and yanked the leather over his hands. This job was his life. He'd come to accept his craving for danger as a flaw in his character that wouldn't be fixed. His desire for the chase was an almost physical pain if not satisfied. The lure of risk and the thrill of capture were as necessary to him as the blood running in his veins. He was a man unfettered by obligations, and happy for it.

"Leave town," he ordered. Lily was suspicious of him, and he'd exploit her fear to his advantage, even if it pained him. "There's nothing for you in Frozen Oaks, Miss Winter."

She gaped at his sudden announcement. "I beg your pardon."

"You heard me."

Sam's eyes widened in betrayal at the harsh tone, and Jake glanced away. He was proud of the work he'd done over the years. He was proud of his career. Though he knew what he was doing was necessary, he wasn't experiencing that same pride this instant. Terrifying women and children went against his nature.

He reached into his pocket and closed his fingers around the penny he'd been carrying all these years. Why carry the past around in his pocket?

He extended his hand toward Peter. "This is for the next time you're near the penny candy."

"Thanks." Peter grinned, instantly mollified.

He ruffled the boy's hair. "Share with your brother."

Catching Lily's gaze, he set his jaw. "Once you've had a decent rest and a good meal, you'd best leave this town, Miss Winter."

His villainous skills were rusty. He sounded as though he was asking her to tea instead of giving her a piece of advice that may very well save her life. Though he knew what he was doing was for the best, he was trapped, in that moment, into playing the villain.

Her iridescent blue eyes grew puzzled. "Why must we leave?"

"Emil has gotten tangled in some trouble. You'd best keep the youngsters away from that."

"What kind of trouble?" Lily searched the room as though Emil might spring out from behind the settee at any moment. "Why should I believe you? I don't even know your name."

"Jake." He replaced his hat. "Frozen Oaks might be a ridiculous name for a town, but it's still a dangerous place. Don't trust anyone, Miss Winter."

"Even you?"

"Especially me."

She gave him a side-eyed glance that had him squirming like a schoolboy brought to the carpet. He glanced away from the curiosity in her shrewd gaze. After years on the job he'd become adept at reading character, and Lily struck him as a woman of unshakable integrity. While he admired the wholesome honesty in her striking blue eyes, this was no place for a tenderfoot.

"Why warn me away if I can't trust you?" She tucked the rebellious strand of hair behind a delicate, perfectly shaped ear. "Isn't that a bit contradictory?"

The teasing warmth in her smile whittled away at his resolve. He had to warn her away because if he was worried about her safety, he couldn't concentrate on his job. Because if he didn't stop Vic from selling those guns, more men would die on either side of the Cherokee war. Because simply being near her was a dangerous distraction.

Instead he said, "If you stay in this town, you're in danger. You were hired to keep those children safe. If something were to happen to them, could you live with yourself?"

She blinked rapidly. "No."

"Then trust your gut, Lily Winter."

"Trust my gut, but not you."

He let out a gusty sigh. She had the kind of pure innocence about her that made a man think about a different way of life.

His breath hitched. The unexpected thought shook him to the core, and he forced the weakness aside. In order to do his job, he'd erected an icy wall around his emotion. Strong feelings were a distraction. He was a man who gave one hundred percent to the job, and there wasn't anything left over for anyone else. That sort of man was no good for raising a family.

He wouldn't be ensnared by the way her pale eyelashes fluttered against her soft cheeks.

"I'm not the man for you, Miss Winter. Never forget that."

"Surely there's someone in Frozen Oaks who can be trusted," Lily demanded. "I doubt the entire town is inhabited by thieves and brigands."

Nothing had gone as planned, and she was unexpectedly frustrated by the gunfighter's insistence on frightening her. While she appreciated his profession required a good bit of intimidation for success, she wasn't in the mood for subtle threats.

She'd created a neat and orderly world for herself. She followed a strict schedule. She never walked alone after dark. She never spent more money than she earned. This unexpected plunge into intrigue had set her on edge.

A humorless smile stretched across the gunfighter's face, and he adjusted his hat over his forehead. "Be cautious with your challenges, Miss Winter. You never know who might pick up the gauntlet."

"I didn't realize I was challenging you."

"A beautiful woman is always a challenge."

She flushed beneath his appraising glance. "You've been away from civilization for too long, Mr. Jake. The description is too generous."

"Look in the mirror, Miss Winter. And don't forget to watch your back."

The next instant he was gone. Lily gaped at the space he'd recently vacated.

"What's a gauntlet?" Peter asked.

"A glove," Lily said. "Throughout history, challenges have been issued by throwing down a glove. The challenge is accepted when the other person retrieves the glove."

She pressed two fingers against her temple and shook her head. Without the distraction of the gunfighter, she took stock of her surroundings. The last thing she recalled, she'd been standing outside. Her unlikely rescuer had carried her into the hotel and an overdone parlor of some sort.

Every window, wall and chair had been dressed in varying autumnal shades of damask fabric, flocked wallpaper and dangling fringed tassels. Clearly the decorator was enamored with the extravagant theme. A little too enamored. The jumble of patterns was giving her a headache.

At least her charges didn't seem any worse for wear. Peter gazed adoringly at the precious coin clutched in his palm.

Massaging her forehead, Lily vaguely recalled the gentle brush of the man's fingers. Had she imagined the encounter? That couldn't be right. Nothing about Jake had struck her as comforting, and yet that was exactly how she felt—comforted. The man had an oddly enthralling effect on her.

She straightened her spine and crossed her ankles.

That sort of thinking wouldn't do at all. From what she'd heard from scores of women passing through the boardinghouse, men were rarely the sensible choice. Men who carried guns in towns that outlawed weapons were the least sensible of all.

At least her head had cleared and she no longer felt as light-headed. The tantalizing aroma of roasted beef drifted from the restaurant, and her stomach rumbled.

Sam perched next to her on the settee. "I like him. He's nice."

Apprehension rippled through Lily. "How long was I unconscious?"

Her instincts warred with her common sense. Jake was clearly a gunfighter. He'd come close to threatening her into leaving. Perhaps *threatening* was too strong of a sentiment, but he'd been very stern in his warning.

"You weren't passed out for long." Peter splayed his hands. "A few minutes."

She'd always trusted the instincts of children. She wasn't so certain anymore. Although she couldn't blame Peter entirely. She retained the same conflicted feelings about the man. The heat of the parlor slicked her skin with sweat and she removed her coat. Conflicted or not, she wasn't lingering over the odd encounter. She couldn't imagine the circumstances where they'd cross paths. They'd likely never see each other again.

She resolutely ignored her minuscule prick of disappointment.

Open double doors led to a larger, wood-paneled lobby. Voices sounded and Lily craned her neck to hear.

"Don't put yourself out, Miss Regina," the first voice spoke.

"I'll handle this," a second female voice said. "If

there's a strange woman in the hotel, Vic will want a full accounting."

Lily stood too quickly and her legs wobbled. Her head spun and she braced one hand on the settee until the moment passed.

"It's a hotel," the first voice muttered. "They're all strangers here."

A pretty dark-haired woman with striking blue eyes, who was not much older than Lily, appeared in the doorway. Her extravagant burgundy day dress with its layers of satin ruffles marked her as the most likely suspect for decorator of the parlor.

"This room is for paying guests only," the woman declared, twitching an olive-colored damask drapery into place. "If you're not paying, you'll have to go."

Something about the woman was familiar, and Lily studied her closer. "Do I know you?"

"The name is Regina Dawson. I don't believe we've met before." The woman squinted. "Wait a second. What's your name?"

"Lily Winter."

Regina fiddled with the perfectly tied wine-colored bow beneath her chin. "I know that name. Are you from Chicago?"

"St. Joseph."

"I rented a room at a boardinghouse in St. Joseph two years ago." A deep crease appeared beneath the netting covering the woman's forehead. "The nasty old biddy who ran the place was always spying on my comings and goings."

"That would be Mrs. Hollingsworth."

Dawning recognition spread across Regina's face, highlighting her rouged cheeks. "Weren't you the maid or something?"

"Not the maid, exactly," Lily mumbled.

Though her memory of Regina was vague, the unexpected sight of someone she recognized temporarily weakened Lily's knees. She latched on to the comfort of a familiar face as though it was a lifeline. While she was perfectly capable of looking out for herself and the children, knowing a local resident when visiting a strange town was always beneficial.

Regina laid a hand across her chest, highlighting a bodice that was cut a tad too generously for such an early hour. The sight sparked a long dormant memory. Mrs. Hollingsworth hadn't approved of Regina. The landlady had even locked Regina out one evening when she'd returned after curfew. Lily had snuck her in the through the kitchen.

"Clearly you're lost." Regina swept across the room and grasped Lily's forearms. "No woman with any sense of self-preservation travels to this part of the country on purpose."

"It's a long story," Lily said with a sigh.

Even with their opposing temperaments, at least Lily had discovered someone who could assist in unraveling the mystery of Frozen Oaks.

"You look a fright, and your hair is mess. Did you sleep in that dress?" Regina clucked. "Let's get you a warm drink and put some color into those cheeks. One mustn't be caught looking like a member of the kitchen staff. The management is liable to put you to work."

Instantly aware of her disheveled appearance, Lily smoothed the strings of her crushed bonnet between her thumb and forefinger.

Her head snapped up. *The outlaw.*

"Did you see a man around here earlier?" Lily asked, hoping her tone conveyed nonchalance.

She gazed at her forlorn little bonnet with its faded daisy trim. Not that she cared if the man found her appearance more suitable for the back stairs than the front parlor, but she couldn't shake her inherent curiosity.

"Only Jake." Regina shuddered delicately. "Best avoid him. As I recall, you're too trusting by half."

Her dismissive tone raised Lily's hackles. "You didn't mind my trusting nature when I snuck you in after curfew."

"Exactly my point. I shouldn't be trusted. You're far too naive for your own good." Regina linked her elbow through Lily's and led her toward the foyer that opened to the restaurant. "Come along and I'll tell you everything you need to know about Frozen Oaks while we unravel this long story of yours."

Lily bit her tongue. There was no use getting her back up. She'd be gone by morning, and Regina appeared to have moved beyond sneaking through kitchen windows after curfew. Judging by the expensive material of her dress, she'd done quite well for herself over the years. Lily hooked her fingers over the frayed edge of her worn cuff.

"Wait." Lily dug in her heels. "These are my charges, Sam and Peter. They're the reason I'm here."

"Charmed." Regina's nose wrinkled. "They're very quiet for children. I like that. After you freshen up, the dining room is that way."

She crossed the foyer without a backward glance.

"You're prettier than she is," Sam grumbled. "I think she's jealous."

Peter nodded his agreement. "You're much prettier."

"Miss Dawson is obviously unaccustomed to children," Lily said with as much diplomacy as she could muster. "But since she might know something about your grandfather, I suggest we accept her invitation."

Brushing at her rumpled skirts, she urged the children forward. The unexpected twinge of vanity startled her. When had she ever worried about her clothing or her station in life? Her recent faint had obviously muddled her head. She should be counting her blessings instead.

Over the years, scores of people had passed through the boardinghouse. Though the transient nature of the business had prevented forming close relationships, delivering countless stacks of linens up and down endless flights of stairs had finally proved beneficial.

"Don't just stand there loitering," Regina called from the dining room. "My curiosity about your new role as a schoolmarm must be sated. Not to mention I'm famished."

"I don't like her." Peter's eyes took on a mutinous gleam. "I don't like her at all."

Though Lily was inclined to agree, she held her tongue. "Regina can be a touch abrasive."

"If we're gonna live here," Sam said, "we're stuck with her."

"This has been a trying day for all of us." Lily stifled a grin at Peter's grim expression. "We'll all feel better after we eat."

The hotel restaurant was crowded with heavy furniture and shadowed with thick burgundy velvet curtains blocking the windows. Over half of the chairs were occupied. The majority of the patrons were men, their heads bent together in conversation, their voices low. An enormous stone fireplace dominated the far end of the room with a crackling blaze. The establishment struck Lily as something of a lair. A den of iniquity where deals were struck—deals that began in infamy and ended in blood.

An unconscious shudder rippled through her. She was worse than Peter with her wild, ghoulish imaginings.

Following Regina, the three wove their way between the packed tables toward a secluded enclave.

The siblings discovered a checkers set and Lily excused them to play. Distracted by the game, the two were perched on wingback chairs covered in hunter green crushed-velvet fabric set before the fire.

"You'd best be careful around here." Regina patted her hand. "That Jake is bad news. He has the whole town quaking. Even Vic avoids him when he can."

"He didn't seem so bad." There'd been a grim, almost grudging sort of compassion to his warning. Not to mention Lily was starting to feel peevish toward Regina and her increasingly transparent insults. "Surely you exaggerate."

"Wait a second, it's all coming back!" Regina clapped her hands. "You're orphan Lily. You're the one who stayed on with Mrs. Hollingsworth after your father died. No wonder you're chaperoning those boys. You were something of a legend amongst the boarders. Anything must be better than working as an indentured servant in that gloomy old boardinghouse with Mrs. Grouch."

The shock froze Lily so completely that the sense of chill was almost physical. Never for a moment had it occurred to her that she was the subject of rumors. Having her personal tragedy reduced to backstairs gossip stung more than she cared to admit. She wasn't some tragic figure to be pitied—a curiosity amongst the boarders.

Biting the inside of her lip, she gathered herself, forcing her attention back to the current problem. There were far more serious issues at stake than the discovery of her humiliating, heretofore unknown, reputation. Despite the warmth of the room, she wrapped her arms around her body and rubbed her upper shoulders.

"I haven't quit." Lily glanced at the two siblings. Speaking about them in the same breath as dollars and cents felt like a betrayal. "The children were recently orphaned. I'm chaperoning them until their grandfather arrives."

"All the way from St. Joseph? The train tickets alone must have cost a fortune. How well are you being paid?"

"Well enough, I suppose. A judge arranged everything."

"Judges dump strays into orphanages. They don't search for long-lost relatives. Mommy and Daddy must have left behind quite a lot of money to pay all those bills."

"They are not strays!" The crude language shocked Lily into silence for a beat. "They are children. With thoughts and feelings."

"Whatever you say. I've never been much for children."

"Apparently not."

A harried server wearing a stained apron loosely wrapped around her gaunt frame set two cups of coffee before them. The server darted away without a word of greeting. Lily caught a brief glimpse of the spill of gray hair escaping from the bun at the nape of the server's neck before the kitchen door slammed.

"Thank you, Ida." Regina raised her voice and flicked an irritated glance in the woman's direction. "I'm almost relieved to discover that you didn't accompany the children out of the kindness of your heart.

Charitable people make me nervous. I always wonder what they're hiding."

"Why would charitable people be hiding something?"

"Because nothing is free in this life."

"Except for the grace of God."

"I'll take your word for it." Regina's lips twisted and she flicked a crumb from the table. "Tell me again how much you're getting paid to play nursemaid?"

"It's not like that." Lily's relief at discovering a familiar face was rapidly waning. "Mrs. Hollingsworth is selling the boardinghouse. When I return to St. Joseph, I'll have enough money saved for the second half of the down payment."

She'd considered all her options and taking over the boardinghouse was the obvious, sensible solution for her future. She'd have a source of income that no one could ever take away from her. She'd never have to depend on anybody for anything. Autonomy was the most sensible choice of all.

"Exactly my point." Regina threw up her hands with a grimace. "I only knew Mrs. Hollingsworth for a few weeks, but I can tell you this—she'll never sell that place. The old bat is stringing you along. Did you threaten to quit or something? Is that why she suddenly had a change of heart?"

Not this time. Lily stiffened her jaw. She wasn't letting Regina's cynical chatter worm its way into her head. This time was different. The landlady's rheumatism was growing worse, and she'd been pining over the idea of a small cottage located nearer to where her son lived. Surely people who pined didn't simply change their mind on a whim.

"Hmph." Regina cupped her well-manicured fingers

around her porcelain coffee cup. "I'd need the paper-work in hand before I believed a word of anything that woman said. Surely you have everything in writing."

"We have a verbal agreement."

"You're being foolish." Regina's gaze flitted over Lily's faded calico dress with its sad, frayed sleeves. "You're better off spending the money on a new dress. You can't bait a trap with moldy cheese."

"I beg your pardon."

Regina waved her hand. "I'm only joking. Don't look so shocked."

"I'm not baiting a trap for some hapless male," Lily snapped. "I'm making a prudent investment in my future."

Despite her bluster, the barb stung. Why must the term *foolish* be used so often in reference to her decisions? *Foolish Lily. Naive Lily.* She'd worked hard. She'd paid her dues. She'd considered all the alternatives and arrived at the judicious choice. There was absolutely no reason for her to be sitting here defending herself.

Regina reached out and covered Lily's hands. "This world is run by men. Men only do business with other men. If you want success beyond that silly little board-inghouse, you'll need a husband."

A sharp pain throbbed behind Lily's temple. Regina's solution wasn't any better. A woman was better off count-ing on herself. Love was never the sensible choice. Nothing tangible was secure save for the brick and mortar hold-ing the roof above her head and the land beneath her feet.

People could come and go all they pleased. She didn't need their company, only their business. She glanced at the two heads bent over their checkers game and a wave of sorrow nearly engulfed her. Love inevitably led to loss. She couldn't endure that sort of pain again.

"I need to find someone," Lily began. She'd grown heartily weary of the current subject. Despite the outlaw's warning, she saw no reason to doubt Emil as a guardian. "The children's grandfather was supposed to meet our stagecoach. He's late."

"Who is he? I know everyone in Frozen Oaks." Regina flashed a spiteful grin. "And all of their secrets."

"His name is—"

A blast of glacial air indicated the arrival of another customer. As the gentleman approached their table, Regina's face lit up. Curious, Lily studied the newcomer. His extreme fairness caught and held her attention immediately. The gentleman's pants were striped in shades of charcoal, his waistcoat was checked in burgundy, and he'd topped his outfit with a black suit coat. The only blemish to his neat appearance was the tail end of a blue bandanna trailing from his pocket.

Though not exactly uncomely, everything about him was slightly off. He was at least a decade older than Regina, with a wide smile that stretched his loose jowls. His light blond hair was neatly trimmed, but shot with gray, washing out the color. Despite his jovial expression, there was sharp edge to his pale blue eyes.

Regina rose to her feet, rattling the table and sloshing her coffee.

"Vic," she exclaimed, her voice breathless. "This is my friend Lily Winter. Lily, this is Vic Skaar. Vic owns the hotel and the lumberyard. He'll own the whole town before long."

The man grasped Lily's outstretched hand in a bone-crushing greeting. "A pleasure, Miss Winter."

Lily stifled a grimace at his clammy palm. "Mr. Skaar."

Regina scooted closer and Vic smoothly evaded her advance. Glancing between the pair, Lily frowned.

"Call me Vic," the gentleman said. "What brings you to our quaint town, Miss Winter?"

He winked at her, a curious twitch of his left cheek that didn't completely close his eye. His greeting was so at odds with the exchange she'd shared with the gunfighter, she paused a moment before answering.

"Are you all right, Miss Winter?" Vic hoisted an eyebrow. "I didn't mean to ask such a confusing question."

"I'm fine." Lily straightened. "I'm just visiting."

"How fortunate for us."

The look on his face was cloying and hinted at the suggestion of something more. Lily sharpened her gaze. At the boardinghouse, she'd struck down more than one overly ardent suitor who thought the maids were providing more than fresh linens. She wasn't completely naive.

"My visit is brief," she replied firmly. "Just until the children are settled."

Much to Lily's chagrin, Regina had noted Vic's interest. The other woman's face took on a hard look, jarring Lily's fragile nerves. Though Regina's cloying affection struck Lily as contrived, the other woman was clearly warning her away.

"When are you leaving?" Regina demanded.

"The evening stagecoach," Lily cut in quickly, seeking to ease Regina's disquiet. "I've escorted Sam and Peter on the last leg of their journey. We're waiting on their grandfather. He's late."

Regina was the one person in town she knew, and Lily was loath to damage the relationship until she discovered Emil's whereabouts.

Vic followed her gaze and caught sight of the siblings in deep concentration over their checkers game.

"What's the gentleman's name?" he asked. "Maybe I can help."

"Emil Tyler."

Vic's grin faltered. "That might be a problem, Miss Winter."

Chapter Three

Emil has gotten tangled in some trouble.

Jake's declaration ricocheted around Lily's brain. Had he been implying something more sinister? The idea sent her strained nerves clamoring. What sort of trouble could an elderly man tangle with?

"Emil missed the gentlemen's weekly poker game." Regina chuckled, though she didn't sound particularly amused. "Emil never misses a poker game. No one has seen him in a week. Come to think of it, I heard he had a dustup with that gunfighter, Jake, a few days back."

Vic bestowed Lily with another of his odd half winks. "You'd best watch your back, Lily. With Emil gone, those two boys are ripe for the picking. Even I saw their luggage stacked outside the livery. One look at the brass fittings on their steamer trunks and everyone will know we have a couple of rich orphans in our midst. Folks around these parts will slit your throat for an acre of land, let alone a juicy bank account."

"Stop." Regina playfully slapped his arm. "Vic, you're frightening the poor girl."

With a gasp Lily half stood from her chair, then thumped back down. Only last week the *St. Joseph*

Star had featured a story about gravediggers desecrating corpses in search of valuables. Greed drove people into all sorts of despicable acts. With Emil missing, how difficult would it be for someone to claim guardianship of the boys and drain their inheritance?

Vic pried Regina's fingers loose from his coat sleeve. "A fellow like Jake is dodgy. Considering his argument with Emil, maybe you should speak with the sheriff. A pretty girl looking out for two young, helpless boys needs protection."

Panic rose in the back of Lily's throat. She was physically weak and shaken, and her thoughts were muddled; clearly she hadn't yet recovered from her earlier faint. The room wavered and shimmered and she blinked her eyes back into focus.

"You've had a long day," Regina said. "You're not thinking straight. Someone has to look out for those boys."

Hollow and bewildered, Lily gazed at the youngsters. Even if she was wrong, dare she put them at further risk? She'd made a vow to guard their safety.

Jake had claimed he was enjoying the view. What if he'd dispatched Emil and was targeting the boys? She'd best act quickly.

"Jake can be quite charming," Regina said. "You wouldn't be the first woman taken in by him."

Certainly, he'd played the gentleman. But then he'd practically ordered her to leave.

Lily pressed two trembling fingers against her aching forehead. If her fears were unfounded, there was no harm in checking.

"You're right. I'll speak with the sheriff." Her thoughts jumbled, Lily gathered her reticule and stood.

"Do you mind if the children stay and finish their game? I'd rather not upset them."

"Anything to help." Vic grinned. "Since you'll miss your stagecoach, let me extend my hospitality. We have plenty of rooms available at the hotel."

Regina's expression shifted. "Perhaps it's safer for all three of them if they return to St. Joseph as soon as possible."

"Nonsense," Vic declared. "Sheriff Koepke will set this to rights."

"The sheriff can sort this out with Lily and the boys safely tucked on the stagecoach." Regina's voice took on a prickly edge. "There's no use staying in Frozen Oaks if Emil isn't coming back."

Lily hadn't taken the gunfighter seriously, but she wasn't making the same mistake twice. After donning her coat and assuring Sam and Peter that she'd be back soon, Lily followed Vic's directions across the street. *Trust no one*, Jake had said. *Frozen Oaks is a dangerous place.*

He wanted the three of them on that stagecoach and away from the safety of town for a reason. All of Regina's sly innuendos about the siblings' inheritance came rushing back. Sam and Peter were wealthy, vulnerable. Her steps slowed. Was she overreacting? Had she read too many of Peter's dime novels lately?

She picked up her speed once more. Right or wrong, something was suspicious about Emil's absence. She wasn't naive orphan Lily. She certainly wasn't taking any chances. Emil hadn't been seen in a week, which meant he'd gone missing only days after accepting guardianship. With their grandfather absent, only one last obstacle remained between the boys and someone who might want to exploit them for their inheritance.

She discovered the sheriff where Vic had predicted, sipping whiskey and playing cards in the saloon. Lily wrinkled her nose against the stench and forged onward. The lawman was wiry and small, barely larger than Sam, and had the bulbous pink nose of a gentleman who spent more time in the saloon than in church. He reminded her of a puppet with his exaggerated features and slim body. He was also her best option at the moment.

The sheriff caught sight of her and winked. "What can I do for you, little lady?"

Lily rolled her eyes. Was winking some sort of odd affliction amongst the men of Frozen Oaks?

"I'm concerned about the disappearance of Emil Tyler."

"Old Emil? He'll turn up. I don't get paid to go looking for folks just because someone has their apron in a twist."

The pain in her temple throbbed once more. This day had gone entirely too long.

"I think the gunfighter might be involved," she said.

"Jake?"

Lily nodded.

"Don't go messing with that one. Even Vic steers clear of him."

"So I've heard."

"What do you think he's done?"

"I saw Jake watching Emil's barbershop. Emil has disappeared. It stands to reason the two may be connected."

"Get me some proof, lady. Right now, all you've got is an old fellow who wandered off. For all we know, he ain't right in the head. Old fellows get odd like that."

"Speaking from experience?"

"Huh?"

"Never mind." Lily bit out the words through clenched teeth. "I'll find the proof myself."

Jake yanked open the lumber-mill door and searched the dimly lit interior. He glanced over his shoulder, then shut the door. Lily Winter had been trailing him for two days. Though his admiration was grudging, he had to concede she was rather good. She'd nearly caught up with him a couple of times.

Clearly she thought he was involved with Emil's disappearance. There'd been no developments on that front either. No one was talking. His entire network had gone quiet. A sense of anticipation permeated the air, as though everyone in town was waiting for something to break.

A sound caught his attention and he spun around and met the muzzle of a quaking gun.

A pair of familiar, pretty blue eyes peered over the barrel.

"I was just wondering when something might happen." Jake automatically raised his hands. "I thought I lost you at the livery."

"You knew I was following you?" She tossed her head. "How long have you known?"

"I had a clue, yes. A lady in the bathhouse is bound to cause a stir."

A violent shade of pink suffused her cheeks. "That was an accident. I was following you and not paying attention to my surroundings. Thankfully, the bathhouse was empty."

The empty bathhouse had been more than fortunate. When he'd first caught wind she might be following him, he'd baited the trap. She'd followed him inside, then exited rather rapidly.

"Since you're here," Jake continued, "how about you tell me why you're following me?"

"Vic said you had an argument with Emil. Why didn't you mention your disagreement when we talked before?"

"Vic is lying." Jake held his hands in a placating gesture, stalling for time. "I'm only trying to help you, Miss Winter. You should also know that the sheriff is following you."

"A coincidence. I went to him for help when we first arrived."

"Then he's letting you do most of the legwork. He waits until you follow me, and then he follows you."

"I'm inclined to believe you're lying about that, as well. The sheriff doesn't strike me as being much of a go-getter."

"You've been here for two days, Miss Winter. Have you discovered anything else that's odd about the inhabitants of Frozen Oaks?"

"Answer my questions first," she demanded. "Did you kill Emil?"

"No." At least the question was finally out in the open. "And we don't even know if Emil is dead. He's missing. There's a difference."

A myriad of emotions flitted across her face, a hint of sorrow and something more—a touch of anger. "People don't just go missing. Either they disappear because they want to, or something bad has happened to them."

"I'm trying to help you, Lily. If Vic is attempting to turn your suspicions on me, there must be a reason." Jake didn't have much time. If Lily was here, the sheriff wasn't far behind. He searched their surroundings and strained his ears, hearing only the scuffling of a mouse scurrying along the walls. "Don't you find something odd about this place?"

"I don't follow."

"Isn't it curious that there's no lumber in the lumber mill? According to town gossip, the Frozen Oaks lumber mill once did a thriving business."

She tipped back her head and gazed at the empty rafters. "Not anymore."

"Precisely, Miss Winter. The lumberyard is empty. The hotel rarely has guests, and there's room in the livery for plenty of horses. That doesn't bode well for Mr. Skaar."

"Why the sudden interest in Vic?"

"I'm trying to warn you. Don't be fooled by Vic. There are things about him you don't know."

"I'm done waiting. Those children deserve answers. Someone around here knows something. You're the obvious suspect."

Jake grappled with his own frustrations. He'd been too slow in acting. He'd only become concerned with Emil's absence when the boys had arrived unannounced on the same day Vic had become a housebreaker. But if Vic had already dispatched Emil to erase his gambling debt, what was his interest in the grandchildren?

"I know you're afraid," he said. "I'm only interested in Sam and Peter's safety, and yours, as well."

She raised the gun above her head and wiped her forehead on her shoulder. Dust motes swirled in the dim shaft of light streaking through a gap in the paneling.

He took a step forward and she scurried back. "I'm warning you. You better not try anything, mister. If the sheriff is following me like you say, he'll be here soon."

"Where'd you get the weapon?" he asked.

She raised her chin a notch. "That's none of your concern."

"Have you ever fired a gun before?"

"I can pull a trigger."

His stomach pitched. There was nothing more dangerous than a greenhorn with a pistol. "Fair enough. But I think you need a little practice. You're lining up your shot by the notch at the end of the barrel."

"Isn't that how you're supposed to line up the shot?"

"There are actually two points that line up. When you squeeze the trigger, squeeze slowly. The kickback will pull your shot off target."

"Yes."

"Yes what?"

"You asked me before if I'd noticed anything odd about the people living in Frozen Oaks. My answer is yes. Regina fawns all over Vic, even though I don't think she truly likes him very much. The sheriff is more interested in discovering a straight flush than in trying to figure out why one of his local residents has gone missing. The strangest of all? The local gun for hire is teaching me to fire a weapon. While I'm pointing a gun at him."

"Trust me, Miss Winter. I'm looking out for your best interest."

"Trust you? How can I trust anyone? I have two young children who deserve a home. They deserve a family. Someone around here must know something. If you don't start talking, I'm going to start shooting." She raised her eyes heavenward. "Don't worry, I'll line up both sights."

"You won't shoot a defenseless man."

"No. But then, you're not a defenseless man, are you?"

She wasn't nearly as tough as she appeared. He'd conned his way through enough situations to recognize the signs. If the boys were in danger, she'd shoot. Without that incentive, he doubted she had the nerve. He only had to prevent her from accidentally firing the weapon until he regained control of the situation.

"I'll tell you what I know." He lowered his hands. "Rumor has it that Vic lost money to Emil in a poker game. A lot of money."

"Vic has money to burn. How much could he lose to a kindly old grandfather?"

"You've never met Emil, have you?"

A lock of her straw-colored hair drifted across her cornflower blue eyes. "If you didn't kill Emil, where is he?" She blew a breath, fluttering the strands aside. "Do you know what happened to him?"

"No, I don't. But I have a few ideas. Some suspicions. Why don't you put down the gun and we can discuss my thoughts?"

"Not likely."

If only he could simply tell her the truth. At this point, she'd never believe him anyway. This was the part of the job he loathed. After five years of running with thieves, corrupt lawmen and killers, he'd lost his ability for gentlemanly speech. He had no convincing words to soothe her with. And for the first time in his career, he desperately wanted those words.

He shook off the hesitation.

She was a distraction. The boys were vulnerable. Nothing more, nothing less. The sooner she left, the better. If the accusation in her melancholy eyes sparked his guilt, that was the price he paid for keeping her and the boys safe.

He took another step forward and she stumbled back once more.

"Don't come any closer." Her breath came in quick, shallow gasps. "I'm warning you, the sheriff knows all about your interest in the inheritance. He'll take you to jail. Once we find proof that you're responsible for Emil's disappearance, jail is where you'll stay."

An inheritance? The ramifications socked him in the gut. Vic didn't want to erase his debt, he wanted a new influx of cash. All the pieces instantly made sense: Emil was missing. His grandchildren were the beneficiaries of an inheritance. Lily Winter was the only thing standing between the boys and someone who might take advantage of them.

He'd underestimated the depths of Vic's depravity and played right into his hands as the villain of the piece.

Carefully considering how to regain Lily's trust, Jake took a cautious step forward. "If the sheriff is on his way, why don't you give me the gun? Your breathing is too shallow. You'll faint again if you don't calm down. We'll wait for him together."

"Don't patronize me. Stop playing the charming gentleman and go back to being an outlaw."

"Lily, we both know the sheriff isn't coming to your rescue. You can't hold a gun on me forever. You might as well let me go." He took a step closer. "There's another stagecoach this evening. If you're worried about the boys' safety, then leave now. Take them far away from here."

"Stop treating me like I'm a simpleton." Her gaze darted around the cavernous warehouse and landed on him once more. "You must have a reason for wanting me on that stage."

"You're not a simpleton. You're right to be cautious. But you've stumbled into the middle of a dangerous situation. I don't want you hurt."

Her stance lifted the floodgates on his past once more. She'd put herself in harm's way for the boys unless he prevented her.

"I don't understand you." Lily's arms sagged and the barrel of the heavy gun tipped down. "Why didn't you take the boys when I fainted?"

"Think about what you're saying, Lily. I'm not the one you need to fear."

"Tell me something. Anything. Give me one reason why I can trust you. Those children need their grandfather. I need to go home. I'm begging you, let me have one piece of proof that gives me a reason to believe what you're saying."

"I don't have any proof. Not yet."

She drew herself up to her full height, as though a scant inch made any difference. "Then we're at an impasse."

"There is one thing."

Lily glanced at something behind him and panic skittered across her face. "Look out!"

Pain exploded in his head. Jake pitched sideways. His legs weakened and collapsed beneath him. Landing on his back, he stared at the face hovering over him.

Sheriff Koepke clasped a shovel in his fisted hands. "This fellow will be spending the next few weeks in jail, miss. He won't be bothering you anymore."

"You can't arrest him," Lily protested. "He hasn't done anything."

"You were holding a gun on him. He must have done something."

"We were, uh, we were only talking."

The blow had knocked the strength from Jake's limbs. His hands and feet tingled and his vision dimmed. After clumsily flipping him onto his stomach, the sheriff secured his wrists with metal shackles.

The sawdust itched Jake's nose. A pair of delicate half boots drifted into his vision. A lock of her hair dusted his cheek.

"Did you have to hit him that hard?" Lily exclaimed softly. She touched the knot forming on the back of his head. "You've knocked him senseless."

"That was the idea, missy."

"What's the charge?" Panic coated Lily's voice. "Why are you arresting him?"

"Don't you worry your pretty little head. We got this all taken care of. Found some stolen goods in this man's rooms over at the saloon. He'll be locked up tight for a good long time."

Nausea rose in the back of Jake's throat and his head throbbed. They'd set him up. There was nothing in his room but a saddlebag and a change of clothes. The sheriff jerked him upright.

He stumbled and Lily steadied him.

"You can't do this," she said. "He was going to help me."

"You'll have to find someone else. This fellow is gonna be busy helping himself."

She smelled of lilacs and her eyelashes fluttered like butterflies. He'd been mired in the job too long. There was so little good left in the world, he'd forgotten people like Lily existed. She was the whole reason he'd become a US marshal. If something happened to her, he'd be to blame.

Sheriff Koepke dragged him toward the door, a difficult task given the disparity in their sizes. A kind of rage Jake hadn't felt in years welled inside him. He would be trapped in a jail cell for the foreseeable future.

Lily pressed her fingers over her mouth. "I'm so sorry. I thought you were lying when you said he was following me."

"I know." The images at the edge of his vision shimmered like mirages. "Forget about Emil. Take the children back to St. Joseph."

"I can't. He's their grandfather. They don't have anyone else."

The sheriff heaved him onto the street and he glanced over his shoulder. Lily clung to the door frame.

She'd never survive in Frozen Oaks alone.

Chapter Four

The sight of Jake being dragged away to jail dominated Lily's thoughts. The snow had ceased falling and sunlight glinted off the fresh layer of white. The restaurant was empty, the fire down to embers. The siblings remained huddled over their checkers game.

She had no doubt Jake was many things, but he certainly wasn't a thief.

He'd known from the start she'd never shoot him. He could have turned the tables on her at any time. Though he was the obvious suspect in the disappearance of the children's grandfather, she'd changed her mind about him after their last encounter.

Why had he urged her to leave instead of taking the upper hand? Why not abscond with the boys when she'd fainted? He'd had a second opportunity when she'd held a useless weapon on him.

She folded her arms on the table and buried her head in the circle.

Events had transpired too quickly, and she hadn't considered all the separate details. Something was off, but she'd been too determined to prove she wasn't naive orphan Lily to notice. She'd seen that odd mixture of regret and longing in the outlaw's eyes before the sheriff had hauled him away.

She'd come to rely on the constants in her life. The barn swallows that nested beneath her window each spring. The familiar lonely ache in her chest each Christmas Eve. The smell of coffee brewing each morning. She'd never been able to wake fully without coffee, a trait she'd inherited from her father.

She stretched out her arms and cupped her hands around the steaming cup before her.

The coffee grinder she'd left back at the boardinghouse was her most treasured possession. As soon as she was old enough to reach the counter, the job of brewing had fallen to her. The one thing that had made her feel part of the family. She'd pour a measured scoop into the top and crank the handle. Then she'd open the tiny drawer and inhale the scent of fresh-ground beans. The aroma was inexorably intertwined with memories of her family. She'd never been able to separate the two, though she'd desperately tried.

Sam exclaimed victory and kinged a checker piece.

She needed a plan. She needed action. She needed an escape from all the drab autumnal colors oozing from the hotel parlor into the gloomy dining room.

Peter turned toward her. "What are we going to do now?"

"I don't know yet. But don't worry. I'll think of something."

The sheriff had jailed the gunfighter before he'd revealed his evidence. Either way, she'd removed Jake from her list of suspects in Emil's disappearance. Despite Vic's and Regina's attempts to frighten her, he'd never once exploited his advantage.

A part of her had thought Emil might return. They'd

been delayed on their arrival; who was to say Emil hadn't been delayed by the weather, as well? But with more days come and gone, her hope was dwindling. Which left her with one option: return Sam and Peter to St. Joseph and to the guardianship of the judge. And yet something held her back. She wasn't prepared to declare Sam and Peter orphans just yet. Her stomach clenched. They deserved better.

Vic appeared in the dining room and an insidious sense of misgiving gripped her. When he smiled, the pink of his gums contrasted dramatically with his white teeth and colorless pallor.

He sidled over to her table and flashed her one of his odd half winks. "May I join you?"

He kept his thumbs hooked in the pockets of his elaborate waistcoat. That single piece of clothing must have cost a fortune. Every inch of the expensive fabric was decorated with colorful, intricately embroidered peacocks.

"I'm afraid I was just leaving." Lily sprang to her feet. Vic's obvious wealth should have excluded him from any interest in the inheritance of a couple of orphans, but he'd been awfully eager in turning her attention toward the gunfighter. "Please tell Regina how sorry I am that I missed her this morning."

Though Lily doubted his attention was personal, she tossed in the reminder of his sweetheart. He struck her as the sort of man who preferred conquests to relationships.

"Certainly," he said. "You seem agitated. Is something amiss?"

"Not at all. Except I wasn't given Emil's address since he was supposed to meet us at the livery." She scrambled for an excuse for her abrupt departure. "Do you know where he lives? Perhaps the children and I can discover a clue to his disappearance."

"What a curious little thing you are. If only you could stay longer." Vic took her hand and kissed the back of her knuckles. "Emil owns the barbershop across the street. His rooms are on the second floor."

Lily resisted the urge to wipe her knuckles against her skirts. "Thank you."

"Oh, and, Miss Winter, you can catch this evening's stagecoach after all."

Hope bloomed in her chest. "Then you've found Emil."

"No."

"I don't understand."

"The sheriff has granted me temporary guardianship of the Tyler children."

"He can't do that." Her blood instantly chilled. "I don't understand. The judge in Missouri was very specific. The children are to be delivered to their grandfather."

Vic splayed his hands. "You're in Nebraska now, Miss Winter. You're under the laws and jurisdiction of this state, not Missouri. That means the sheriff is the authority."

Glancing at Sam and Peter's worried expressions, she offered a reassuring smile that didn't quite reach her eyes. "*Jurisdiction* seems like an awfully big word for the sheriff. Are you certain the change in guardianship was his idea?"

"Regina says you were being paid." Vic reached into his pocket and retrieved a fat wad of bills, then licked his thumb and rested the pad on the top layer. "I'll settle the debt."

She stumbled backward. "There's no need."

"I insist." He peeled off enough bills to cover Lily's salary for six months. "For your trouble."

Sam stood and she gave a quick flick of her hand, urging silence. "That's very kind of you, but I'd be shirking my duties if I left the children."

"Oh, dear." Vic's pale lips turned down at the corners. "I'm not certain you have much choice, Miss Winter. You've involved the sheriff once already."

She snatched the bills and clutched them against her stomach. She needed him gone, she needed time to think, and Vic wasn't leaving unless he thought he'd won.

"This is very generous of you." She lifted her eyebrows toward Sam and Peter, willing them to follow her lead. There'd be time enough for panicking later. "A trip to the mercantile is in order. The children were well-behaved on the trip. They deserve a reward."

Anything to stall for time and escape the hotel.

"It was a pleasure meeting you, Miss Winter. I hope you'll visit our little town again one day."

"I doubt I'll be back."

"You might be surprised."

"My stay has certainly been filled with unexpected revelations."

If he caught the implied insult, he let the discretion pass. Absently whistling a lively tune, he strolled from the dining room once more. As soon as he was out of sight, Lily shook out her hands.

Sam and Peter rushed forward.

"Are you leaving us?" Sam demanded. "Where will we stay?"

"I don't like him," Peter said. "I don't want to stay here without you."

Perhaps it was his odd pale coloring, but there was something about Vic that struck her as sinister.

"Don't worry." Lily hugged them close. "I'll sort this out."

With his peacock waistcoat and colorless skin, Vic would make an excellent villain in one of Peter's novels. She certainly didn't trust his motivations. There was no way the sheriff had come up with the idea of taking over guardianship. If the word *jeopardy* was outside of his vocabulary, he certainly wasn't throwing around words like *jurisdiction* and *authority*.

She mentally checked off the people she'd met in the past few days: Regina, Jake, Vic and Sheriff Koepke. For such a small town, Frozen Oaks sure had its fair share of shady characters. Last week she'd been fully prepared to leave the boys with their grandfather and return home immediately. After spending several days in this peculiar town, she'd grown reticent. Truth be told, she'd feel no better about leaving the boys and returning home if Emil walked through the door that instant. She certainly wasn't handing them over to Vic Skaar and his saloon-frequenting sheriff.

Sitting here stewing about her predicament solved nothing. "Who wants to go on an adventure?" Lily asked.

Her question was met with obvious enthusiasm.

She tucked the bills into her reticule. She didn't plan on keeping them, but she couldn't exactly abandon that amount of money on the dining room table either. Once outside, Lily directed them toward the red-and-blue pole of the barbershop. As she'd noted the day before, the windows were shuttered. The whitewashed storefront needed a fresh coat of paint, but Emil was probably waiting for better weather.

"What's this place?" Sam asked, unwrapping a peppermint.

"Your grandfather's shop. He's a barber. Did you know that? Apparently he lives upstairs."

"My dad said he was a vagabond who couldn't stay in one place if his shoes were nailed to the floor." Sam finished off the candy with a decisive crunch. "Can we go inside? I mean, I'd like to see where we're going to live."

"The door is probably locked." Melancholy stirred in her heart. Of course Sam and Peter were interested in seeing their new home. But was this their home? From the moment they'd stepped into Frozen Oaks, nothing had been certain. "I suppose there's no harm in looking."

A narrow space between the buildings held a staircase leading up to the second level. Boot prints showed in the fresh layer of snow. They overlapped each other, as though a man had come and gone from the apartment.

Emil has gotten tangled in some trouble.

All she had were rumors and gossip. She knew well enough the lack of truth they contained. She was poor orphan Lily after all.

"Hold the railing. The steps might be slippery."

They traversed the narrow stairs and crowded onto the landing. She shook off her apprehension. Probably someone had come to check on Emil when he didn't open his shop. She touched the handle and the door swung open.

Before she could stop them, the siblings rushed inside.

Lily chased after them. "Wipe your feet. Don't track snow."

The person who'd been here before them had not

been as thoughtful. Footprints tracked across the wood floors. Crouching, she swiped at the marks. The melted snow had dried, leaving only dirt behind.

The space was neat and tidy, though sparsely furnished. The woodpile was well stocked, and Emil's belongings were scattered about. There was a pipe and a tin of tobacco along with a stack of newspapers. Though clearly occupied, the space was oddly impersonal. The rooms might have belonged to anyone, save for the feather Christmas tree sheltering a stack of gifts propped on a table in the corner.

The walls of her room at the boardinghouse were covered in drawings and postcards. The windows had been decorated with curtains she'd sewed. Even her floors were covered in hand-knotted rag rugs. While she recognized through her experience at the rooming house that men were less likely to personalize a space with their possessions, Emil's home felt cold and detached. There was certainly nothing warm and welcoming for the children.

Well, almost nothing.

The feather tree was the only touch of homey decorating, which was even odder still considering how early it was in the season. She'd never known anyone who put the tree out before December. After crossing the distance, she rummaged through the brown-paper-wrapped packages. The labels included both Sam's and Peter's name.

The two caught sight of her discovery and scurried over.

Peter held a package near his ear and shook it. "These are for us."

Squinting, he held the box to the light streaming from the second-story window.

Despite the general lack of preparation for the arrival of two youngsters, their grandfather had, at least, bought them presents. Why purchase gifts and then abscond? Feeling guilty but determined, Lily riffled through a stack of books on the side table. She discovered several dime novels featuring Deadwood Dick on the cover. Deeper in the pile, a black-and-white cover displayed a tall man with a hat pulled low over his eyes. The title read *Gunman for Hire*.

While Sam and Peter explored the open kitchen on the far side of the room, she followed the path the tracks had taken into the small apartment. Once again the arrangement struck her as odd. Where did Emil suppose his grandchildren would sleep? There was only the single bed that hardly looked big enough for a grown man.

The trail ended before a bureau set along the far wall beneath a double window. She ran her finger across the top and came away with only the barest hint of dust. Uttering a brief prayer for forgiveness, she opened the top drawer. A handkerchief box, the lid open, rested in the corner. Several coins were scattered along the bottom.

The years slipped away and she was five years old again. Each night when her father returned from work, he had emptied his pockets of coins and dollars into a similar box. She glanced at the footprints once more. The intruder had known exactly what he was looking for.

Though rifling through a stranger's belongings went against her nature, she opened the second drawer and discovered a stack of folded blue handkerchiefs. Her heart kicked in her chest. She'd seen the same handkerchief before.

Lifting her head, she gazed out the window. Emil's

bedroom directly overlooked the hotel and the board-walk, where a wooden chair sat empty.

I like the view.

She squeezed her eyes shut and pictured Jake's boots. Pointed tips. How could she forget? She'd stared at them propped on the boardwalk rail for nearly twenty minutes. The footprints in the snow had been square-toed.

"Oh, dear."

She had a bad feeling Emil's troubles were wrapped up with a man who wore a peacock embroidered vest and winked without closing his eye.

She closed the lid with a snap and hastily exited the space.

Sensing the change in her mood, Sam scooted closer. "What's wrong?"

"Nothing is wrong. Everything is fine. When we return to the hotel, pack your belongings. We might have to leave in a hurry." She knelt before Sam and Peter and held their hands. "I want you to know that no matter what, I'll always look out for you. I won't let anything bad happen."

Peter clutched his package. "Can we keep the presents?"

"Yes. We'll take them with us."

She reached for the doorknob and discovered the metal casing was bent and hung loose.

Sam paused on the threshold. "What do you suppose happened to Grandpa Emil?"

"I don't know. But I know someone who can find out."

Jake prowled the narrow jail cell. The building wasn't much to look at. A squat brick structure set slightly north of the town. Only three cells flanked the back wall, a cot in each. Obviously Frozen Oaks was a quiet town without need of more lockups. The walls were rough-hewn and covered with maps and wanted posters. A tattered American flag had been haphazardly pinned between two corners.

He should have told Lily the truth. He'd been trying to protect her and instead he'd put her life in greater danger. Impotent fury settled in his chest. He'd made mistakes in his career before, especially in the beginning.

He'd never felt this powerless.

He tested the bars once again, though more to vent his frustration than discover a weakness. The cell wasn't particularly sophisticated, but he was without tools. The sheriff had even stripped him of his shoes and belt.

The door swung open and Lily appeared in the entry.

He blinked a few times, wondering if he was hallucinating. Had the blow Sheriff Koepke delivered rattled his brain? She was just as he remembered. Her blond hair surrounded her face in a lustrous halo. Her coat was an indistinguishable shade of brown, but the hem of her bright yellow dress peeked out from beneath the wool.

His jaw hung slack. "What are you doing here?"

"I'll explain later. Where are the keys to the cell?"

He motioned with one hand toward a narrow cupboard on the wall.

Lily and her cheerful smiles were a jaunty dash of liveliness in a desolate world. Entombed in a Nebraska winter for eight weeks, he'd begun to think the wind and snow had extracted all the color from the world. The barren landscape and drab buildings along with the constant haze had taken their toll.

With brisk efficiency she flipped open the door and retrieved the keys. "Where are your shoes?"

Being caught in his stocking feet left him feeling exposed and oddly defenseless.

"On the bench by the door."

"Hmm." She snatched one of his boots and studied the sole. Relief flitted across her face. "Just as I thought."

"What did you think?"

"Never mind. What about your gun belt? You'll need that, as well."

"The belt is hanging on the hook above your head, but they took my guns."

Jake doubted Sheriff Koepke planned on giving them back.

Jingling the keys, she approached his cell.

He braced his hands on the bars. "What are you doing?"

"I'm releasing you."

He couldn't have been more surprised if she'd declared she was riding an elephant in the Sahara. "You can't. That's against the law."

"What does an outlaw care about breaking the law?"

Good point. "I don't want you in trouble with the sheriff."

"It's my fault you were arrested," she stated matter-of-factly. "I'm correcting the wrong. I'm letting you out."

"That's not how the law works." He scrubbed a hand down his face. "Give me the keys."

"Why?"

"Because if I open the door, you didn't break the law. I did."

"You're a terrible outlaw." She dangled the keys through an opening in the bars. "No wonder you got yourself arrested."

"You have no idea."

He awkwardly groped at the lock, turned the key and yanked open the door. "Why are you doing this?"

Unbearably relieved he'd purchased new socks the previous week, he took a seat on the bench and tugged his boots over his stocking feet.

"I've been doing a little investigating," she said, crossing her arms over her chest.

"Oh, no."

"Oh, yes. I've discovered a few things about Vic Skaar."

Jake's attention sharpened. "What does Vic Skaar have to do with breaking me out of jail?"

"I searched Emil's rooms above the barbershop today. Someone had already been there."

A cold sweat broke out on his aching forehead. "Promise me you're done with sleuthing, Miss Winter. It's far too dangerous."

"I won't promise you anything. Whoever searched the barbershop knew Emil wasn't there. He knew Emil wasn't going to catch him. Don't you find that suspicious?"

Jake wrapped his gun belt around his waist. He tightened the buckle, then strapped the second tie around his thigh.

The empty holster weighed on his nerves. "And you think you know the identity of this mysterious housebreaker?"

"Don't pretend you don't know who. The ruse doesn't suit you. The view you were enjoying the other day faced the barbershop. When I saw Vic at the restaurant, he had a blue handkerchief in his pocket. I found the same blue handkerchiefs with Emil's belongings."

While Jake admired her investigative skills, he didn't

want her involved in the case. "Coincidence. There's only one store in town. Why break into someone's room for a handkerchief?"

"The place was dusty. Vic is clearly fastidious. He searched the rooms, wiped his hands on the handkerchief, then stuck it in his pocket out of habit."

Jake stifled a groan. "You're too smart for your own good."

Keeping her out of danger was going to be impossible at this rate.

"Don't mock me." Furious color suffused her cheeks. "I think Vic had something to do with Emil's disappearance. I believe he may be after Sam and Peter for their inheritance."

"What brought you to that conclusion?"

He didn't doubt her, but he was curious about her reasoning.

"Vic just informed me that the Tyler children were now a part of this jurisdiction, and the sheriff has decided that Vic Skaar should assume their guardianship."

"Those are some awfully fancy words for Sheriff Koepke."

"My thoughts exactly."

Jake rubbed the back of his neck. He'd had some time to think while he was locked up. Whatever Vic was searching for, he hadn't found the item. Jake had watched Vic exit the building looking grimmer than when he entered. There was still something missing from his motivations. If he'd been responsible for Emil's disappearance over his poker debt, why search his rooms? Dead men didn't collect debts.

A sudden realization dawned on Jake. Vic hadn't found out about Emil's grandchildren until after he'd searched Emil's rooms. He also hadn't discovered what he was searching for, which meant he needed a new plan.

Lily, Sam and Peter had dropped into his lap like a gift. Vic and Emil were definitely tangled in some trouble.

None of that explained why Lily wanted to bust him out of jail. Especially considering she'd practically put him there.

"Why are you here?" Jake asked. "I still don't know what you want from me."

"I think that's obvious. You're a gun for hire, aren't you?" She extended the pistol she'd held on him earlier, the muzzle down. "Here's a gun. I want to hire you."

Chapter Five

Jake flushed. This certainly complicated matters. More for safety than for an acknowledgment of the offer, he accepted the gun.

After flipping open the chamber, he spun the cylinder.

Empty.

Clearly the ancient weapon hadn't been cleaned or fired in ages. Probably a relic from an elderly relative.

"This gun isn't much use without the bullets," he said.

"I know." Lily scowled. "I forgot about the bullets. I didn't think having a loaded gun around the children was very safe."

"It's not much of a defense either." While he was grateful she'd relinquished the weapon, he wasn't finished with his lecture. Lily holding a gun was about as natural as a peacock in a rowboat and just as precarious. "You and I need to have a long and detailed conversation about personal safety and protection."

"Until then—" she looked him up and down, as though measuring the strength of his resolve "—you may assume the responsibility for the gun."

Lily Winter took too much for granted. She was far too trusting. What if he was actually an outlaw? What then? She'd just handed a gun to someone she thought was a killer for hire. He could easily shoot her. If he had the bullets, and if the gun's workings weren't rusted with age. But that wasn't the point.

"The gun is mine," he said. "For now. And we're not associating. I haven't agreed to anything."

She reached for the weapon and he yanked it out of reach.

"You're stealing my gun?" she cried. "That's some gratitude for breaking you of jail."

"I didn't ask for your help."

Her expression turned wintry. "I'll pay you."

"How much?"

"Fifty dollars."

"Not enough."

Her eyes narrowed. "You never intended to accept!"

"I needed to know how much you could afford."

With an abundance of caution, Sheriff Koepke had barred all the windows in the cramped space. Sunlight persevered, casting blocks of shadows on the floor, illuminating Lily's expressive face. He shouldn't goad her, but there was something magnificent about how the sliver of light piercing the barred window lit her blue eyes.

The color reminded him of the feathers on the crown of a barn swallow. The kind of blue that brought to mind the endless summer days of his youth. When he and his brothers had slipped away from their chores and splashed in the stream behind the old barn—before their mother's death. He'd felt as though his life had been cleaved in two, and everything before her death had dropped into oblivion. He'd thought those memories had vanished from his consciousness, but for some inexplicable reason, Lily and her charges had inspired their reappearance.

The door swung open, snapping him back to the present.

Sam and Peter scuttled inside. They were bundled head to toe against the cold, wrapped like colorful mummies.

The older boy, Sam, tucked his hands in his armpits and shivered. "I don't think he saw us."

Peter slammed the door and leaned against the wood panel. "He's coming!"

"Why aren't you at the hotel?" Lily rushed to meet them. "How did you find me?"

"I didn't figure you'd take a gun to the mercantile," Peter replied. "We watched you from the window on the landing."

Sam released his fingers from the warmth of his armpits, skipped past Jake and stuck his face through the bars. "How come the gunfighter isn't in there? I thought you said he was in jail."

Peter joined his brother. "Do you think a killer carved his initials in the bricks? Do you think there's ever been a hanging in Frozen Oaks? Do you think there's ever been a jail bust? Do you think Billy the Kid was ever locked up in here?"

"Enough of that morbid talk!" Lily snatched the boy's arm and dragged him back a pace. "You can't be here. We mustn't arouse suspicion."

"But it's Sherriff Koepke." Peter grasped his brother's other arm, putting the boy in an odd tug of war. "He's coming."

Jake stilled. "No games. Did you actually see the sheriff?"

"We're telling the truth."

"We heard everything," Sam eagerly added. "The sheriff and Vic were talking. Vic is coming to the jail-house after he has dinner with Miss Regina and smooths her ruffled feathers."

"Why is he coming to the jail?" Jake prodded. "Did he say?"

Lily shot him a quelling glance. "Don't encourage them. We don't have time for questions. They need to leave."

"I'm not encouraging them, and time or not, this information is vital."

Possibly even lifesaving. Vic was obviously interested in the boys and their inheritance. Lily was either part of the prize or a hindrance. Jake needed to know which before he made his next move.

"Vic said that he and the sheriff are going to take care of the prisoner," Sam continued. "Then he'll finally have everything he wants."

"Did either the sheriff or Mr. Skaar see you?" Lily interrupted. "Are you certain he doesn't know you were listening?"

"We were silent as mountain lions," Sam offered cheerfully. "We were hiding outside his door. Don't worry, we were real quiet. He didn't even know we were there."

"Why on earth were you spying on him in the first place?"

"Because we found this," Sam declared. He retrieved a folded *St. Joseph Star* newspaper from the waistband of his trousers and pointed at a block of text in the social commentary section. "Regina and Vic left this on the table when they finished having lunch with the sheriff. Read the second paragraph."

Lily grasped the paper. "'The wealthy heiress to the Carter Smelting Corporation and her husband perished in a cholera epidemic while building a children's school in the South African Republic. Their sole living heirs have been transferred to the guardianship of their paternal grandfather, Emil Tyler, of Frozen Oaks, Nebraska.'" She flourished the paper. "You can't trust anyone these days. Who puts that sort of thing in writing? Have reporters no sense?"

"That's our proof." Sam nodded. "That creep from the hotel is after us for our fortune, and the sheriff is helping him."

Lily blanched. "I'm afraid I've come to the same conclusion."

Pacing, Jake weighed his options. There was no good reason for her and the boys to be here. The barred windows prevented a hasty exit that didn't lead directly to the street. There was no back way out of the jail, which meant Lily and the boys were trapped. If the sheriff suspected a double cross, they'd both be in jail.

Peter rose on his toes, hooked his fingertips over the sill, then peered through the barred window overlooking the street. "He's almost here. You don't have much time."

"Lily—" Jake began.

She shoved him backward into the cell. "Stay there. Act like a prisoner."

Startled by the unexpected maneuver, he tripped over the threshold and sat down hard on his cot. She closed the swinging bars until they latched, though she didn't turn the key in the lock. He sprang from the mattress. The hay stuffing had long ago mildewed, and the stench was overpowering.

"Lily, you have to listen," he demanded. "We don't

have much time. Take the boys to your home in St. Joseph. There's a stagecoach scheduled this afternoon."

He'd wire the marshal's office in St. Joseph and have someone waiting at the next station. Someone who'd look out for the trio. Jake tugged on his beard. All he had to do was escape the jail without implicating Lily.

"No." Lily splayed her hands. Something akin to panic flitted across her face. "We can't separate. How will you find us? How will we find you? We must stay together. Besides, Vic isn't a fool. He'll be expecting us to leave by the obvious routes. He's practically ordered me to board that stagecoach. I took money from him. I made him believe I was leaving."

"Good. That's good. That buys us some time. He won't come for the children until then."

The fear in her eyes gave him pause. She was frightened, all right, but not of him. She was terrified of being left on her own.

"I promise," he said. "No matter what happens, I won't abandon you."

She and the boys had become his most pressing concern. The mystery of the stolen guns had to wait.

"You can't guarantee that. No one can. What if the sheriff discovers the cell is unlocked? What happens then?"

He reached through the bars and touched her shoulder. She didn't flinch this time. "Don't worry, I'll manage."

Lily placed her hand over his. Her fingers were delicate and pale against the rough cotton of his shirt. She stared up at him, her eyes full of a trust he hadn't earned, and a faith he didn't deserve.

"I'm putting our fate in your hands," she said.

"You have to promise me something. Don't tell a soul that you're leaving with me, not even Regina."

He didn't trust anyone in this town, especially someone associated with Vic.

The boys stared at him with mirrored expressions of horror and wonder.

Sam's mouth hung open, then snapped shut. "We're going to travel with an outlaw. A real, live outlaw. You're the best chaperone ever, Miss Lily."

"I know this all seems quite unusual." Lily patted Sam's head. "I assure you, I know what I'm doing. I've hired this man as our escort. Your grandfather is, uh, temporarily indisposed. There are some mitigating circumstances that make the added safeguard of a hired gun prudent."

"I have no idea what you just said, but I'm not scared," Sam replied, his voice breathless. "I'm excited. This is better than *The Captives of the Frontier*. I'd rather stay with you than that creepy pale guy."

"Well, don't be excited either. This is a very serious situation." She strode across the room and replaced the key, then secured the cupboard. "We need a plausible reason to be here."

"No, you don't," Sam declared. "I have a better idea. C'mon, Peter."

"Not so fast." Lily blocked their exit. "Where are you going?"

"We'll distract the sheriff so Jake can break out of jail."

"Absolutely not," she said. "Too dangerous."

"This is no time for a lecture," Sam pleaded. "We'll create a distraction. Just like in *The Fourth Bullet*. Then you can break the outlaw out of jail."

"I'm siding with Lily." Jake shook his head. "Absolutely not."

Sheriff Koepke was too unpredictable for this nonsense. If the man sensed trouble, he was liable to accidentally shoot them all and ask questions later. He wasn't much of a marksman in the best of circumstances.

Lily prowled the cramped space. She peered through the barred windows and tapped her front tooth, no doubt reaching the same conclusion as Jake. The cottonwood trees planted for shade had lost their leaves for winter, providing little cover between the jail and the hundred yards to the edge of town. With the sheriff on his way, he'd never make the distance unseen.

"Wait!" Peter hollered. "The sheriff has stopped walking. He's talking with Regina. They've turned around. Looks like they're heading back to the hotel."

Jake exited the jail cell and blew out a gusty breath. "All right. You three need to leave. Now. You can't be seen here any more than necessary."

"Oh, no," Peter groaned. "We're too late. He's coming back again."

"Leave," Jake ordered. He grasped Lily's arm and turned her gently toward the door. "There's no other way. The sheriff can't know we're working together. And stop breaking outlaws out of jail. It's not safe."

She was a menace. A beautiful, distracting menace. Forcing her to leave was for her protection, but letting her go went against every fiber of his being.

"You're the safest choice I have." She stubbornly refused to move. "I know what I'm doing is right. You shouldn't be in jail in the first place."

"You don't understand the danger. Go back to the hotel. I'll figure a way out of here and meet you there."

"I don't believe you. The moment we separate, who's to say what you'll do? We stay together."

She didn't completely trust him. As a US marshal, he admired her skepticism. Corrupt or not, the sheriff was the law in town, and Koepke was smarter than his vocabulary indicated. If he alerted Vic of trouble, they'd never make their escape out of Frozen Oaks. All Jake could do was offer an excuse for their presence, and hope the sheriff bought their lie.

"We're running out of time," he said. "When the sheriff arrives, tell him the boys wanted to see the prisoner."

"I'd believe that." Sam rubbed his chin. "My friend Thomas had a button from a man who was hanged in Wichita. He let us see it for a penny."

"That is positively morbid." Lily grimaced. "What is so fascinating about all this blood and gore? There's a lovely book I heard about from one of the ladies on the train. It's called *Heidi*."

"I'd rather read *Huckleberry Finn* and see a tooth from a dead guy. Jimmy said he had a tooth from a bank robber but I never saw it. I think he was lying."

"All right, that's enough. No more talk of souvenirs from hanged men. It's disrespectful."

"Then they shouldn't have gone and gotten themselves hanged."

Jake hooked his fingers on the open cell door and considered his options. If the jail remained unlocked, there was an excellent chance Sheriff Koepke wouldn't notice.

Lily gathered the boys and hustled them toward the front of the building. The three of them huddled, their heads bent together, whispering. The hairs on the back of Jake's neck stirred. He had a bad feeling about their conversation. Sam and Peter kept glancing over their shoulders at him, then nodding.

Lily approached the cell and Peter angled his body near the window, watching as the sheriff approached.

She held out her hand. "If you're too stubborn to let me bust you out of jail this instant, at least give me the gun."

"Why?"

"For the same reason you refuse to leave. If the sheriff discovers a gun after my visit, he'll know I gave you a weapon. If you can't keep me safe, I'll need something stronger than my wits for protection."

Guilt socked him in the gut. He rummaged beneath the mattress, crossed the distance once more and held the empty gun loosely in his right hand.

She caught his gaze, her expression somber. "I'm really, really sorry for what's about to happen."

"What—"

The words had barely left his mouth when Peter called out.

"Now!"

Lily yanked open the cell door.

The squeak of hinges indicated the sheriff's arrival.

"Don't come any closer." Lily shrieked. "This is a jailbreak."

Jake's stomach pitched. In an instant his last hope of coming up with a safe plan disintegrated. Six months. Six months of work out the window. Lily had just willfully implicated herself in a jailbreak. At best, if they were caught, the boys would wind up alone and unprotected. At worst, Lily was liable to be shot by some overzealous posse.

Time seemed to slow, and he glanced at the open door.

There were no good options. "This is a hostage situation, all right!" he hollered.

In for a penny, in for a pound.

He pointed the gun at the ceiling. "Hands over your head!"

Lily's chest seized. She'd taken a dreadful risk. The gunfighter was staring at her as though she'd lost her marbles, and the sheriff was scratching his head.

She caught Jake's gaze, desperately hoping he'd read her frantic appeal. Her plan was sound. This would work. She'd break him out of jail and make a run for the next town, where they'd explain themselves.

In an instant Jake wound his free arm around her stomach and dragged her back against him. "I've got hostages. Women and children."

Lily stiffened. "But that isn't—"

"Easy there." The sheriff held his hand over his right ear. "You'll have to speak up, son."

Jake squeezed Lily's middle. Not enough to hurt, but enough to get her attention.

"I'm in charge of the plan now," Jake whispered harshly against her ear. "If we get out of this alive, our talk about personal safety and defense just doubled in length."

Sam and Peter had raised their hands along with the sheriff.

"Are we hostages, too?" Sam's eyes grew as round as saucers. "I didn't know we'd get to be hostages. That's even better."

"This is not an improvement," Lily whispered back. "I need a moment to think."

She'd told the children she had a strategy. While this

wasn't precisely what she had in mind, they didn't have much choice but to follow Jake's lead.

"I can be a hostage." Peter shrugged. "I don't mind."

"I can't believe you agreed with their plan." Jake's fierce scowl could have melted the icicles from the eves. "I thought we decided involving the children was too dangerous."

"I expanded on their idea," Lily said under her breath. "Lower your voice. The sheriff is hard of hearing, not stone deaf." She elbowed him in the stomach and bellowed, "Jake says unhook your gun belt and let it drop to the floor."

She'd planned on sharing the burden for his escape, but Jake had ruined that approach. She doubted the explanations she'd conjured would convince the law if they were caught now. Jake had just implicated himself in a jailbreak *and* a kidnapping. Taken together, those were hanging offenses.

"That's all he said?" The sheriff scrambled to comply, his gaze darting between them. "Seemed like he said more."

"Don't rile him up," Lily declared. "Now kick the gun this way."

The belt skated across the floor and landed near Lily's feet. Stooping, Jake snatched the leather and hung it on a peg next to the door.

He retrieved the pistol from the holster and scoffed. "This is mine."

Sheriff Koepke had the decency to look abashed. "Your pistol was nicer than mine."

Jake kept hold of Lily's useless weapon, and stuck the second loaded gun in the back of his trousers.

Though her revolver was empty of bullets, she was grateful he kept the muzzle pointed away from her. He shoved her behind him, an odd move for a kidnapper, but she doubted the sheriff was taking notes.

"You've lost your mind." Lily fisted her hands in the material of his shirt and rose up on her tiptoes. "This is a terrible idea. You can't go around kidnapping women and children. If it looked like we were in on the jailbreak together, I might have explained things."

He held her back with his outstretched hand. The sinewy muscles on his exposed forearms temporarily distracted her.

"You can't explain a jailbreak." He glanced over his shoulder and pinned her with a hard look. "I'll say it again, that's not how the law works. Just follow along. You began this charade, remember?"

"Yes, but my plan was different. We were together," she grumbled. "I was bearing part of the responsibility."

The sheriff strained forward. "What's that you're saying? What are you two gabbing about?"

"I'm warning this lady," Jake said, "that if she makes any false moves, I'll lock her up and throw away the key."

He accompanied the announcement with a fierce stare that dared her to refute his claim. Though her heartbeat picked up rhythm, his threats were empty. They'd gone this far—there was no turning back. Jake stepped away and Lily immediately missed his warm refuge.

She glanced at the children, who were watching the events unfold as though they were watching a stage performance.

Jake motioned toward them. "Make certain they stay out of trouble."

Gathering them close, she leaned forward. "Don't be frightened. Mr. Jake has everything under control."

"He sure does," Sam declared. "This is just like one of Peter's books come to life."

"Just in case, stay behind me. If anything goes wrong, take care of yourselves and don't worry about me."

Peter straightened. "No can do. A cowboy always looks out for the lady."

"Thank you." Lily dropped a kiss on this knit cap. "You're the bravest cowboy in Frozen Oaks."

Jake tossed a burlap sack over the sheriff's head, and the sheriff yelped. An apple core tumbled over his shoulder and hit the ground with a thud.

Lily tilted her head in question.

Jake shrugged. "He brought me lunch. I didn't finish the apple."

With the youngsters safely tucked by the door for a hasty escape, Lily wrapped her scarf around the sheriff's ears, hoping to muffle the sound further. Once she'd finished, she stepped back to admire her work.

"You're a dreadful hostage." Jake caught her upper arm and placed his lips near her ear. "You could have at least acted a little cowed."

His breath tickled her ear and she shivered. Turning her head brought their faces mere inches apart. Her gaze dipped to his lips. This really wasn't the time or the place, but she found herself imagining him without the whiskers and the long hair. His cheeks were high and chiseled, and the dip in his beard indicated a cleft in his chin.

For all she knew, he might be wretchedly ugly, though she highly doubted the possibility. No one with eyes that beautiful could be completely unattractive. Not that his looks mattered. She was simply making an observation.

Those beautiful coffee-colored eyes narrowed. "Are you listening to me? I was hoping you'd act more like a hostage when the sheriff is watching."

"I'll do no such thing." Focusing once more, she dragged him as far away from the sheriff as she could. "How can you escort us to St. Joseph when you're wanted for kidnapping?"

"At least this way you're safe from some vigilante posse. What was your plan?"

"The sheriff arrested you on false charges. I was breaking you out of jail. We could have explained the whole thing as a mistake on my part. How I couldn't stand to let an innocent man rot in jail."

"You knew the charges were false?" His expression was incredulous. "How?"

"Because you're not a thief. And my idea wasn't the worst. You just had to trust me."

"Well, it's too late now. Besides, there was no guarantee they'd have believed you."

"Yes, but I'd have felt far less guilty if we were both implicated."

Jake lowered his chin and lifted his eyebrows in an expression that could only be described as long-suffering. "I will never, as long as live, understand you."

The sheriff shook his head, trying to disengage the sack. "What's going on? Let me outta here."

"What are we going to do with Koepke?" Jake jerked a thumb over his shoulder. "He'll raise the alarm as soon as we let him go."

"Then lock him in jail for now. Serves him right. He'll know what it feels like to be jailed for a crime he didn't commit."

"Fair enough."

Grasping the sheriff by the shoulder, Jake hauled the struggling man into the vacant cell and shut the door. Lily scurried forward and gave him the key, then retreated once more. Even behind bars she didn't entirely trust the sheriff.

Jake stalked toward her and halted inches away. "The next time you make a plan, I'd like a briefing. If something had gone wrong, there were too many civilians in too small of a space. There was no way to control the situation."

"Civilians?" She frowned. "That's an odd way to refer to us."

For the first time she noted the smooth skin on his forehead. Since he normally wore a hat, she'd never really gotten a close look at his hairline. He was younger than she'd first suspected.

"Innocents. Civilians." Jake reached for his hat. "What does it matter?"

"I know you're still in here." The sheriff struggled to remove his head covering. "You'll never get away with this."

With the sheriff behind bars, Sam and Peter emerged from the shadows. Peter edged closer and jabbed his thumbs in his ears, wiggled his fingers, then stuck out his tongue. Sam joined him and followed suit. Since the sheriff was blind to their antics, they added a merry jig and some silly pantomimes to the routine.

"Stop that nonsense right now." Lily snapped her fingers. "Get back over here this instant."

"What?" The sheriff nearly doubled over in an effort to see. "What's going on out there?"

"Nothing," Jake hollered. "Keep quiet."

He turned and reached for his coat, trapping Lily between his body and the wall. The tension in her chest grew. Something was wrong with her breathing. He was as immovable as an oak, and a myriad of conflicting emotions tumbled insider her. He was an outlaw but she trusted him. He was infuriating and stubborn, yet oddly kind. Her instincts defied reason. The world had gone topsy-turvy from the moment she'd stepped off the stagecoach. She might as well hang on for the duration and hope something made sense later. For the first time in her life, she tossed aside reason.

There was also absolutely no way a man with eyes that gorgeous could be ugly.

"Miss Winter." Jake lowered his voice into something akin to a growl. "I'm going to find someplace safe for you and the boys, then I'll come back and square things here."

Lily tipped back her head. She caught his chin and her teeth slammed together, sending a sharp, stinging pain through her head.

She muttered an apology and caught his gaze.

"You'll be the death of me yet," he mumbled, gently rubbing the spot on her head though his own chin must hurt, as well. "Try and stay out of trouble for the next few minutes. I need a rest."

"Don't worry." His self-mocking grin sent a wash of tenderness through her. "I won't let anything happen to you."

"From here on out, my little protector, I'm in charge. My rules. My plan. My orders. No arguments."

Chapter Six

"We're a team," Lily stated. The wash of tenderness drained away beneath his domineering stance. "My idea was not without merit."

Perhaps making a deal with an outlaw wasn't the most prudent decision. What other choice did she have? She'd simply work around his more overbearing tendencies.

"This isn't a scene from a dime novel," Jake said. For the first time since she'd met him he appeared weary, almost defeated. "Bullets always miss the hero on the page. In real life, guns are lethal and far less discerning."

Her throat tightened. She glanced at Peter and Sam. Peter hastily retracted his tongue.

The children. Jake's admonishment neatly put her in her place. She'd put the children in danger. Part of her *had* been picturing a scene from a dime novel. The other part had been certain Jake would keep them safe. Despite his bluster and rough appearance, she had no doubt he'd protect them. With his life, if necessary.

During the two days she'd been observing Jake, she'd learned a few things about the man. There was something innately kind about him. He held open the door for those exiting behind him. He tipped his hat even when ladies crossed the boardwalk to avoid him. He always smiled at Ida, the server at the hotel restaurant, even when she spilled coffee on his table.

He might play the dangerous gunfighter, but there was an unconscious kindness about him that he couldn't quite camouflage. She doubted he even noticed his telling slips.

Given his fierce scowl, this didn't seem like the time to confess her growing trust. "What next?"

"Let's talk outside. I'm tired of whispering."

"Sam, Peter." Lily jerked her head toward the door. "Outside, please."

Peter placed his hands over his mouth and muffled a giggle. The sheriff had worked free from the scarf around his ears and she hustled the children out the door before he freed himself from the sack.

"For the sheriff's benefit," Lily said, placing her hand on Jake's chest, "don't forget to act like an outlaw."

"I'll do my best." He hoisted his dark eyebrows. "As long as you agree to act like a hostage."

"Agreed."

Jake half led, half dragged her through the door. Once outside, Jake caught Lily's arm and tugged her around the corner of the building.

Sam and Peter had collapsed in a fit of giggles.

"That was fun!" Peter exclaimed.

"Can we still be hostages?" Sam hopped from foot to foot. "I want to still be a hostage."

"Pretend hostages." Lily corrected. "Please pull your hat down over your ears. You'll catch your death."

"It's not that cold. The snow is even starting to melt."

"Be that as it may—" she adjusted the muffler "—you still need to stay bundled."

Jake stowed her useless gun and replaced his pistol in his holster, then strapped the handle into place. "Please don't put yourself or the children in danger again," he said, his voice taking on that exasperated, long-suffering tone again. "It's very distracting."

Peter cocked his thumb in Jake's direction. "I wouldn't complain if I was you, Mr. Jake. At least you're out of jail."

"Yeah." Sam nodded eagerly. "Sounded like Vic was gonna shoot you between the eyes and bury you in a shallow, unmarked grave where the coyotes would dig up your bones and gnaw on them."

"Sam!"

"All right," Sam grumbled. "But I'm siding with Peter. Jail is worse."

Jake braced his hand against the wall and hung his head.

Lily touched his shoulder. "Are you all right? You look ill."

"I'm fine."

"Your voice sounds a bit strangled."

"I'm considering our situation."

"I planned on escaping to the next town where we'd explain the misunderstanding. I hadn't thought much beyond that point." She caught a glimpse of his expression. "You still look ill."

"Just thinking," he said, his voice strained. "You were right about one thing. We should return those boys to Missouri. I've been watching Vic for a while now, and I don't trust anyone within fifty miles of here. We've got no proof he's done anything wrong."

"But—"

"I believe you, don't get me wrong. There's no good reason for Vic to take an interest in those children, which means trouble for all of us."

"If we travel far enough away from Frozen Oaks, maybe we can find someone who'll believe our story." Lily paced, her boots crunching through the snow. "Someone who'll believe that Vic is setting you up, that he's a danger to the children."

A range of emotions passed over his face. Lily had seen hints of compassion in him. She must appeal to that part of the gunfighter. He'd only leave them if he thought he was putting their lives in danger. Which meant she had to clear his name, and quickly.

"We can stay ahead of a posse until Steele City." Jake scratched the back of his neck. "I'm not worried about that. Which means the boys are safe with me for the next few hours. After Steele City, I'm a wanted man who'll put your lives in danger. I'll see that you're out of the sheriff's jurisdiction, then we'll separate."

Exactly what she feared. The moment he'd declared them hostages, she'd known this might happen. "No. I won't do that. I won't risk your hanging for something you didn't do."

"I can take care of myself."

"We can clear your name in St. Joseph." She clung desperately to the idea of keeping them together. As long as they stayed together, she could counter any accusations the sheriff made. "Promise you'll stay with us until then."

There was no way she was implicating him in a kidnapping, but she'd sort out the details later. Right now they simply needed to make the next destination.

"We don't have time to argue," Jake said. "We've only got a few hours until Vic discovers I've escaped.

While I doubt anyone will hear the racket the sheriff is making from this distance, I'd rather not take any chances that someone might wander too near." He lifted his head and adjusted his hat. "Can you ride?"

"Uh-huh." Lily focused on a spot behind his left shoulder. "I'm a passable rider."

Before her mother and brother had died, and before her father had sold the house, they'd kept horses. Benjamin was the better rider. No surprise there. She hadn't ridden in over a decade, and her skills were rusty. None of which she planned on sharing with Jake.

Something in her hesitation must have shown, because his eyes narrowed.

"I need to know that you're telling the truth," he said. "Because we have to leave town. Quickly. The St. Joseph and Western Railroad runs out of Steele City. It's a single line all the way to St. Joseph and runs mostly through Kansas. Once you cross the border, Sheriff Koepke can't follow."

"Legally," Lily added. "We can't assume he won't follow illegally."

"Agreed. If we ride hard, you can make the evening train. They'll be looking for me, not for you or the children. I'll fix the damage on this end."

"How?"

"Let me worry about that." He faced Sam and Peter. "What about you two? Can you ride? Are you up for this? We'll be riding hard."

"Our parents traveled all over the world." Peter's eyes glimmered as though he'd discovered a half-buried skeleton in the woods. "We can ride horses, camels, and Sam even rode an elephant once."

"Excellent." Jake propped his hands on his gun belt

and frowned. "We just have to figure out how to make it to the livery without anyone seeing us."

"No, we don't." Lily lifted one shoulder in a careless shrug. "Who's to say you weren't released from jail properly? Skulking about will only draw attention to you. If we walk with conviction, no one will pay us any mind."

That took him aback. As he considered her suggestion, a tiny thrill of victory zipped through her.

"You're right," he said. "The only person I need to avoid is Vic, possibly Regina. You three are in the clear. As long as no one sees us together, and no one notices us leaving town, we're past the worst."

"I am right." Her chest swelled. For once she wasn't foolish, naive Lily. "The children and I packed and hid our belongings at Emil's barbershop. We'll collect our bags and meet you at the livery."

"Remember, if anything goes wrong, you were my hostages. Just stick to that story."

"I will."

She wouldn't. But he was correct about one thing— this was no time for an argument. "We'll meet you at the livery in twenty minutes. Don't forget—walk with conviction."

Jake waited until they were out of sight and reentered the jail. They were safe for the moment, of that he was certain. Lily had cleverly played along with Vic's announcement, which meant he was expecting her to leave on the evening stage. Vic was too arrogant to assume anything else.

Jake shut the door behind him and winced. Sheriff Koepke hollered and banged on the bars with a chair left in the cell. He caught sight of Jake and went still.

Jake crossed his arms over his chest. "You and I need to talk."

"About what?" The sheriff glanced at him askance. "Where is the girl and them two boys?"

"Not your concern."

The sheriff lowered his chair and plopped onto the wooden seat. "What do you want?"

"Where is Emil? Is he dead?"

"I don't know. But I don't think so."

"Why not?"

"Because Vic is real jumpy."

"Then the rumors are true." Jake searched his memory for all the crumbs of gossip he'd collected over the past two weeks. "How much did he lose to Emil in the last poker game?"

"The hotel for certain."

Jake blew out a low whistle. "He bet the hotel?"

"Yeah. And Regina is hopping mad. He promised her that after they were married, the hotel was hers. She already acts like she owns the place. Did you see what she did in the parlor? I never seen so much fabric. Looks like my grandmother's sewing room."

"Anything else?"

The sheriff removed a slender cigar from his breast pocket along with a box of matches. "Money."

"How much?"

"I don't know."

Jake leaned against the sheriff's desk, stretched out his legs, and crossed his ankles. "What about the stolen guns?"

"What guns?" The sheriff appeared genuinely surprised. "I don't know anything about any stolen guns."

That was interesting. Apparently the sheriff wasn't

privy to all Vic's schemes. Keeping the sheriff ignorant of his most nefarious moves was probably a wise move.

"Vic isn't earning all his money at the lumberyard," Jake said. "Surely you know that."

"He does all right." The sheriff puffed his cigar to life. "He can lose a little money in a poker game now and again. Don't make him no never mind."

The sheriff removed his cigar from his mouth and studied the tip. Jake grimaced.

Keeping the sheriff in the dark was more than wise—the decision was genius. "There's no lumber in that yard, or hadn't you noticed?"

"I guess, now that you mention it." The sheriff exhaled a billow of smoke. "Business has been slow. Things were a lot better before Steele City got the St. Joseph line. The customers have dried up since then."

The railroad depot had been finished for over a year. Enough time for Vic to become desperate. "Your boss picked the wrong town to occupy."

"He didn't think that in the beginning. He paid that fellow a lot of money to make Frozen Oaks the last stop on the line. Steele City got the depot instead. The guy from the railroad was named Steele. They named the town after him. I guess that meant more than a bribe alone."

"Vic should have changed the name." Jake snorted. "Frozen Oaks is a silly name for a town."

"You got that right." The sheriff chuckled. "I wouldn't mention it to Vic, though. He's still sore."

"I have other business with Vic." Leaning back, Jake braced his knuckles behind him on the desk and considered what he'd learned. "You must know something about what's going on in this town."

"I get paid to look the other way."

"Sometimes a man can't help but see things, even if he's not supposed to."

"I already told you what I know. Vic lost the deed to the hotel, and Regina is spitting mad. She gets visitors all the time. Likes to show off."

Which explained Vic's lapse into housebreaking. He was searching for the hotel deed. Another reason to believe Emil was still alive and had gone into hiding. Which was good for Emil and disastrous for his grandchildren.

The full implication sent a flush of pure, hot rage through Jake. That old fool had gone into hiding and left his grandchildren like lambs to slaughter. Lily and the Tyler children never had a chance. She'd walked right into a trap.

He'd been too focused on Vic and the guns, and he'd missed the real crime unfolding. "Vic was looking to recoup his losses. That's why he talked you into granting him guardianship?"

"Yeah. But you didn't hear that from me. You got no proof of nothing. Everything is on the up and up. Regina read a bunch of legal stuff in one of them law books. She got enough fancy-sounding words to make the paperwork sound legitimate. Between you and me, I think she's the smarter of them two."

"I've heard enough." Jake pushed off from the desk. "Thank you for your time, Sheriff."

"Wait a second, ain't you letting me out?"

"Can't do that. I need a head start. It's two days to Omaha." Jake doubted even the sheriff was dumb enough to take the bait, but he might as well try a little misinformation. He snatched the newspaper and slid it through the bars. "A little reading material while you're waiting."

The sheriff's furious hollering followed him out the door.

Once outside, he tucked his hair inside his coat and turned up his collar, then set his hat low on his forehead. Head bent, his hands stuffed in his pockets, he stepped onto the boardwalk. As long as he stayed clear of Vic and Regina, he could keep an eye on Lily and the boys.

He crossed the street and leaned against the corner of the hotel, then waited. He didn't have to wait long. Lily and the boys exited the barbershop and made their way down the stairs.

As he pushed off to follow, the door swung open beside him. He slipped around the corner and waited. After the footsteps faded, he stepped into sight once more.

Regina.

Even from the back he recognized her. No one else in town wore that shade of emerald. Especially not around Frozen Oaks. Regina might be smarter than Vic, but her taste in men left something to be desired. Jake would never understand what she saw in him.

On a hunch, Jake crossed the street and followed her. She ducked into the telegraph office and emerged only a moment later, stuffing a sheaf of telegrams into the fur muff she carried. Once she cleared the doorway, Jake slipped inside and let his eyes adjust.

The telegraph operator was a nondescript middle-aged woman with a dishwater-blond topknot and a plain gray dress. She glanced up from her work.

"May I help you, sir?" she asked.

"You haven't gotten any dispatches from Emil Tyler, have you?"

"The name doesn't sound familiar." The woman set

down her quill and knocked over her ink well in the process. "Oh, dear me. Look at that."

She hastily mopped up the mess, darkening her white handkerchief an indigo blue.

"Emil Tyler." Jake concealed his impatience. "Owns the barbershop."

"No. I can't say that I've had any dispatches from someone by that name. 'Course, I'm not the only one who works here. You could ask one of the other ladies." She pinched the soaked rag between her thumb and index finger and dropped the mess in the wastebasket. "We're all ladies running the telegraph machines. Western Union figures we're cheaper than men. They're right, you know."

Not in the mood for small talk, Jake gave a curt nod. "Thanks."

He stepped onto the boardwalk and froze.

Regina had cornered Lily and the boys.

Chapter Seven

With Sam and Peter eagerly trailing behind her, the three of them had made their way to the barbershop unimpeded. The town was quiet, the boardwalk deserted for the noon meal. Lily gathered their bags and paused. A stack of correspondence sat on a side table. On impulse, she stuffed the mail into her bag. While the chances of discovering a clue were slim, they were running out of possibilities.

"All right." She faced the children. They each carried a single small bag. "How are the two of you holding up?"

"We're doing great."

"This is neat."

Lily sighed. At least their enthusiastic embracing of the situation was better than fear.

She looked them up and down. They'd dressed in double layers with their hats pulled low over their ears and yards of knitted scarves wrapped around their necks. The weather was cold, but not frigid, and there was barely a breeze stirring the air. As long as she kept a close eye on them, they shouldn't come to any harm.

"Stop worrying," Sam said.

"I'm not."

"You're chewing on your lip and frowning."

Lily touched her cheek. "I guess I am worrying. Just a little. I was hired to keep the two of you safe, and I've involved you in a jailbreak and a cross-country escape on horseback. Believe me, if I thought there was another way, I'd never put you two through this ordeal. I don't trust Vic Skaar. I still think we have a chance of finding your grandfather. I'm not giving up just yet. I will never do anything unless I truly believe my actions are in your best interest. I promise."

Sam grew serious. "Kids aren't as dumb as adults think. For the first few months after our parents died, we did nothing but travel. We traveled across Africa, we traveled across the ocean, we traveled across America. The whole time I felt like a burden. I never felt like that before. I never understood what it was like when nobody wanted you. For the past week you've been fussing over us. I never thought I'd miss my mom fussing over me, but I do. She was trying to show us she cared. That's how I know you care. You just keep fussing over us, okay? And we'll keep pretending like we're annoyed."

"I will. I promise." She drew them both into a hug. "Your parents must have been very special people, because they raised two very special children."

Peter pulled back. "We'd best get going or Mr. Jake will be champing at the bit."

She stuck out her hand. "All in."

Peter set his hand over hers, and Sam followed suit. "All in!" they shouted in unison.

Lily opened the door and searched the empty street. "It's as quiet as a Sunday morning during church service."

Halfway down the stairs, she paused. A movement

caught her attention and she glanced at the hotel across the street.

"What is it, Miss Lily?" Sam asked.

"Nothing." She shrugged. Must have been a trick of the light. "We'd best not dawdle."

Peter paused before the mercantile window and Lily recalled the money from Vic in her reticule. She ushered them inside.

"Choose quickly," she said. "Something small. Remember, we're traveling light."

They both purchased a bag of marbles. Outside once more, Lily breathed a sigh of relief. Thus far, everything was going neatly according to plan. A few more steps and they'd be safely tucked inside the livery. She'd nearly reached the door when a familiar voice called out her name.

"Hand me your bags." Lily halted and glanced askance at Sam. "Whatever happens, let me do all the talking."

There was no reason to panic. Absolutely no reason at all. Willing her pulse to slow, she took a deep, steadying breath. Just an ordinary day in Frozen Oaks.

Turning slowly, she faced Regina. In deference to the cold, Regina wore an emerald cape lined with dark, supple fur. The outfit featured a matching hat and muff in the same luxurious materials. The ensemble seemed rather extravagant for an afternoon in Frozen Oaks. Lily gave a mental shrug. Then again, almost everything Regina did appeared a touch extravagant.

"Lily, how fortunate I ran into you," Regina said.

"Isn't it?" They hadn't run into each other at all. Regina had practically chased them down. "Your cape is beautiful."

"I do miss the amenities available in the city." Regina touched the fur on her collar. "A few luxuries make town living bearable."

"Yes, well, I…you… Love the color," Lily blurted at last. Oh, dear. She sounded like a babbling idiot. There was absolutely no reason for this nervous twittering. There was nothing odd in strolling around town. What was the use of walking with conviction if she didn't talk with a little conviction, as well?

Lily spread her hands in an encompassing gesture. "Green is your color."

As conviction went, her conversation was lacking.

"Thank you." Regina puckered her brow. "That shade of brown is definitely not your color. You should wear pink. Nothing too bright. Something subtle and pastel."

"Pink." Lily stifled a grimace. She loathed pale pink. "Yes. I'll remember your advice the next time I purchase a dress."

Definitely not a lie. Recalling a piece of advice did not mean she intended to take the guidance.

Regina flicked a glance at Sam and Peter. "Vic told me all about how the sheriff has appointed him guardian. You must be so relieved. Vic was a close friend to Emil. I'm sure it's what he would have wanted. Although I sincerely hope Vic doesn't expect me to get involved. You know how I feel about children. Better to be seen than heard and all that. I'm certain Emil will make an appearance soon enough. Anyway, are you leaving today? Looks like you're all packed and ready to go."

"Just taking my bags to the livery."

"It's a little early for the stagecoach."

"I like to be prepared."

"Well, I suppose in your line of work, you're used to packing up. Given Mrs. Hollingsworth's temperament, I'm sure you don't want to be away from home for long." Regina pulled her hand from her muff and wiggled her gloved fingers. "Maybe we'll run into each other again someday."

"Maybe."

Lily heaved a sigh and turned.

Sam tugged on her sleeve. "That was a close one."

"Too close," Lily said. "Let's walk past the livery, then circle around back."

Walking with as much conviction as she could muster, they made their way to the end of the block, then walked to the back of the building. Lily slipped inside first and held her index finger over her lips for silence, then motioned them forward.

An almost imperceptible sound came from behind her. Something touched her shoulder and she shrieked. "Jake!"

A large hand came over her mouth and solid wall of male muscle pressed against her back.

"Yes," he said. "It's me. Probably we shouldn't alert the whole town."

He released his hold and stepped back.

Lily whipped around. "Then don't sneak up on me."

She pressed a hand over her pounding heart. She shouldn't be peevish, but skulking about had made her jumpy. Not to mention, for such a large man he could move with remarkable stealth.

"What did Regina have to say?" Jake asked.

Lily reared back. "How did you know Regina talked with us?"

"I was keeping watch." He scratched his forehead and glanced away. "Just in case Koepke sounded the alarm."

There it was again. That innate sense of protectiveness. More and more she pondered what had driven him into living as a gunfighter. Perhaps she'd been reading too many of Peter's novels, but something about Jake didn't fit her preconceived notions. His speech was too refined, and his conversation too intelligent.

"Regina wanted to say goodbye," Lily said. "But I had the feeling she was making sure I was leaving town."

"I'm not surprised. She doesn't like the competition for Vic's attention. Single, pretty women don't last very long in this town. Vic has a wandering eye, and Regina ensures he doesn't have any temptation."

A spark of pure feminine pride jolted through Lily. He'd called her pretty. And not in that calculated way the men staying at the boardinghouse had said it. The sly nod and wink as they tested the waters. They tossed around premeditated flattery in the hopes of scoring an extra slice of pie at dinner or a walk in the moonlight.

Jake's compliment had been haphazard and off the cuff. There was an unabashed sincerity in his delivery.

Peter rubbed his hands together. "What's the plan? We're wasting time."

"I've arranged for four horses," Jake said. "Sam and I will ride the two horses from the livery. Lily and Peter can ride my horses. They're better trained and better suited for inexperienced riders."

"I'm experienced." Peter huffed.

"Yes, you are," Jake conceded. "You can help look out for Lily."

She might have protested the insult but Peter puffed up again and crossed his arms over his chest. He was so proud to be called out for the task, she couldn't disappoint him.

"Thank you, Peter," she said. "You'll be my special helper."

"Don't worry about anything, Miss Lily. I'll watch out for you."

"Excellent," Jake said. "Let's put this plan in motion."

The three of them appeared to know exactly what to do. While they fetched saddles, bridles and horses, Lily paced the corridor between the stalls in the livery.

There was absolutely nothing sensible about this plan. The least sensible part of the whole crazy mess was that she'd been an integral part in the proposed strategy. If someone had told her a week ago she'd be on the run from the law with a hired gun, she'd have accused them of reading too many penny dreadfuls.

The plan was much more like something her brother, Benjamin, might have conjured. Anticipation stirred in her chest. Was this how Benjamin had felt before one of his adventures? For the first time in her life she felt a kinship with him. The thought of breaking a rule used to always leave her horrified. This time a curious sense of expectation filled her. Perhaps there was bit of her father's blood in her after all.

The stall door slid open and Lily jumped, then calmed when she realized Jake had returned.

"The livery owner owes me a favor," Jake said. "He doesn't know where we're going, and he's agreed to look the other way when we leave. We've caught a fortunate break." He waved them into the center corridor and indicated three stalls. "Those two horses are mine. The other two belong to the livery."

"How will we return the horses?"

"I'll send word when we reach Steele City. He can retrieve them there. He's been well compensated for any trouble we might cause. We'll be long gone by the time anyone traces the horses."

"As long as we're not breaking any laws."

"Says the woman who planned a jailbreak."

"That was different!"

Jake, Sam and Peter finished saddling and bridling the animals while Lily chewed on the ragged edge of her thumbnail and fretted. The initial excitement of the escape had worn off, replaced by the worry over her limited horsemanship skills. She didn't have to prove her aptitude, she simply had to stay mounted until the next town. This wasn't a dressage show on a Saturday afternoon. There were no winners and no ribbons.

As Sam tightened up the girth, Lily tugged on Peter's sleeve and pulled him aside. "Do you have any pointers? Any tips on riding?"

Peter looked her up and down. "Hang on tight and don't look down."

"Anything more? Anything less ominous and terrifying?"

"Your horse will follow the others. Keep the reins slack and just follow the rest of us." He patted her shoulder. "We'll keep an eye out for you. You'll be fine."

Wonderful. She was begging advice from an eight-year-old. What was next?

Jake assembled the horses and Lily and her charges stared at him in anticipation.

"We've got an hour's ride, maybe an hour and a half. We're taking a well-traveled shortcut along a creek bed, but we'll still encounter some rough terrain. Follow my lead. If you get into trouble, ask for help." He finished that last sentence with a pointed gaze at Lily. "Once we reach Steele City, I'll take care of the horses. Lily will buy the three of you train tickets, and I'll keep watch. If you're approached, be honest. Say I used you to escape from jail, and then I let you go. It's plausible enough.

Even if Vic's influence reaches beyond Frozen Oaks, your story is rock solid."

"But what about you?" Lily demanded. "What will happen to you?"

"I'm a wanted man, remember? I'm a kidnapper. We can't be seen traveling together until I clear my name."

Her stomach plummeted.

"Whatever happens, Miss Lily," Sam said, "we'll look out for each other. You just keep fussing."

"I will." Once again she marveled at the children Mr. and Mrs. Tyler had raised. "Don't forget to tuck your sleeves into your gloves or the wind will chap your wrists."

Sam accepted the reins to a horse, and his brother followed him to a wooden block in the center of the paddock.

Lily faced the bay gelding she'd been assigned. She knew it was a bay gelding because Jake had told her so when he'd handed her the horse's reins.

"What's his name?" she asked.

Jake ran one hand down the horse's muzzle. "Paris."

"Very romantic."

"After the town."

"In France?"

He grinned. "In Texas."

Peter had already mounted and he sidled his horse nearer. "Did you kill your first man in Paris, Texas? Is that why you named your horse after the town?"

"No." Jake chuckled. "I named him after the town where I was born."

Lily couldn't contain her shock. Certainly he'd been born someplace. He hadn't been dropped in a blanket from the beak of a stork. He had a mother and father. He might even have brothers and sisters.

The horse bumped against Jake's sleeve in an affectionate gesture. There was a clear respect between animal and man. Another piece of his curious character. She never trusted people who abused animals. Jake clearly took good care of his horses.

With Sam and Peter astride their horses, Lily took her turn at the mounting block. She could do this. She'd done this before. Too bad her horse back home had been much, much smaller. She'd inherited Benjamin's pony when he'd outgrown the animal. That pony had been petite and stubborn. No matter how hard she kicked, she'd never gotten the animal to move any faster than a bumpy canter.

Aware that the three of them were watching, she approached the mounting block with conviction. That was where her false bravado ended. Her movements ungainly and awkward, she stuck her foot in the stirrup and pushed off. After two more attempts, Jake grasped her around the waist and tossed her into the saddle.

She adjusted her skirts over her legs.

Jake rested his hand on her ankle. "Are you ready for this?"

"Absolutely."

"You're certain?"

"Yes. Don't worry. You should be worrying about the children instead of fussing over me."

The realization brought her up short. He was fussing with her.

Jake gave her ankle a squeeze. "You're quite a woman, Lily Winter."

"I'm a very ordinary woman."

"Not to me."

He released his hold but his touch lingered. She loosely grasped the reins and tossed her head. There was no way she was leaving Sam and Peter to the mercy of Vic Skaar. Even if that meant risking her neck on this wild ride across the country.

She glanced down and her stomach heaved. The distance to the ground seemed to have doubled. She stared straight ahead and concentrated on the cottonwoods in the distance. The horse shifted and she flinched. The muscles in her back and shoulders tensed and she unconsciously tightened the slack. Well trained, her horse shifted backward. Lily loosened the reins.

If only she'd been an excellent rider like Benjamin. Then again, her brother had been fearless. She glowered at her gloved hands fisted over her reins. Something of her brother's talent must have been transferred to her. They had the same parents. It didn't seem fair that she hadn't even gained a modicum of his abilities.

Jake led his horse before them as though he was a general mustering his troops. "I'll lead. The boys in the middle. Lily will take the end. The trail we're following is a shortcut used by plenty of other folks, and the path is well cleared. The temperature is a different story. I want your scarves wrapped around your faces, and your ears covered. I've got an extra jacket and hat for you, Lily."

He tossed up a canvas coat. She shrugged into the arms, then reached for the hat. The brim fell over her eyes. She pushed it back and secured the strings beneath her chin, grateful for the extra warmth. The coat lent her the feel of armor. She was protected against the cold—against harm. Jake's comforting scent enveloped her, that curious mixture of leather, wool and gunpowder. She'd be fearless like her brother.

Jake considered them for a long moment, and she feared he was changing his mind. After an eternity, he held up his fisted hand. "This motion means we're stopping. If you have any problems, if you're cold, if you're tired, if you're having trouble with your mount, raise the signal. Understood?"

"Understood," the three repeated in unison.

"No one has set up the alarm, which means, worst case, we've got two hours before they can give chase. I've weighed all the options, and the boys are safer in Steele City than here."

Lily frowned. More often than not, Jake had the bearing of a soldier rather than a gunfighter. Had he fought in one of the Indian skirmishes? According to the newspapers, there were still battles being fought in the Oklahoma Territory.

Perhaps he'd been a soldier for hire. She'd heard the army wasn't above hiring extra muscle when dealing with an Indian uprising. Nothing terrified settlers more than the thought of an attack.

Even as she pondered this strange anomaly in Jake, he opened the gate and led them all from the corral. Her stomach pitched and she jerked in the saddle. When Jake glanced her way, she forced her hips to relax.

Peter twisted in his saddle and gave her the thumbs-up.

She returned his gesture with a weak smile.

Her rolling gait must have passed as horsemanship, because Jake mounted, appearing satisfied with her abilities.

He tucked his bandanna around his neck, tightened his hat over his ears and kicked his horse into a trot.

Sam and Peter followed suit.

Lily's horse, as the boys had predicted, trotted along after them. With each step her teeth clattered together and her head ached. Just when she thought her brains would rattle out of her head, Jake urged his mount into a canter.

Lily's shriek was muffled by the scarf wrapped around her neck. Her heart leapt into her throat and she leaned forward, grasping a handful of mane hair along with the saddle horn. The sudden wind in her face brought tears to her eyes.

The first twenty minutes passed in pure agony. She clenched her teeth together until her jaw ached. Her backside grew numb and her legs throbbed. Ahead of her, Sam and Peter rode beside each other, shouting encouragement, easily swaying in the saddle. Jake appeared as though he was a part of the horse. He bent close over the animal's neck and the two moved as one.

Her aching muscles cramped and she soon lost the feeling in her fingers. Tears streamed down her face. Mostly from the sharp wind, but not without a little misery mixed in.

The second twenty minutes she found something of an awkward rhythm. Sheer exhaustion had sapped all the fight from her muscles, as though her body was being dragged along unwittingly.

After a particularly harrowing journey down a deep gully and back up the other side, with her horse slipping and lunging over the snow-packed bank, Jake slowed. He pivoted in the saddle, one fisted hand on his knee.

"Everyone all right?" he called. "Do we need to rest?"

"Not us," Sam and Peter shouted in enthusiastic unison.

The little beasts. Lily tugged her muffler higher, the knitted threads stiff with her frozen tears. They appeared as though the last forty minutes of riding had invigorated them. She threw back her shoulders and shook her head, not trusting her voice.

Jake studied them each in turn before giving a sharp nod, then reined his horse around.

They kicked into a canter once more, jarring her bones into a clatter of agony. For a moment she considered flinging herself from the saddle and ending the misery. The fall would be brutal, but with so many other bumps and bruises, the pain would hardly be noticeable.

No.

She wouldn't be the weakest person in the group. She wouldn't hold them back. Gritting her teeth, she leaned forward and ignored the ache in her legs and the fog enveloping her brain.

Not much longer.

She'd endure.

She was made of sterner stuff.

At least Jake had been correct about the terrain. The dry creek bed was well traveled. The leafless cotton trees offered a web of branches overhead. The sky was overcast once more, the day a hazy shade of soot. A blanket of snow covered every surface for as far as the eye could see.

A flock of turkeys, startled by Jake's horse, scattered across the path. Sam and Peter split apart. Peter's horse narrowly missed trampling a large gobbler. Feathers flailing, the gobbler took off in awkward flight and smacked into the muzzle of Lily's horse.

The animal bayed and pitched, rearing on its hind legs, using its forelegs and sharp hooves to defend itself from the unexpected attack.

Lily shrieked.

She frantically clutched at the saddle horn but the past forty minutes had sapped her strength. Her feet slid from the stirrups and she bumped over the cantle. The next instant she was tumbling through the air.

She landed on her backside, and the blow knocked all the air from her lungs. The frightened gobbler clawed over her in its frantic escape, scratching her leg.

She desperately clutched at her throat. Something was wrong. She gasped for breath but her lungs were empty, useless. The sky overhead grew dim. She was going to die on this miserable trail after all.

Chapter Eight

Jake whipped around. Sam and Peter had maintained their seats, darting in opposite directions around the frightened turkeys. He caught sight of Lily's rearing horse and a wild anguish surged through him.

She plummeted backward. Limbs flailing, she landed flat on her backside. The horse danced away from the chaos. Feathers flying, the turkeys scattered off the trail. In three short strides Jake was by her side.

Hastily dismounting, he knelt over her. She'd clearly gotten the wind knocked out of her. Her eyes were wide and frightened and she was gasping for air. Her hands clawed at her throat.

Quelling his own panic, he rested his hand on her chest. "It's all right, Lily. Calm down. Take a big deep breath. The biggest breath you've taken."

She reached for him, clutching his wrist. The two brothers leapt from their horses and crowded around.

Jake glanced up. "Let's give her some space. She needs some air."

"That happened to me once," Sam said. "Felt like I was gonna die."

Lily's eyes widened in frantic panic.

"Shut up." Peter punched his brother's shoulder. "You're scaring her."

Jake lifted her head onto his bent knee and rubbed her chest in soothing circles. "Breathe. Everything is all right. You're fine. That's it."

Gasping and wheezing, she sucked in great gulps of air. Utterly helpless to ease her suffering, he smoothed her hair and murmured soothing words. The deathly pallor of her face was gradually suffused with bright red color. Several moments later she coughed and struggled to sit upright. Jake supported her back and helped her into a sitting position.

She collapsed against his chest and took several heaving breaths. "I felt as though I was suffocating."

"You got the wind knocked out of you."

Without being asked, the brothers had gathered all the horses and stood a distance away. Jake studied the hazy edge of the horizon. They were still a good twenty minutes away from Steele City. He bit the tip of his glove and tugged it free, then gently brushed the backs of his knuckles along Lily's icy cheeks.

Her eyelashes glistened with tears. He reached between their bodies and unbuttoned his coat, then tucked her deeper into his warmth.

She shivered and turned her head into his chest. A curious tenderness took hold of him. Her head rested in the hollow below his neck, and she wrapped her arms around his waist. She fit against him as though they were meant to be together.

"I'm better now," she said, her voice weak. "I can ride."

"I'll be the judge of that. We'll wait here. I'll build a fire and get you warm, then we'll make our way into town."

"We'll miss our train." Her teeth chattered. "I'm not quitting now."

He hadn't experienced that sort of fear since the day his mother had been shot. He'd buried all his tender feelings in an icy grave somewhere near the vicinity of his heart. Seeing Lily hit the frozen ground had ignited a fire, thawing the protective barriers.

The fear shattered him. He needed that protection. He needed that distance. When emotions were involved, people made mistakes.

He was too close. He'd become too involved, and there was no escaping. There was nothing he could do while they were sitting out in the open. They wouldn't be safe until they were off the trail and in town. Until then, he ran the risk of being run down by a posse.

"You'll catch the next train," he said.

She shivered. "My hands are numb."

"Take off your gloves. They'll warm faster."

The next instant she had her icy fingers pressed between the layers of his sheepskin lining and canvas shirt.

He hissed. "We should have stopped earlier. You're freezing."

"I'm fine. Don't make such a fuss."

He hugged her tighter, infusing her with his warmth, and she burrowed closer.

When he'd stopped earlier, she'd seemed all right. Had he been wrong about the children, as well?

"Sam, Peter," he called. "Let me check your hands."

The two exchanged a glance, looking at him as though he'd lost his mind. They dutifully held out their mittened fingers.

"You're fussing, aren't you?" Peter said. "You're as

bad as Lily. I didn't think I'd be fussed over while I was riding with an outlaw."

Sam and Peter dropped down on either side of him.

Peter held out his hand. "Look. I'm fit as a fiddle. Probably Lily is just cold because of how she gets sick. You know, like on trains and stuff."

"You can't get sick riding a horse," Sam said. "That's just stupid."

Keeping one hand hooked around Lily, Jake pressed the backs of his knuckles against each of their cheeks. They weren't nearly as chilled as the woman he held in his arms.

"Gather some firewood."

"Won't someone see the smoke?"

Jake glanced at Lily. "Plenty of people build fires this time of year. If I'm caught, I'm caught. We'll sort out the details later."

"We'll tie up the horses." Sam gave his brother's shoulder a nudge. "There's plenty of brush by the stream."

Without fully realizing what he was doing, Jake rocked Lily in his arms, rubbing her back and willing heat into her chilled bones.

"Why do you trust me?" he asked.

"Hmm," she mumbled against his chest. "What was that?"

"Why do you trust me? You shouldn't, you know."

"You're a good man. You can't help yourself. You open doors for ladies. You pick up after yourself. You put yourself in danger to save us."

He loosened his grip.

She twisted sideways. "I'm sorry. Did I say something wrong?"

"Nothing."

Nothing except he'd better fix his act before he tried another clandestine case. He was giving too much away without even realizing his mistakes. Lily's exaggerated perception had caught several of his quirks. What else was he inadvertently revealing?

With quick efficiency, Sam and Peter built a fire. They stacked the larger kindling in a pyramid, and stuffed leaves and brush at the base. Their time with their missionary parents had served them well. Jake directed them to the matches in his saddlebag. They'd proved they were adept enough to handle them.

Sam scratched the flint and the fire sparked into life. An instant later, heat from the fire enveloped them. Sam and Peter sat cross-legged, their hands stretched toward the flames.

Lily sighed. "That feels positively delightful."

He sat back and held her away from him. "How are you otherwise? Is anything hurt? Have you broken any bones?"

"I'm perfectly healthy." She gathered the collar of his borrowed coat around her throat. "If I ever see that turkey again, I'll roast him for dinner."

Her color had returned and her eyes sparkled. She stood and crossed to the horses. He focused his vision, searching for any sign she'd been injured. She dug something out of her saddlebag and returned. There must have been a better way. He should never have led a bunch of greenhorns on such a dangerous ride.

She flopped down beside him once more. "You didn't have any other choice."

"What?"

"I know what you're thinking." Leaning to one side, Lily tilted her head and met his gaze. "You're blaming yourself. You might as well quit beating yourself up.

What other choice did we have? If we had stayed, we'd have handed over the custody of Sam and Peter to Vic. I'd rather freeze to death than let them suffer that fate."

"There must have been a less dangerous way."

"Then you would have thought of it." She scooted nearer. "I can say all the right words, but they're just words. I can't make you believe them."

Jake cupped the back of her neck and tucked her against his side. "I've never met anyone like you, Miss Winter."

"Really? Must I keep reminding you that I'm quite ordinary? You, on the other hand, are the strangest outlaw I've ever met."

"How many outlaws have you met, Lily Winter?"

"Just you."

"Then there's no way to know if I'm strange or not."

Her muffled laughter puffed against the skin at his throat. "You have an answer for everything, don't you?"

"Not everything."

Nothing in his career had prepared him for this encounter. Over the years he'd hardened himself to the anguish of others. He'd had to. There were victims. Of course there were victims. All crimes had consequences. He knew that better than anyone. Despite that, or perhaps because of his unique insight, he'd always remained aloof from the suffering.

"We should go." Lily rubbed her ear against his shoulder. "We can't let them capture you. We can still make St. Joseph, even if we miss the train tonight."

"I've gotten out of tighter scrapes," he said. "I'll get out of his one."

"You were in Frozen Oaks because of Vic, weren't you?"

"What makes you think that?"

"You're a gun for hire. He's the only man in Frozen Oaks with enough money to care."

"You missed your calling." Jake stared into the crackling flames. "You should have been a detective."

"Did he hire you for something?"

"No."

All the work he'd done had been for nothing. He'd have to start the case over from scratch. Returning was out of the question.

He'd always prided himself on his honor. Everything he'd done up until this point had been little more than playacting. The danger had always been his and his alone.

Not anymore.

He was more danger to them with his current identity. There was no way of shedding his role until he contacted his superior. There wasn't anyone in Steele City he trusted.

Though the sky was overcast, the muted light showed the weary circles beneath Lily's eyes. Exhaustion was catching up with her, sapping her strength. She wasn't the only one adept at reading the clues. He took careful note of the little telltale signs—the slight drooping at the edge of her mouth, the increasing pallor of her porcelain skin.

The longer he lingered between Steele City and Frozen Oaks, the more likely it was he'd be captured. He'd made a fool of the sheriff, and the man wasn't likely to forgive and forget. If Jake's fortunes held, he'd be able to contact the US Marshals before they hanged him for kidnapping and the jailbreak. If his fortune didn't hold, well, he had no one to blame but himself.

"We've wasted enough time." Lily struggled away

from his embrace. "We don't have much longer before the sheriff is sprung. We all need a good meal."

She made to push off and winced, then cradled her arm against her side.

"What is it?" Her face had taken on a pallor that sent Jake's stomach clenching. "You've been hurt."

"It's nothing."

When he reached for her arm, she flinched away.

"Show me."

"No."

"Show me or I'll fire this gun into the air and alert everyone from Steele City to St. Joseph of our location."

"You wouldn't."

He reached for his holster.

"Stop!" she called. "You don't play fair."

"That'll teach you to hitch your wagon to an outlaw."

She reluctantly extended her hand. "It isn't broken."

"I'll see for myself."

He examined the fragile bones of her wrist. A darkening purple bruise marred her pale skin.

"Just as I thought," he said. "You've sprained your wrist. You can barely ride with two hands, let alone one."

"I said that I was fine." She scrambled upright and swayed on her feet. "I can ride."

He leapt beside her and steadied her. "You're exhausted. You're unsteady on your feet."

"I'm not giving up. How much farther?"

"Lily, I'm a grown man. I can make my own decisions. We're resting until I'm certain you can make the rest of the trip."

"I'm a grown woman, and I can make my own decisions, as well. I say we're moving forward."

"You can't ride with a sprained wrist. End of discussion."

The two brothers had followed the volley of words between them, their heads turning in unison. Sam raised his hand as though they were in school and he was requesting a turn.

"Yes, Sam." Jake sighed. "What is it?"

"Why don't you and Lily ride together the rest of the way?"

Lily perked up. "I like that idea."

"She doesn't weigh very much," Sam continued. "Her horse is still fresh. We can't make the same speed, but we can come close."

"Yes," Lily said, grasping his lapels. "Please."

The brothers crowded around him and hopped up and down. "Please."

"Easy there." Jake held up his hands. "I told you, I have to think of the safety of everyone in this group."

"Including your own," Lily implored. "You said it yourself. A posse is liable to shoot first and ask questions later. We'll need to be off this trail and in town before those children are safe."

The longer he stayed out in the open, the more likely his capture. Justice was swift and resolute in this part of the country. If caught, there was little chance of him escaping a possible hanging. By the time word reached his commander back in Washington, he'd be wearing a stone hat in the lonely corner of the cemetery.

Lily took his hands. He hadn't replaced his glove, and she'd removed one of hers. The warmth of her hand was comforting.

She gazed up at him, her eyes pleading. "I didn't mean to trap you in this position. I saw a way to break you out of jail, and I seized the opportunity. Sam and

Peter weren't safe in Frozen Oaks. Until we find their grandfather, you and I are all they have."

She was forthright, brave and not a little headstrong. A trait that both annoyed and enthralled him. How had her staunch, unflagging belief in the goodness of others survived? She wasn't sheltered or naive. He didn't doubt she'd seen tragedy in her life. Her gaze was shrewd, her disposition fearless. She'd known loss. The more he knew of her, the more curious he became about the forces that had shaped her.

"Your plan was clever and unexpected," he said. "If you ever decide on a life of crime, promise you'll look me up."

"Be careful who you challenge."

"Now you're using my words against me."

"I never promised to fight fair."

"You'll turn up safe and sound in St. Joseph," Jake said. She also had an overdeveloped sense of responsibility. "Sheriff Koepke had no reason to throw me in jail. He might even keep the jailbreak a secret. Jailbreaks are bad for reelection."

He didn't believe his own words, but it was a small fib, and he figured he'd be forgiven since his intentions were good.

"Which means we have to reach Steele City and catch the train. That gives you time to put distance between you and the sheriff. Just until the search quiets." She glanced away. "I'm sorry about the trouble I caused you. When I first came to town, I made a lot of incorrect assumptions. I didn't know where to turn, and I believed the wrong people."

"You were fed a bunch of lies from people you thought you could trust. You're a person who looks for the good in others. That's a fine trait. You're a kind human being who expects the best out of people."

He considered telling her his true identity and discarded the idea just as quickly. He'd waited too long. She'd never believe him. He had no proof and no way to back up his claim.

The wind picked up, tugging at her skirts and tangling through her hair. The brothers had come up with an excellent solution. Lily didn't weigh much. She'd be no burden for his horse. Lily's horse could be led by one of the children.

"Mount up," he called.

Lily's face flooded with joy. "Thank you."

"Don't thank me yet. We've still got twenty minutes of hard riding ahead of us."

Her joyous expression morphed into a grimace. "I'll manage."

He mounted first, removed his foot from the stirrup and reached for her. He guided her knee and hooked her right leg over the saddle horn, maneuvering her to sit sideways in his arms. She glanced over her shoulder; her nose was pink with cold, and he tugged her muffler over the chilled flesh.

She wrapped her arms around his middle and clung to his waist. "I can't sit like this."

"You're not used to riding. The change in position will help your sore muscles."

"I'll fall off."

"I won't let you."

He circled her waist beneath her ribs and grasped the reins, then kicked his horse into a gallop. She gasped and tightened her arms around his middle, then buried her face in his chest. As the horse's hooves chewed up the miles, her trembling gradually abated and the warmth of their bodies melded.

Her absolute trust invoked a fierce protectiveness. He wasn't letting anything happen to Lily or the boys. Even if that meant risking his own life.

They arrived on the outskirts of town and Jake led them to a ramshackle abandoned hut he'd discovered on an earlier scouting mission. Only three walls and part of the roof remained. The dirt floor was covered in matted leaves and filth, but at least the space offered a modicum of shelter against the elements.

They dismounted and gathered near one of the crumbling walls.

"The train depot isn't very far," Jake said. "I'll buy the tickets and return for the horses."

As long as they were ahead of the posse, the four of them might as well continue moving forward. After Lily had fallen from her horse, he'd known he couldn't leave the trio until they boarded the train. He'd ensure they were safe, even if that meant sacrificing his own security.

"No," Lily said. "You're too recognizable. Let me buy the tickets. No one will take notice of me, but people might recall a big, scary fur trapper."

"You might be right." Jake tugged on his beard. "Do I really look scary?"

"Well, not scary perhaps. But intimidating."

That was good. He was supposed to be intimidating. Why did the realization bother him so much?

He hesitated. Losing sight of her, even for a moment, sent a shaft of pure fear straight through him. After checking his pocket watch, he glanced over the horizon. He took out a scope and searched the tree line.

There wasn't much cover. If a posse had formed, he'd see the movement.

Everything about this felt wrong. He was a lawman; he should be turning Lily and the boys over to the law for protection. Except he was out of his territory, and he didn't have anyone he could trust. The weeks he'd spent in this part of Nebraska had shaken his faith in his fellow lawmen. Delivering her to the sheriff in Steele City might be the same as delivering her into the hands of Vic Skaar.

Was he willing to take the risk?

Jake stared into the wide, innocent eyes of the two boys and made his decision. "All right. You buy the tickets."

He handed her a wad of bills and she shook her head. "I can't take this," she said.

"You've got a long journey ahead of you. You'll need every cent."

"All right." She hesitated another beat. "Thank you."

"How is your hand?"

She flexed her wrist. "Good as new."

She reluctantly took the money. Her chin trembled almost imperceptibly before she set her jaw. He'd already recognized a fierce pride in her that mirrored his own. Neither would risk showing more vulnerability than the other.

This would be so much easier if she weren't quite as intuitive. Her mittens were threadbare and too small for even her small hands. Probably a pair left over from childhood. He had a curious need to tug the mittens free and press a kiss against her knuckles. He wanted to be whatever heroic version of himself that she'd invented in her imagination.

Standing here wasn't getting them any closer to their

goal. "I'll expect you in thirty minutes. That gives you time to walk to the train depot and back. Thirty minutes, then we come looking for you."

"You stay out of sight."

As far as she knew, he was a gunfighter. She should be more concerned for her own safety than his.

After the first twenty minutes of waiting, his pacing took on a frantic edge. He checked his watch and muttered. He should have gone himself, no matter how memorable and intimidating his appearance.

Since that awful day at the bank, he'd seen a larger plan. He'd stepped outside himself and into something greater. The work he did, though often solitary, was part of a larger purpose. In an instant the world shrank and only the four of them remained. He'd fought so hard in grand gestures, he'd nearly forgotten the true nature of his work. Lily and her charges reduced his obsession to its purest form.

She'd flipped his purpose. He was supposed to be fighting men like Vic to save innocents like Lily. In order to maintain his focus, he'd carefully kept those innocents abstract in his mind. That's what had killed his mother—a hesitation. He couldn't hesitate in his work. The people he fought for were always a manifestation of the victims at the bank. Lily had turned the abstract into a flesh-and-blood person. If he wasn't careful, she'd remove the barriers he'd erected between his feelings and his work.

He couldn't let that happen. His focus was vital. Losing that focus left him exposed and vulnerable. He needed that distance.

Jake looped the reins around his hands. "Let's look for Lily."

"All right," the two agreed readily.

The three of them secured the horses and set off in the direction Lily had taken. They'd barely taken a dozen steps when they caught sight of her rushing forward. She was breathless and he thought he noticed a slight hitch in her step.

"I have good news and bad news," she said. "Which would you like first?"

Chapter Nine

Jake did not look pleased. Given that Lily had turned him into a kidnapper, he had reason to be annoyed. Granted, given his job, he'd probably been in tighter scrapes before. Still, through no fault of his own, he was a wanted man for a crime he hadn't committed.

Jake set his jaw. "Tell me what's happened. What took you so long?"

"We didn't miss the train. Bad weather has all the trains delayed. Everything west of here is running behind."

"How long?"

"At least two hours."

Jake rubbed his eyes with a thumb and forefinger. "That's too much time. Vic will have discovered the sheriff by then, and word will be out."

"Maybe we're overreacting," Lily said. "I got the distinct impression that the sheriff didn't care very much what happened to me."

"We've humiliated him. We locked him up in his own jail." Jake paced the rotted floorboards of their temporary shelter. "I'll wait around until the train leaves, just to ensure there's no trouble, then I'll head north."

YOUR PARTICIPATION IS REQUESTED!

Dear Reader,

Since you are a lover of our books – we would like to get to know you!

Inside you will find a short Reader's Survey. Sharing your answers with us will help our editorial staff understand who you are and what activities you enjoy.

To thank you for your participation, we would like to send you 2 books and 2 gifts – **ABSOLUTELY FREE!**

Enjoy your gifts with our appreciation,

Pam Powers

SEE INSIDE FOR READER'S SURVEY

For Your Reading Pleasure...

We'll send you 2 books and 2 gifts
ABSOLUTELY FREE
just for completing our Reader's Survey!

YOUR READER'S SURVEY
"THANK YOU" FREE GIFTS INCLUDE:
▶ **2 FREE books**
▶ **2 lovely surprise gifts**

▶ DETACH AND MAIL CARD TODAY! ▶

PLEASE FILL IN THE CIRCLES COMPLETELY TO RESPOND

1) What type of fiction books do you enjoy reading? (Check all that apply)
○ Suspense/Thrillers ○ Action/Adventure ○ Modern-day Romances
○ Historical Romance ○ Humor ○ Paranormal Romance

2) What attracted you most to the last fiction book you purchased on impulse?
○ The Title ○ The Cover ○ The Author ○ The Story

3) What is usually the greatest influencer when you <u>plan</u> to buy a book?
○ Advertising ○ Referral ○ Book Review

4) How often do you access the internet?
○ Daily ○ Weekly ○ Monthly ○ Rarely or never.

5) How many NEW paperback fiction novels have you purchased in the past 3 months?
○ 0 - 2 ○ 3 - 6 ○ 7 or more

YES! I have completed the Reader's Survey. Please send me the 2 FREE books and 2 FREE gifts (gifts are worth about $10) for which I qualify. I understand that I am under no obligation to purchase any books, as explained on the back of this card.

102/302 IDL GLDJ

FIRST NAME

LAST NAME

ADDRESS

APT.#

CITY

STATE/PROV.

ZIP/POSTAL CODE

© 2016 ENTERPRISES LIMITED
® and ™ are trademarks owned and used by the trademark owner and/or its licensee. Printed in the U.S.A.

HLI-816-SFF15

READER SERVICE—Here's how it works:

"You can't do that. The longer you delay, the more likely they are to catch you."

"I let you plan the first part of this escape—you can't have the second part."

Lily crossed her arms over her chest. The throbbing in her leg had left her peevish. The turkey had scratched her in its escape. She'd taken a closer look in town, and the wound was deeper than she'd thought. A fact she didn't plan on sharing with Jake.

"Stop being difficult and listen," she ordered.

"All right." A smile twitched at the corner of his mouth. "I'm listening."

"We're cold, we're tired, and I'm starving. When the sheriff puts up the alarm, they'll be looking for a woman and two children, and a man with a beard. We have to ensure that's not what they see."

"I can shave off my beard. How do you propose to change your looks?"

"First off, Sam and I will go into town, rent a room and gather our supplies. You and Peter will meet us there. I did a little scouting—that's what took me so long. There's a back staircase into the hotel. Keep your head bundled and your hat on. The less people see of your face the better."

"Agreed."

"There is one more thing that will make this charade perfect." Lily knelt before Sam. "You know what that is?"

"I think so." Sam's expression turned mutinous. "Do I have to?"

"I know I'm asking a lot of you," Lily said. "You don't have to do anything that you don't want to. But your part could be the difference between success and failure. In order to keep our cover, we can't be seen in any combination of the people the law will be searching for."

Sam dragged off her cap, revealing two coiled braids, then removed the pins holding them in place. They flopped over her shoulders.

Jake gaped. "Sam is a girl."

"My name is Samantha." She crossed her arms and glared. "How long have you known?"

"From the beginning," Lily admitted. Revealing the truth was a weight off her shoulders. "The judge gave me some paperwork. Your name was listed as Samantha."

"Hah," Sam declared. "You cheated."

"Yes, I cheated. You're a rather convincing boy." Lily gave Sam a quick squeeze around the shoulders. "We're all making sacrifices. Now, come along, we don't have much time."

"If you knew I was a girl, why didn't you say something before?" Sam remained skeptical. "Why did you go along?"

"I was trying to respect your privacy." Lily held out her hand. "Are you ready for some shopping?"

"I suppose," Sam grumbled. "Don't you even want to know why I was pretending?"

"Why were you pretending?"

"Because it's safer for girls if people think they're boys. And also because boys get to do more stuff. Plus, I don't like dresses."

"I can't argue with any of that. All right, we still need to drop off the horses at the livery." Lily straightened. "We'll meet Jake and Peter at the back door of the Steele City Hotel in one hour."

"I haven't agreed to your plan yet," Jake said. "I reserve the right to back out if I think there's even a hint of danger."

"Agreed."

The snow was soft and slushy. Steele City was much larger than Frozen Oaks, which suited her purpose. Since the sun hung low on the horizon, she walked quickly. She discovered a sign for a tailor advertising ready-made clothing and ducked inside. After fifteen minutes of searching and haggling, she and Sam left with their arms full of paper-wrapped packages. Her pockets were also considerably lighter, but she'd worry about that later.

She couldn't bring herself to use Vic's money. The bills felt tainted.

The next stop was the mercantile. She paused in the doorway and inhaled the familiar scent of snap pickles and lemon floor wax. She and Sam made several more purchases. By the time they reached the hotel, their arms were overflowing.

She procured a suite since they'd all need to clean up and change. The clerk who reached behind the counter for the key barely flicked a glance in her direction. With the train depot marking the final stop on the St. Joseph and Western Railroad Line, strangers were probably a common sight.

Reaching into her reticule, she nearly choked out a sob as she handed over the cost of two adjoining rooms. She'd spent nearly the entirety of the rest of the down payment for the boardinghouse. So much for her being sensible. She'd started this trip to make money, and nearly the whole of her second payment had been frittered away.

Throwing back her shoulders, she made her way to the suite. She and Sam dumped their packages and closed the shades, yanking on the fringe tassels until the room was darkened.

Sam lit a kerosene lamp.

Lily paused. "Where did you find matches?"

"Jake gave them to us to build a fire."

"Be careful you don't burn yourself."

"Stop fussing."

After peering into the corridor, Lily slipped through the passage and waited by the back staircase.

She checked the watch pinned to her bodice and heard a knock on the door at the precise time she'd indicated. Jake was nothing if not punctual.

She waved them inside. "Quickly. Did anyone see you?"

"No one set up the alarms," Jake replied. "If that's what you're worried about. The horses are at the livery."

"Good."

She ushered them down the narrow corridor to the first set of doors of their adjoining rooms.

Her plan was sound. Once Jake saw them outfitted in her purchases, he'd have no objections. She'd be home by tomorrow. In an instant the rush of anticipation dissipated and an unexpected melancholy took hold instead. Despite the fact that she was returning home, she couldn't shake the nagging sensation that the changes taking place in her life were permanent.

All the traveling had left her weary and irritable. Perhaps her exhaustion explained why the thought of spending the rest of her days carrying linens up and down stairs no longer held the same appeal.

Sam leapt onto the bed and bounced. "This place is great."

"Stop bouncing." Peter threw himself backward onto the mattress. "I'm tired."

Sam shook the bed again.

"Don't tease your brother," Lily admonished. "This day has been trying, and we're all exhausted and peevish."

"This day has been amazing," Peter said. "I broke an outlaw out of jail, I was a hostage and I escaped a posse."

Lily groaned. "I sound like the worst chaperone ever when you put the events in that order."

"Nuh-uh." Sam shook her head. "You're the best."

She pictured holding the deed to the boardinghouse in her hand and waited for the familiar thrill of pride. Nothing manifested. Instead, she pictured nonstop mountains of dishes and never-ending piles of laundry.

She forced all thoughts of drudgery from her head.

What other future did she have? She wasn't an adventurous person. She was a homebody. Running with outlaws and hiding from the law should not, under any circumstances, be thrilling. Yet the unexpected kick of excitement remained. There was something of her father's blood in her after all. She didn't know whether to be ecstatic or horrified.

Jake doffed his hat, and Sam and Peter explored the adjoining room. A cheerful fire burned in the grate and Lily arranged her purchases on the bureau.

"Sit," Jake ordered abruptly. "Have something to eat. Warm yourself. We've been traveling hard. You deserve a rest."

"I'm afraid if I slow down, I'll collapse into exhaustion and never wake again."

"At least have something to eat."

She and Sam had gathered tinned peaches, a loaf of bread and a hunk of cheese from the mercantile. They'd also procured a tin of crackers and jar of homemade jam. She tossed a protective blanket over the bed and arranged their feast.

All four of them were famished, and they lapsed into silence as they ate. The stress of the day had taken a toll. Outside a sleety snow had started to fall. The flakes tapped against the windowpanes. Inside, the room was warm and cozy. With her stomach full, the tension from her shoulders eased.

"Good eats," Sam said. She sat back and patted her stomach. "What now? Where do we go next?"

"We're traveling back to St. Joseph. That's where this all started. We'll speak with the judge."

"Grandpa is dead, isn't he?" Peter ducked his head. "That's why he didn't come to meet us."

"You mustn't think like that." Lily moved to sit next to him and wrapped one arm around his shoulders. "We don't know for certain what happened to your grandpa. For now, all we know is that your grandpa chose a very odd town for his home, and that he's taken a trip without telling anyone. There wasn't anything in his rooms or in the barbershop that indicated where he might have gone."

Peter's brown eyes shimmered. "What will happen to us if Grandpa Emil really is dead?"

"When we return to St. Joseph, we'll speak with the judge who located your grandpa in the first place. He might have more information. Either way, he's the one who will decide your future."

"Is it bad that I'm not sad about Grandpa?" Sam asked, her eyes wide and unblinking. "I don't remember ever meeting him."

"No," Lily said. "I'd feel the same as you. It's rather difficult to be sad about someone you've never met, isn't it? Even if they're family. There's nothing bad about that."

"Yeah." Sam's expression seemed to lighten. "You're right. It's like reading about someone in the newspaper."

Lily glanced at Jake, and he gave a nod of encouragement.

"And we don't have to live with that pale guy?" Peter asked.

"Absolutely not."

"Good. I didn't like him."

"I'll tell you this much," Lily continued. "I'm not giving up yet. This is merely a setback. People rarely disappear. Your grandfather must have left behind a clue. We'll talk with the judge—we'll hire a Pinkerton detective if we have to. Once we're back in St. Joseph, there'll be no more running and hiding from men like Vic Skaar."

"That was fun!" Peter declared. "Better than any book I ever read."

"And also dangerous. I should not have put you in danger."

"I don't think that was your fault, Miss Lily," Peter said matter-of-factly. "I think that was Emil's fault for not being where he was supposed to be."

Her throat tightened. How typical of children to reduce the complex into a few simple words. "That's very kind of you to say."

"What happens now?"

"Mr. Jake is going to escort us back to St. Joseph. He's going to make certain the two of you are safe."

She wasn't giving up on him yet. He'd fight her because he thought his presence was a detriment. She'd find a way to convince him otherwise.

"And you," Sam said. "Jake will make sure you're safe, too."

Her heart beat in sudden, painful jerks. "Yes, and me."

No one had looked out for her in a very long time. Not since her mother had died. Her father's grief had been all-consuming. She didn't blame him; everyone grieved differently. Yet she relished the sense of team work the four of them shared. She enjoyed feeling as though she was a part of something.

She was no longer a burden. She wasn't the one left behind. She was truly a part of the circle.

"Is the money why Vic wanted to be our guardian?" Peter asked. "Are we in danger, as well?"

"I don't think anyone wants to harm you." She paused. They were children, but they also deserved the truth. "Because of the newspaper article, people will know about your wealth. They'll know you're vulnerable." Vic's words rang in her ears: *Folks around these parts will slit your throat for an acre of land.* Lily shivered. "I simply think it's best if we take precautions. I'd rather not involve the local sheriff. Not until we can sort out what happened at the jailhouse. That means we'll have to travel incognito."

"You mean in disguise?"

"Yes, something like that. The sheriff from Frozen Oaks is looking for a scruffy-looking gentleman who may or may not be traveling with a woman and two boys. That's why, for the next leg of our trip, we'll be traveling as a family. A mother, father, son and daughter."

Sam clapped her hands. "I don't mind traveling as a girl because I'll be in disguise."

"That means we're all going to alter our appearances just a touch. Sam and I picked out everything we need."

"Then Mr. Jake is coming with us? He's not going north like he said before?"

Lily held her breath.

"Yes," Jake said. "I'm coming with you. We're better off staying together."

He hadn't contradicted her before, but she hadn't been certain of his cooperation until he said the words. Thus far, he'd kept all his promises. He wouldn't lie to the children.

Sam looked between the two. "What happens when we return to St. Joseph? If we can't find Grandpa?"

"We'll cross that bridge when we reach it."

Lily expelled the breath she'd been holding. They'd all be together until St. Joseph—after that everything changed. When they returned, Sam and Peter would be in the care of the judge once more. They'd be wards of the state while Emil was missing.

They'd be orphans.

She clenched her hands together. She'd petition the judge for guardianship. At this point, she knew the children better than anyone else. She was growing to love them. Certainly the judge would see the benefits of letting them remain together? Even Mrs. Hollingsworth wasn't cold enough to object.

Mostly, they needed to find Emil. Until they found the children's grandfather, their fate was unresolved.

Holding out her arms, she took Sam's and Peter's hand in turn. "We have each other. We'll do the best from there."

"You won't leave us, will you?" Peter appealed. "You'll stay with us until we find Grandpa Emil?"

"Yes," Lily said. "I promise."

She'd find a way to keep that promise, no matter what happened.

She'd be alone again after that, but she was accustomed to being alone.

A soft knock sounded on the door. Jake swung it open and paused. There was something different about Lily's expression. A hint of sadness he hadn't noticed before.

"Is everything all right?"

"Yes," she said, brushing past him. "But we don't have much time to put everything in order."

While Sam and Peter perched on two chairs, Jake leaned forward and trimmed his beard in the mirror. Clipping off his whiskers felt as though he was coming out of hiding. He'd grown accustomed to the shelter of the beard. Sure, when he'd first met Lily he'd pined for the days when ladies didn't cross the boardwalk when he approached, but he'd forgotten what he looked like. He'd forgotten who he was on the inside *and* the outside.

She'd seen right through him. One day he'd tell her the truth. Would she trust him then? Would she trust him after she discovered he'd been lying to her?

Lily planted her hands on her hips and glanced at them. "What have the three of you been doing for the past twenty minutes?" She waved toward a clock on the mantel. "The train is late, not indefinitely delayed."

"You're fretting." Jake grinned in spite of himself. "We're definitely behaving as though we're a family. You've already started nagging me."

"I never!"

"I'm teasing you, Lily. Relax." He checked his neatly trimmed beard. "Do you think this enough of a change?"

"No. Not even close. Why are you so attached to looking like a fur trapper?"

"You keep saying that. Don't I look like a dangerous gunfighter?"

"You're quite frightening." She rolled her eyes. "Either way, the beard has to go."

The banter reminded him of his own parents. The memories of happier times had dimmed, yet Lily had flooded the past with light. His parents had married young. His mother had barely turned sixteen and his father was seventeen. Neither family had been particularly pleased with the pairing, but young love had prevailed, and he'd been born the following year.

Despite all the grim predictions about his parents' future, they'd survived and thrived. They'd argued, too; their love had been fiery. But he didn't recall them staying angry for long.

Those same protective feelings welled up inside him. He remembered his own father, and felt as though a window had opened inside his soul. After his mother's death, his father had changed. A child at the time, Jake hadn't understood those changes. They'd all lost someone. There were times when he felt as though his father had forgotten that. There were moments when he'd wanted to shout his own loss. For the first time in his life, he looked at his mother's death from his father's point of view.

At last he understood. His father had been fighting his grief *and* his guilt. He'd been fighting against what he saw as a failure. He'd failed to protect his family.

Jake and his father had drifted apart, as though his mother had been the magnet holding them together. She would have been devastated had she known her death had caused such a rift. They'd each grieved in their own way, and neither had understood the other. Lily wasn't his wife, and Sam and Peter were not his children. They'd known each other only a few days. He'd be shattered if something were to happen to one of them.

That's what had happened to his father. He'd been shattered.

Jake stared in the mirror and made a vow to return home in the next year. He'd see if there was anything left of their relationship on which he could build.

Running a hand down his beard, he stared into the mirror. "I do look like a fur trapper."

"I can cut your hair for you." Lily spoke softly. "If you'd like."

He'd grown his hair long for the notoriety. He'd gone into Frozen Oaks wanting to be noticed. He needed to catch Vic's attention. It seemed fitting that he was cutting his hair for the opposite reason. The time had come to peel back the layers. He didn't know what he'd find beneath them, but he was done hiding.

"Yes," he said. "You can cut my hair."

She didn't appear triumphant, only relieved.

She sat him on the chair and grasped a stool he hadn't noticed from the corner. After rummaging through the stacks of packages she'd bought from the mercantile, she emerged with a drape and whisked the material over his upper body. He slouched in the chair and she stood on the stool, rising on her tiptoes to reach the top of his head.

Sam's face screwed up. "Have you ever cut anyone's hair before, Miss Lily?"

"Yes," she said, her brow knitted in concentration. "I cut my father's hair."

"Do you still cut his hair?"

"Not anymore." The scissors remained suspended in the air near Jake's ear. "He died."

"What happened?" Sam asked.

"Sam," Jake spoke. "That's not a polite question."

"I don't mind talking about him." Lily rested her hand on his shoulder. "When I was fifteen, my mother and older brother contracted rheumatic fever. I did, as well. They, uh, they didn't survive. I did. After that, my father took a job with the railroad munitions crew. There was an accident at the jobsite, and he was killed."

"When was that?"

"Five years ago, give or take. He never quite recovered from losing his wife and son. They isolated everyone who was sick during the outbreak. The illness had spread rapidly, and people were dying. Everyone was scared. I think he was always sad that he never got to say goodbye to them."

"Then you lost everyone," Peter said. "Just like us."

"You have each other, remember."

"And you have us," Sam said.

She pressed her bent knuckle against her eye, holding back a tear. "Yes. I have you."

Jake reached across his chest and caught her hand, pressing her fingers against his shoulder. He'd sensed a sorrow in her, but he hadn't realized how deep it ran.

"I'm sorry, Lily," he said. "That must have been very difficult."

Peter lay on his stomach on the bed, his chin cupped in his hands. "Do you miss them still? I wonder sometimes. I wonder when I'll stop missing my parents."

Lily's throat worked and she squeezed his hand.

"You never stop missing them," Jake said. "But missing them gets easier over time."

"You're right." Lily cleared her throat. "I never

thought about grief that way. The burden of missing them never grows lighter, but your strength grows stronger over the years. The sorrow is always there, but the grief is more bearable."

"Good," Sam said. "Because I don't want to feel like this forever."

"You can be sad as long as you need." Lily straightened. "Everyone grieves differently. There's no right or wrong way to miss someone."

"I never thought about it that way either." Peter rolled onto his back and folded his hands on his stomach. "The woman at the children's home in St. Joseph said that we should be happy they were in a better place."

"You want them to be with you. There's nothing wrong with that." Lily ran her fingers through Jake's hair. A shiver of awareness rippled down his spine. "We'd best get on with this haircut."

Before he could change his mind, she was snipping away. She'd pulled the rug aside and shorn hair fluttered onto the wood floor. Lily heated a pot of water near the fire and immersed a towel. With her thumb and forefinger, she gingerly retrieved the towel and let the excess water drip into the pot.

The towel steamed. She pinched opposite side and flapped the edges.

"Tip back your head," she ordered.

"Why?" He squinted one eye. "What are you doing?"

"Softening your whiskers."

"You're not shaving my beard. Cutting my hair will be enough."

He hadn't seen his face in ages, and he was worried about her reaction. He'd never given his looks much thought before. He was sure thinking about them now.

"Your beard will grow back in a week," she said. "Don't be childish."

"All right, but I can shave my own face."

"I don't trust you." The steamy warmth of the towel billowed toward the ceiling. "I saw how well you trimmed your beard. You barely clipped the edges."

Her eyes were soft and appealing.

"All right," he said. "But at the first drop of blood, I'll take over the duty."

"Deal."

They'd kept the curtains closed over the windows and Sam had lit two of the kerosene lamps.

Since there was no way to tip back his head comfortably, she knelt before him and brushed the hair from his forehead. Her touch was gentle, featherlight, and his heartbeat quickened. He was vitally aware of her, the gentle puff of her breath, the soft pulse in the hollow of her throat.

Her eyes were only inches from his, her pupils large, the wintry-blue color barely visible beyond the edge. Even before he'd become a US marshal, he'd rarely paid for a shave. The extravagance seemed unnecessary since he was perfectly capable of wielding the blade over his own skin.

She foamed the lather and spread a layer over his face.

Arching his neck, he was vulnerable against her touch. She tucked two fingers beneath his chin and turned his head to the side. With deft strokes she shaved the right side of his neck, the soft scrape of the blade the only sound in the room. A lock of hair drifted over her cheek. Her brows knitted together in concentration; she tugged her lower lip between her teeth. Turning his head the opposite direction, she rested her left hand on his shoulder for balance.

There was an intimacy to the act. Once again he was back in Texas. There were clothes flapping in the breeze. His mother and father were sitting on the porch with their heads bent together, laughing over some joke only the two of them shared. He'd forgotten their casual tenderness. His mother had been the only one who brought out the warmth in his father. Without her, he'd become a closed man. Aloof. Not unkind, but something had gone missing from him after his wife's death.

Lily stuck out her lower lip and blew a breath, stirring the hair off her forehead. Instead of his mother and father, he and Lily sat on the porch. Not the porch of his home in Texas—somewhere different, with hills rolling in the background. He pictured the rolling hills of his uncle's horse farm.

Lily wore a yellow gingham summer dress and her skirts tangled around her ankles in the breeze. The picture was so true, so vivid, he sucked in a breath.

"Stay still." Lily drew back. "You nearly lost an ear."

The walls closed in around him and he was trapped once more. He snatched the wrist holding the blade and held the instrument away from his face.

Her eyes widened and the pulse beneath his fingers beat rapidly.

"I'll finish," he said.

"I was only joking about losing an ear." She smiled. "I'm almost done."

He dropped her hand as though it was a flaming-hot poker, then yanked the drape she'd placed over his shirt. The material felt as though it was choking him. "I can take over from here. Take Sam and Peter to the other room. Get them ready."

"Your suit is here. I had to guess on the size. I bought a small sewing kit—I can make a few adjustments. Nothing elaborate."

"Good. Whatever. Go to the other room. Take Sam and Peter. I'll be right out."

"Did I do something?" She cupped his chin, turning his face this way and that. "I didn't cut you, did I?"

Once more he took her delicate wrist, forcing her touch away. "I'm fine. Go."

"I've annoyed you."

All at once he felt like a bully. A schoolyard bully picking on someone weaker than himself to prove that he was tough. "Don't apologize, Lily. You've done nothing wrong. If we're going to make that train, we'd best hurry up."

"All right." With a last look over her shoulder, she ushered the children into the other room. "Knock when you're ready."

Jake swiped the foam from his face and searched for the few whiskers she'd missed. Without wetting the blade, he scraped against the grain and flinched. A drop of blood appeared on his cheek.

So much for shaving himself.

Every time he looked at Lily, he sensed that same familiar, lonely feeling in her. A part of him felt responsible for that look. He couldn't protect her heart, only her safety. She'd feel better once she was home, surrounded by her friends.

Her heart. He almost scoffed aloud. She probably hadn't given him a second thought outside of the help he offered. She'd called him a scary old fur trapper more than once. She needed his help and he'd give what he could, at least until he was caught.

Their charade wasn't foolproof. If they were spotted, he'd simply give himself up and claim he'd threatened Lily. There was no reason for anyone to believe anything different. Until then, he'd play along. If they reached St. Joseph without incident, he'd wire his boss in Washington. His commander was one of the few people who knew the dual role Jake was playing. All he had to do was stay out of Sheriff Koepke's clutches for another day.

Shrugging into the jacket Lily had left draped over a chair, he tugged on the sleeves and tied his neck cloth without looking in the mirror. She'd done an admirable job on the sizing. The sleeves and the shoulders on the jacket fit well. The waist on the trousers simply needed a belt, though the length was a touch too short.

Throughout dressing, he avoided looking at his face. He knew what he'd see: a boyish man barely past his twenty-fifth birthday. He crossed the room and knocked on the adjoining door. She'd probably laugh at him.

He slicked his hair back and straightened his tie, then smoothed his hands down his cheeks. There was no turning back now.

The door swung open. He stepped into the room and Lily faced him.

Her cheeks flushed and her hand flew to her mouth.

He braced for her next comment. "I know I look too young."

"That wasn't what I was going to say at all. You look, well, you look positively handsome."

His heartbeat kicked into a canter and he feared his foolish grin had her wishing he was a bearded, long-haired outlaw once more.

Chapter Ten

Lily couldn't stop staring at the gunfighter. He didn't look like an outlaw at all anymore. He looked exactly as she'd hoped. No, that wasn't right. He looked far better than anything she could have hoped for or even imagined.

His dark hair swept across his forehead and brought out the deep, bronzed hue of his eyes. His chin was strong with a slight cleft. His cheeks were works of art, with strong bones over a slight hollow. Removing the layer of whiskers had removed at least a decade from his age. She'd have thought him in his midthirties before. Now she'd guess his age at midtwenties. He was definitely a grown man, and yet there was a handsome, boyish quality in his full lips and strong jawbone.

Gracious. She waved her hand before her face. The fire sure heated the room quickly.

Flustered and out of breath, she ushered him forward. "Let's take a look at that suit."

She circled around him. The shoulders fit snug and the length of the sleeves was almost perfect. The hem of the charcoal-gray jacket was an inch longer than she might have liked, touching just below his lean hipbones, but that was a small concession considering the suit coat had been ready-made. She'd spent a little more than her budget, hoping the costly materials might further disguise them. The expense and elegance of the cut leant an air of sophistication to him.

She needn't have bothered with spending the extra money. The suit was merely an afterthought compared to the other changes. Even having spent time with Jake, if he'd walked past her on the boardwalk with his trimmed hair and shaved beard, she'd have drifted right past him. She definitely didn't recognize this man.

Her jaw hung slack and she snapped shut her mouth. "You look very nice."

Stepping back, she noted the one flaw. The matching charcoal-gray pants were too short. For that she was almost grateful, otherwise she might have stood there staring at him like a fool for ages. She knelt and flipped up the cuff. The tailor had assured her there was plenty of material in the hem if the slacks needed letting out.

She sat back on her heels. "I can let those out in a tick. We'll hang them over a pot of boiling water and let the steam pull out the wrinkles from the previous hem. You'll be wonderfully respectable in no time."

"My tie is too tight." He stuck a finger in his collar and tugged. "I look like a twelve-year-old boy on his way to church."

"I can assure you, you do not look like a boy."

Her heartbeat fluttered and she snuck a glance at him once more. The difference was astonishing.

She'd donned the dress the tailor had provided for her, part of an order that a patron hadn't been able to pay for. The hem was too long, and she'd folded over the waistline. Cut from indigo velvet fabric, the design was simple but elegant. The sleeves were fitted, and the bodice featured a row of buttons that began at the stand-up collar near her throat, and ended at the V of the waist. The middle was a touch large, so she'd tightened the waist tapes. The skirts were full and modestly bustled. Even Peter had commented that the indigo blue brought out the color of her eyes.

Since she'd remarked on Jake's appearance, she waited to see if he would remark on hers. She'd taken a bit of time with her hair, as well. Since visiting the milliner had been an added expense she couldn't afford, she'd arranged her hair at the back of her neck and pinned a lacey handkerchief over the top, anchoring the corners behind her ears beneath a loop of braid.

Except Jake hadn't noticed.

She lifted one shoulder in a shrug. Oh, well. It wasn't as though she was desperate for the attention of a hired gun. He wasn't a suitor accompanying her to a country dance. They were on the lam from a corrupt law official.

The final player in the charade, Sam, was taking her sweet time in changing.

Lily rapped on the adjoining door. "Are you ready yet?"

"Almost," came the grumbling reply.

Waiting for Sam, the three of them milled around the suite, gathering the supplies and cleaning up the mess they'd made in their preparations. A short while later, stomping feet sounded from the other room.

The door slammed open and Sam flounced in.

She wore a pink gingham dress with a square collar and mother-of-pearl buttons. Her dark hair had been released from her usual braids and rolled into sausage curls that hung loosely over each ear.

Sam's fierce look dared anyone to say anything disparaging. Lily shot a warning look in Peter's direction. He shrugged his shoulders.

Lily approached Sam and straightened her collar, then smoothed one hand over her hair. "You look positively lovely."

"I figured once our parents were gone, I'd never have to dress like a girl again." She crossed her arms and huffed. "I'm only doing this because we're on the run."

"What's wrong with being a girl?" Lily asked.

"Girls only get to do stupid stuff. They have to get married and have children, and they can't go to college, and they can't even vote."

"That's not true. There's no law that says a woman has to get married and have children. There's a women's college in St. Joseph, and more all over the country. Women can't vote, that's true, but there are plenty of people fighting for the cause."

Sam snorted. "I'd still rather be a boy. They don't have as many rules, and their clothes are more comfortable."

"This sounds like a lengthy discussion for another time. If it makes you feel any better, we're all making sacrifices. Your brother has traded his canvas pants for wool trousers, and poor Mr. Jake had to cut his hair and shave his beard."

Only just noticing the gunfighter, Sam gaped. "He looks good. He looks like our dad. But skinnier. You're real handsome, mister. You ought to cut your hair more often."

Jake flushed. "I'll take that as a compliment. You look very nice as well, Sam."

"What about Lily?" Peter puffed up. "Lily looks beautiful, too, and you haven't said anything nice to her. A gentleman should complement a lady on her appearance."

"Peter!" Lily admonished.

"You're quite right, Peter," Jake said. "That was very rude of me. Miss Lily, you look lovely. That color blue looks delightful on you."

Though she recognized his flattery was forced, she appreciated the compliment. "Thank you."

As though he sensed his failure, Jake opened his mouth to speak, then appeared to think better, and remained silent.

Lily donned her coat and ordered the children into theirs. Peter wore his same wool coat but they'd purchased a more feminine cut for Sam.

Their trunks were still sitting at the livery in Frozen Oaks, a problem she'd address at a later date. She'd procured a single satchel and packed the bare necessities. Together they were a mother, father and two children traveling to St. Joseph. Not noteworthy in the slightest.

All in all they gave the appearance of a very ordinary family of modest means.

She lifted the shades and peered outside. A light snow fell from the overcast sky, the flakes large and puffy.

"At this rate," she said, "we'll most certainly have a white Christmas."

"I can't wait for Christmas." Peter sighed. "Christmas in Africa is hot. I want to build a snowman and sit by the fire."

"That sounds delightful," Lily replied.

She stuck out her elbow and Jake stared at her for a long moment. She flapped her arm.

"We're a family," she said. "I believe it's customary for a gentleman to hold his wife's arm."

The outlaw's face flushed and he hooked his hand through her arm. He was wearing a supple pair of brown leather gloves she'd discovered at the mercantile. They'd been another expense, but gentlemen wore gloves and this pair was more in tune with his suit than his thick sheepskin ones.

She checked her watch and her nerves jangled. The train had been delayed a full four hours. By now, Vic had discovered the sheriff and knew that Jake was missing. The next few minutes may very well decide their fate.

With her heart thumping against her ribs, they made their way along the boardwalk unimpeded. Sam and Peter trailed behind them. The weather was keeping folks inside once more. The few gentlemen braving the snow tipped their hats. One or two ladies bestowed an admiring glance on Jake, but Lily quickly scowled them away. He was supposed to be her husband. What sort of brazen woman smiled at another woman's pretend husband?

They arrived at the depot and Lily's stomach sank. The train hadn't arrived.

Jake approached the ticket booth, and the clerk flicked his glance up before returning his attention to the ledger. "No train until tomorrow."

"Are you certain?" Lily quelled her rising panic. "I thought the train was merely delayed."

"The snow is delaying all the schedules," the clerk said. "Nothing is getting through."

"When do they expect another?"

"Like I said, tomorrow." He made a sound of annoyance. "Tomorrow morning. First thing. You're fortunate. This time of year, we don't get many travelers. Plenty of seats left. Just you and the preacher have bought tickets on this stop."

"A preacher?"

"Sure. There's a preacher on his way back to St. Joseph. Visiting some family."

Lily fiddled with the button on her collar. Somehow playing at being married with a preacher on board seemed worse. She glanced at Sam's and Peter's upturned faces and steeled her resolve. She'd rather break the law than turn them over to Vic Skaar.

Though her insides churned, she kept a straight face as they strolled away from the ticket booth. Once out of earshot, she grabbed Jake's sleeve.

"What now?"

"We wait and catch the train tomorrow."

"The town will be swarming with law by then."

"That may work to our advantage. They'll assume we're two towns ahead by now, not sitting around and waiting on a train."

"Do you really think so?"

"No. But what else are we going to do? We'll have a nice dinner, we'll stay the night in our separate rooms in the suite at the hotel, and we'll catch the train at first light."

Lily glanced around and shivered. The longer they stayed in Steele City, the more dangerous the wait for Jake.

He tucked her fingers into his elbow and covered her gloved hands with his own. "This will give us a fine opportunity to practice being a family. And after that hasty escape and picnic, you deserve a decent meal and full night's rest."

An evening's rest sounded good though she doubted she'd sleep. She was far too nervous. As for the food, she pressed one hand against her stomach. She wasn't feeling very hungry at all. She'd taken the time to clean and dress the wound on her leg, but the scrape had been red and blistered.

"I doubt I'll sleep a wink," she said.

Lily nearly fell asleep in her soup.

Her head dipped and Sam and Peter giggled.

Jake steadied her shoulder and she blinked.

"What happened?" Her voice was drowsy with sleep. "Where am I?"

"You dozed off for a moment," he said. "We're at the restaurant, remember?"

She stifled a yawn behind one hand. "I think the day has finally caught up with me."

Their appearance in the restaurant hadn't caused even a stir of recognition. Despite his misgivings with the plan, Lily's predictions had proved true. Cleaned up, with Sam dressed as Samantha, they had disappeared into the crowd. No one paid them any mind.

He glared at the gentleman sitting a table over. Almost no one. Lily attracted all sorts of male attention.

Leaning back in his chair, he studied his make-believe family.

Though he'd never tell her, Lily was the only real impediment. Of the three of them, she looked the most recognizable. Her appearance hadn't changed, only improved. She was absolutely gorgeous. The blue in her dress brought out the many highlights in her hair and made her eyes sparkle.

He doubted Vic would remember the children; he'd barely glanced at them. For a man like Vic, all children were basically the same. The sheriff hadn't gotten a good look at them either. He'd been distracted by their jailbreak.

Lily, on the other hand, had been seen and admired by both men.

She'd also provoked the admiring gazes everywhere they went. He doubted she'd be easily forgotten. A detriment, considering they were trying to blend in.

He'd sort that problem out tomorrow, since she was also exhausted. Her eyes drooped and her head pitched forward once more.

Sam and Peter giggled again.

"Upstairs, you two," Jake ordered. "Face and teeth washed. It's time for bed. We'll be up early in the morning. You'll need your rest."

"Lily is resting now."

Sam laughed and Peter socked his sister in the shoulder. "Be nice to Lily."

"No fighting," Jake said. "Upstairs."

He shot the pair a good-natured scowl and they scurried from the dining room. Jake followed their progress as they thumped up the stairs. Peter had assumed a protective role with Lily.

He stood and offered her his hand. She swayed and he wrapped his arm around her waist. "Not much further."

She leaned heavily against him on her way to the staircase. She was such a delicate little thing, he was tempted to sweep her into his arms and carry her. Such a display would only draw more attention to them, and he stifled the urge.

"My father would have liked you," she said, her voice slurred with exhaustion. "You're smart. He liked smart people."

She'd drifted into a half-sleep state and he doubted she even knew what she was saying.

"I'm sure I would have liked your father, as well."

"He didn't like me."

"Of course he did," Jake absently replied. An ill-kept gentleman who looked as though he'd been on the trail had entered the lobby. Jake carefully turned Lily away from the man's view. "All fathers love their children."

The gentleman approached the counter and asked for a room. He lacked the alert bearing of someone on the lookout for an escaped fugitive, and Jake breathed a sigh of relief. The man wasn't part of a posse. Come to think of it, Steele City had been awfully quiet. He'd expected something more by now. Someone should have raised the alarm. Why wasn't the sheriff canvassing the town?

"He loved Benjamin." Lily yawned behind one gloved hand. "Because Benjamin was adventurous."

"I'm sure he loved you, too."

"Yes. But have you ever had the feeling you're just a poor substitute for the people they really want?"

Jake paused on the landing. Even after his mother's death, he'd always felt as though he belonged. When his father had sunk into melancholy, his family had circled around him, smothering him and his siblings with love.

He turned her face toward the light. "Who made you feel as though you were a poor substitute?"

"No one." She blinked at him, as though realizing she'd revealed too much. "Never mind. I'm tired. It's been an extremely long week. I rarely travel. I'd forgotten how exhausting it can be."

"You've done more than simply travel. You've been under a tremendous amount of strain. Sam and Peter are fortunate you accepted this adventure." He ran his thumb over the delicate lace covering her radiant hair. "Someone else might have left them in Frozen Oaks."

"People should never leave without saying goodbye."

"Sometimes people don't have a choice."

"I suppose."

His mother had been gone for more than a decade, but the ache of her loss remained. There were certain days he felt the sorrow more acutely. Holidays and birthdays were difficult. Sometimes entire days passed when he didn't think of her, and the guilt weighed on him.

Lily cupped his cheek, her eyes glazed. He felt the warmth of her hand all the way to his toes.

"What about you?" she asked. "Does your family still live in Paris, Texas? Do you have brothers and sisters? Where does a gunfighter spend Christmas?"

"I have brothers and sisters. My father is still alive, but my mother died."

The smile faded from her expressive face. "I'm sorry. You must think me very insensitive."

"I think you're exhausted."

She fumbled with the door, nearly delirious with exhaustion, and he gently took the key from her fingers. "Let me help."

Sam and Peter had finished preparing for bed, and had crawled beneath the covers. Lily tucked the sheet beneath their chins and smoothed the hair from their foreheads.

"What happened to your mother?" she asked.

"She was killed in a bank robbery."

"I'm so sorry."

"I was Sam's age at the time. I was pouting that day, making all her tasks more difficult. I wanted to be home playing marbles with my brothers. I didn't want to be in town carrying her sacks from store to store. I was peevish and bored. I didn't even pay attention when the outlaws first entered the bank." He paused, replaying the scene in his head, recalling each vivid detail. He pictured the black-and-white tile floor, the stamped horseshoe on the outlaw's belt buckle. "Everyone else was ducking behind furniture, or scattering away. I just stood there. I looked up and saw the gun, and I couldn't move. My mother reached for me. The movement caught the attention of one of the bank robbers. He turned and the gun went off."

"That must have been horrible for you."

"She died instantly. I don't think she even knew what happened."

"I don't understand you," she said. "Why take up gun fighting? After seeing something that horrible. I can't imagine."

He backed toward the door. "My path is a long story for another time."

"I admit I'm curious about the entire tale."

He turned to go, and caught the sound of her footsteps behind him.

"Wait," she called.

"Yes?"

"I'll never hear your story, will I?" She collapsed against the doorjamb, her hands braced behind her. "You're leaving us, aren't you?"

Jake rested his hand above her head and leaned forward. He caught the faint hint of lilacs once more. Lilies and lilacs—she'd ruined his two favorite flowers. He'd always think of her. Of the way her indigo velvet dress brought out the caramel highlights in her hair and sent her blue eyes shimmering.

"I have to leave," he said. "The delay has made any escape for me too risky. I don't trust the law around here. If I stay with the three of you, I put you in danger. Remember, tomorrow, if anything goes wrong, you and the children escaped from me. You were trying to put as much distance between us as you could because you feared for your lives."

She reached out a hand. "Thank you. For everything. For getting us this far."

"You're welcome, Lily." He considered his next words carefully. "Sam and Peter are blessed to have you. You were never a poor substitute."

"Thank you."

His brow creased. "What are you thinking, when you look at me that way?"

"I'm thinking that you look like a handsome suitor come to call."

"Then I should kiss you good-night."

She stroked his face, running her hand along the line of his jaw. No mortal man could resist the temptation. He leaned forward, pressing his lips against hers in a featherlight touch. She rose up on her tiptoes and wound her arms around his neck. Fighting himself, he reluctantly pulled away.

She touched her lips. "Goodbye, Jake. I never even knew your last name."

He brushed his hand along her silken hair one last time. "Good night, Lily Winter. You and the children are going to be just fine."

Chapter Eleven

Lily woke the next morning feeling no more refreshed than if she hadn't slept a wink. After collapsing on the bed, she'd tossed and turned. All night long she'd been tensed for a pounding on the door.

If the sheriff hadn't begun searching already, perhaps he'd simply given up. Her body ached from their grueling ride, and the scratch on her leg throbbed. She'd known, of course, that Jake would leave. For his own safety, and for theirs. Still, his desertion struck her as a betrayal.

The feel of his lips on hers lingered. Sensible Lily Winter had kissed an outlaw, and she didn't regret her actions.

Peeling back the layer of bandaging on her leg, she winced. With the children sleeping soundly, she dipped a towel in the ewer of water on the nightstand and cleaned the wound again. Once they were in St. Joseph, she'd visit the pharmacy for a salve. By the end of the evening, they'd be well away from Vic and his influence.

Having replaced the bandage, she shook Sam and Peter awake with a renewed sense of purpose. No matter what happened, she wasn't leaving these two. Even if everyone in the world deserted them, they'd have each other.

Thirty minutes later they were all dressed and their bags packed. Lily checked the clock on the mantel. They had plenty of time for breakfast before their train departed.

She smoothed the material over her stomach and took a deep breath. Jake hadn't said goodbye the previous evening. He'd said good-night instead. For some reason the oversight annoyed her to no end. People ought to say goodbye when they were leaving.

She swung open the door and discovered Jake standing on the threshold, his hand raised in midknock.

Her heart jerked against her ribs. Before she could stop herself, she threw herself into his arms and hugged him around the middle. His arms came around her. She let herself sink into his embrace for a moment before pulling away.

He offered her one of his rare half grins. "I hope you don't regret this."

"Not at all. Never." She rushed ahead, her voice breathless. "You didn't leave us. I can't believe you didn't leave us."

"I figured I better stick with you three until my beard grows back." He rubbed the backs of his fingers against the grain of the stubble on his chin. "I'll never get work as a hired gun looking like this."

"You're quite handsome. I like you far better this way."

If she didn't know better, she'd think there was a hint of a blush at her complement.

Twenty minutes later they handed their tickets to the conductor and boarded the train. The station was crowded with people bustling to and fro. Steamer trunks and bags made navigating the depot difficult, but all the commotion provided much-needed cover.

Taller than Lily, Jake scanned the crowd and gave her hand a reassuring squeeze. "Nothing. I don't see anyone searching the passengers."

Relief surged through her. "Then we've made it."

"I won't feel relief until you're back home in Missouri."

They boarded the train and Lily and Sam took a seat across from Jake and Peter. The passenger car was new, the polished dark wood trim gleaming. The bench seats were covered in a deep brown fabric and grouped facing each other. She fisted her hands in her lap and listened for the steady *chug, chug, chug* as the engineer shoveled more coal into the steam engine. The whistle blew and the train seemed to jerk forward.

Her relief was short-lived. A second later the engines seemed to heave, then slow. The passengers sitting around them raised their heads and looked around.

"What's wrong?" a voice called. "Why are we stopping?"

An elderly porter appeared at the end of the aisle, holding his hands in a placating gesture. "Don't worry, folks. We've got a little situation. The sheriff is on the lookout for some folks, and he's going to take a walk up and down the aisles."

Several gasps accompanied his words.

The porter chuckled. "As long as you haven't broken the law, this will only be a short delay."

There were titters following his words.

Stars appeared at the edges of Lily's vision. She felt the same as when she'd faced Jake on the boardwalk that first day. As though there wasn't enough oxygen and she might collapse at any moment.

Jake half stood but she grasped his knee, preventing him from rising.

"Stop," she said. "Don't give up yet."

"We're stuck." He sat back down and shook his head. "It's too late, he's coming this way."

"Who?"

"The Steele City sheriff."

Her ears buzzed and her breakfast roiled in her stomach. "Oh, no."

Jake snatched a newspaper someone had abandoned on the seat across from them. "Don't make a fuss when he captures me. I don't want anyone hurt."

In deference to their situation, Lily had worn a bonnet that day. The hat didn't match the rest of her outfit, but her coat was bland enough she doubted anyone would notice. Jake was almost completely unrecognizable with his clean-shaven face, shorn hair and new suit.

With a sudden jolt she acknowledged the real problem. Her own appearance hadn't altered enough. She'd been focusing on the other three, and hadn't noted the obvious flaw in her plan. Of the four of them, she was the most recognizable.

She scrambled for a solution. As long as the Steele City sheriff didn't get a good look at her, she might escape his notice. She listened for the footfalls and when the sheriff neared, she leaned down and pretended to tie the laces on Sam's half boots.

Jake tipped his hat low over his eyes and made a point of concentrating on the newspaper he held.

Her heart beat a rapid tattoo in her chest. The footsteps paused beside them.

Sam sighed. "I can tie my own shoes."

The footsteps continued past them.

Lily peered up. Jake folded a corner of the newspaper and met her gaze. He gave a slight shake of his head. She concentrated on tying another knot. They'd have to cut the laces off poor Sam's boot at this rate. For the next ten minutes they sat in tense silence.

Outside their window, the porter called the last warning for boarding passengers. The engines began to hum once more and the train whistle blew. She clapped her hand over the back of her mouth, quelling a hysterical giggle.

"I can't believe that worked."

"You're a genius, Lily Winter." A smile stretched across Jake's handsome face. "I wouldn't have believed the story if you told me twice."

"He just walked right by us."

"You were right. Once he saw Sam, he barely spared us a glance. No one is looking for a couple with a boy and girl. We were invisible."

Sam pressed her back against the seat. "I helped, didn't I?"

"You were the most important part of the plan," Lily replied.

"What about me?" Peter crossed his arms over his chest and harrumphed. "I did my part, too."

"Yes. You were very stoic and brave." Lily soothed his bruised feelings. "You both did very well."

The giggle in the back of her throat erupted into a laugh and she pressed her knuckles against her lips.

"I'm sorry," she apologized, "I don't know why I find his ineptness so hysterically funny all of a sudden."

"You're letting go of the tension." Jake folded the newspaper. You've been under too much stress for too long."

A hand landed on her shoulder and she nearly leapt out of her skin.

"I'm afraid you'll have to stand up, miss," a masculine voice spoke.

The preacher sitting across from Jake was flanked by Sam and Peter. With light brown eyes, he was one of those nondescript middle-aged men who tended to fade into a crowd. He'd insisted on letting the couple sit together. Especially when it became apparent that Lily wasn't feeling well.

He and Lily had almost given themselves away when the preacher boarded the train late. Poor Lily had nearly fainted when he'd touched her shoulder. She wasn't looking much better now.

Her complexion had turned an unnatural shade of green. Despite the chill air, a fine sheen of sweat had formed on her brow. Out of habit on the trail, he'd packed a cantina of water. He unscrewed the lid and wetted his handkerchief, then pressed the chilled material against her forehead. She sighed and leaned into his hand. He wrapped one arm around her shoulder and pressed her against his side.

"How much longer?" she asked weakly.

"Why don't you close your eyes and rest? Try and sleep."

"I don't know how anyone could sleep through this awful swaying."

"This train is sprung like a feather bed compared to my last journey," the preacher declared. "And at least we aren't pressed together like sardines. You can't imagine the smell in the summertime."

Lily snatched his handkerchief and pressed the material against her mouth.

If the preacher noticed her discomfort, the observation didn't stop him from forging ahead. "You know, my mother used to love peppermint. Said it settled the stomach."

He peeled back the lapel of his black suit coat and revealed a package of peppermint sticks.

"Thank you, but I think I'll pass," Lily replied.

Jake chafed her upper arm. "Not much longer, sweetheart. Try and rest. The time will go faster."

The term of endearment came easily. Obviously too exhausted and queasy to argue, she collapsed against his side. They were well chaperoned between the preacher and the children, but he couldn't shake the natural comfort of the moment. They might have been a real family. She'd removed her bonnet and he ran his fingers over her silky hair in a soothing motion.

She curled into him, her hand resting on the buttons of his new suit jacket.

He touched the back of his hand to her cheek and alarm bells rang in his head. "You're more than sick because of the motion. You're feverish."

She groaned and shook her head. "I'm fine."

"You're not fine."

The preacher departed at the next town, and Lily's condition worsened. When the server-carriers brought meals for purchase to the train window, Sam and Peter eagerly wolfed down their fried chicken and pickled okra. Lily declined any food.

Growing more concerned, Jake set her away from him and studied her glazed eyes. "You're sick. You need to see a doctor."

"It was the turkey."

"You haven't eaten since this morning. You're not making any sense."

She struggled away from him and lifted her skirts, revealing her calf. Blood oozed through a makeshift bandage.

His chest seized. "When did that happen?"

"When I fell off my horse."

"You said you weren't hurt in the fall. You lied."

"I didn't lie. This didn't happen when I fell. That blasted turkey leapt over me in his escape."

"A small point. Why didn't you say something sooner? Why didn't you purchase medical supplies in Steele City?"

"Stop shouting at me." She rubbed her temples. "My head already hurts."

"I'm not shouting." He lowered his voice. "I'm not shouting, I'm merely concerned."

Jake leaned forward for a better look and she halted him with a hand on his shoulder. "I'm fine."

"You're not fine. We're getting off at the next stop."

Her face flashed in stubborn mutiny, but he was done with letting Lily have her way.

Sam and Peter elbowed closer.

Peter grimaced. "That doesn't look so good, Miss Lily. Maybe you'll get a big scar. My dad burned his leg once, and he had the most amazing scar."

"Ladies don't like scars," Sam said. "She doesn't want her leg ruined."

"What would you know about being a lady?"

She socked him in the gut. "I know plenty."

"Enough," Jake snapped. "Both of you."

At the inherent authority in his voice, they both clammed up.

"Sorry," Sam mumbled.

"Me, too," Peter added. "That scratch looks really

bad, Miss Lily. I imagine your leg hurts something fierce."

"I'll be fine," she replied weakly. "You two needn't worry about me."

The length between stops drew out interminably. Sensing the gravity of the situation, Sam and Peter lapsed into silence. Lily dozed fitfully at his side. He urged her to drink water and bathed her forehead. He was fully prepared to override any objections she might make, but by the time they reached the next depot, a town called Seneca, Lily was in no shape to argue.

Sam and Peter took their bags and he wrapped his arm around Lily's waist. Thankfully the nearest hotel was only a few blocks from the tracks. He hoisted her into his arms and she protested weakly.

"I'm too heavy."

"Hey, there, I won't have you questioning my brawny strength."

His teasing brought a gleam of amusement to her weary eyes. "I'd never dare."

The elderly clerk glanced up from his ledger when they entered the lobby. The hotel was small, probably no more than four or five rooms. Rag rugs were scattered over the wood floors. The lobby was neat and tidy and smelled of a fresh scrubbing. Thankfully, they didn't need anything fancy, just a place for Lily to rest.

"I need a room," Jake called. "And fetch the doctor."

Recognizing the resolve in Jake's voice, the clerk sprang into action. With his round face and layered wrinkles, he reminded Jake of a bulldog he'd owned as a child. The man grasped a key from the row of boxes behind him.

"Follow me," the clerk said.

Sam and Peter trailed close behind him.

Even with his extra burden, Jake took the stairs two at a time. The porter unlocked the door and he rested her on the embroidered counterpane.

"I should have told you about my leg sooner," she said weakly. "But I thought the wound was healing."

"Is Miss Lily going to be all right?" Peter asked.

"She'll be fine. I saw a checkers game set up in the lobby. Why don't you two play a few games while the doctor and I take care of Lily?"

The two eagerly agreed. Once they'd left the room, Jake peeled back the layers of bandages and examined the scratch on Lily's leg. "This has gotten infected."

A piece of the bandage had adhered to the dried blood, and she flinched when he pulled the edge free.

"I thought I would be all right." She hissed. "But the pain just kept getting worse and worse."

The porter delivered a ewer of water, and Jake carefully cleaned the edges. A sharp rap on the door indicated the arrival of the doctor.

As short as he was round, he wore a black suit over his crisp white shirt. His dark hair had been parted in a torturous path down the exact center of his scalp, then slicked away from his face with some sort of pomade.

He knelt beside Lily and frowned. "I do wish my patients would see me sooner. Especially the ladies. They always wait too long." He glanced up. "How did this happen?"

Lily offered a weak grin. "Gobbler."

"Oh, dear." The doctor pressed his hand against the back of her head. "Has she taken a blow to the head, as well?"

"She's not rambling," Jake said. "She had a bit of an accident while we were riding. We startled a rafter of turkeys and she was thrown. One of the gobblers scratched her during its escape."

"The immediate cure is going to sting like a rattlesnake bite," the doctor declared.

Jake sat on the edge of the bed and took Lily's hand.

The doctor balanced a pair of spectacles on his nose. He uncorked an opaque bottle of a noxious-smelling substance and doused a clean rag.

"All right, miss," he said. "Take a big, deep breath."

He pressed the cloth against her leg and Lily shouted and squirmed. She squeezed Jake's hand in a bone-shattering grip. Her back arched, and she groped for his lapel with her opposite hand, her eyes squeezed shut, her face contorted in a grimace.

Jake fought off a sudden urge to sock the doctor in the face for hurting her.

"All right." The doctor removed the cloth and peered over his spectacles. "That's the worst of it. Doesn't look like the infection spread. I think we caught it soon enough. Next time call me sooner."

Jake scowled. "The lady isn't in the mood for a lecture."

"Overprotective husbands." The doctor adjusted his spectacles on his nose. "I guess I'd rather have threatening, protective grizzly bears than the alternative. Ladies are always looking out for the rest of the family, and they forget to take care of themselves. Another day and I'd have had to cauterize that wound."

Lily gave a strangled cry. Jake glared.

"Relax. The both of you." The doctor shrugged. "Sometimes my patients need a dose of the truth in order to take care of themselves."

The doctor dug in his bag and pulled out a tin. "Clean

and dress the wound at least once a day, and put a little of this under the bandage."

Jake accepted the tin. "Anything else?"

"She'll be back on her feet in no time." The doctor grasped her wrist and frowned in concentration. "Her pulse is strong. She's healthy. I'd say she's more exhausted than anything. You folks been traveling much?"

"A little."

That was an understatement. She'd been crisscrossing the country for days.

"Take a day or two and rest." The doctor rummaged in his bag and retrieved more supplies. "Relax. Let her catch her strength. Make sure she eats. I'd say she's a bit underweight." He spread a poultice over the wound, then wrapped the bandage around her calf once more. "Remember. Rest is the best medicine."

He set a clear, liquid-filled bottle on the side table. "This will help her sleep. Looks like Father will be looking out for the young 'uns for a while."

"I'm fine, Jake." Lily struggled upright. "I can take care of Sam and Peter."

The doctor pressed her shoulder, urging her back against the stack of pillows. "Men are more capable than you think. Let your husband take care of the children."

Jake's chest swelled with something akin to pride. He found he enjoyed being addressed as Lily's husband.

"Don't worry," Jake said with a small smile. "I promise they'll survive."

"I'm more worried about your survival. Don't show any sign of weakness, or Peter will take advantage of you." Too exhausted for more instructions, she collapsed against the pillows. "I only need a nap. Twenty minutes and I'll be good as new."

She tugged the blanket over her shoulder and turned on her side.

The doctor waved Jake away from her bedside. "She'll be asleep for hours. There's a nice café in town that serves roast beef on Fridays. I suggest taking your young 'uns there for dinner."

"There's something else as long as you're here," Jake said. "Lily is sick when we travel. Is there anything that will help?"

The doctor scratched his chin. "There's folklore about several cures. I've found ginger works the best. A bit of ginger before a trip will often help settle the stomach. You might try that."

The doctor packed up his supplies and slipped out the door. Jake rubbed his forehead. The delay should have left him frustrated. Instead, there was only a curious lethargy. The incessant need for the chase had abated. The craving for danger that normally gnawed at his gut had dissipated. He looked forward to a checkers game with Peter. He wanted to hear one of Sam's stories. All thoughts of illegal guns faded into the background.

He'd spent weeks in Frozen Oaks without a solid lead—what was another day or two?

He wasn't an overprotective husband, but he'd certainly become an overprotective *pretend* husband.

Chapter Twelve

Lily stubbornly crossed her arms. "I'm not resting anymore."

Jake had been treating her as though she'd contracted the plague, not simply injured her leg.

"You're resting." The implacable set of his jaw remained. "Doctor's orders. You can't be mad at me. Blame him."

Her eyes narrowed. "Where are we now?"

"Seneca."

"That's close." She pictured Seneca on the map. "We're over halfway to St. Joseph. The boardinghouse is on the western edge of town, just across the river."

"We're staying the night, and I'm not arguing."

"But we've already lost a day."

"Then we'll lose another day. We're far enough from Frozen Oaks that I feel safe going into town and listening for any gossip. After seeing the sheriff in Steele City, we can assume Vic hasn't given up."

"That's out of the question." She vigorously shook her head. "What if someone recognizes you? By your own admission, you're a wanted man. What if something happens to you?"

The more time they spent together, the more she worried for his safety. The delay had her on edge. She wouldn't feel secure until they'd spoken with the judge about Vic's claims of guardianship. The man was a constant, troublesome worry. Until his claim was successfully refuted, they were all in danger. Jake most of all. Yet he insisted on behaving as though nothing was wrong.

He propped one shoulder against the wall. "This isn't my usual haunt. No one will recognize me. Especially without my beard and long hair."

"Where is your usual haunt?" She plucked at the stitching on the counterpane, keeping her voice deceptively neutral. "Where do you live when you're not roaming the countryside as a hired gun?"

"Enough talk. It's time for rest."

She made a sound of frustration in her throat. The man was a closed book. He let her peer around the edges, but he never allowed her any closer. She'd caught snippets of his past. His mother was dead, he had siblings, although she didn't know how many. He'd been born in Paris, Texas. The more she learned, the more she sensed he was hiding something from her.

Her eyelids drooped and she leaned back once more.

"Did you take the laudanum?" Jake asked.

Lily stifled a yawn. "A little."

"The doctor recommended a café in town. Sam and Peter and I are going to have dinner. We'll bring back something for you."

"I'm not hungry."

"I'll bring you something anyway, just in case. Doctor's orders."

"Stop blaming the doctor for everything." Another yawn interrupted her protest. "All right. I'll take a short nap, and then we can discuss leaving. I won't relax until we're in St. Joseph."

The twinge of homesickness had turned into an ache. All the uncertainty had left her restless and discontent. She craved something familiar. She craved her own bed. She craved being surrounded by her own things. She wanted her routine back. Yet when she considered those tasks, the future stretched before her in a bleak haze. What did she have to look forward to?

There was no one waiting for her. The friends she'd made over the years were transient. The decision had been purposeful. Since her father's death, she hadn't let anyone close to her. She'd never minded the solitude. Until now. She'd grown close to Sam and Peter, even Jake.

Eventually the laudanum took effect and wiped away all her other arguments. She awoke the following morning feeling refreshed and ready to face anything. The scratch on her leg no longer throbbed, and her stomach rumbled. After washing up and quickly dressing, she went in search of her traveling companions.

She discovered Jake, Sam and Peter in the parlor. They'd pushed the furniture to the side and chalked a circle on the hardwood floor with two flanking horizontal lines.

"You've written on the floor!" she exclaimed, aghast.

Jake glanced up and caught her horrified gaze. "Don't worry. We cleared our game with the management. As long as we clean up afterward, they said we were welcome to play."

Lily sank onto one of the chairs that had been pushed against the wall.

Sam waved her over. "You can play with us."

"I can't." She held up her hands in denial. "I don't know how."

"It's not difficult. We can teach you."

"I'm a beginner." Lily sank deeper into her chair. "I'll ruin your game."

Peter rolled his eyes. "Everyone starts out a beginner. How else are you supposed to learn?"

She couldn't argue with that logic. Pushing aside her skirts, Lily slid from her chair and reclined on the floor. For the next fifteen minutes, the three patiently explained the rules of marbles.

Sam knelt behind one of the lines. "We have to decide who goes first. You shoot your marble and whichever marble lands closest to the line on the opposite side without going over, that person has the first turn."

Sam easily made her shot, and Lily took her place behind the line. Mimicking Sam, she flicked the marble with her thumb.

"Not like that," Sam said. "You need at least one knuckle touching the ground."

"Yeah," Peter chimed in. "You have to knuckle down or it doesn't count."

Lily bit her lip and concentrated on mimicking the way Peter positioned his hand. Her brow knitted, she made her second attempt. She flicked the sphere with her thumb, but only caught the edge. Her marble barely reached the center of the circle.

Sam chucked her on the shoulder. "You'll do better next time."

They each took a turn and Jake's marble landed closest to the line. Sam retrieved larger marbles. When she finished, Peter dumped a pouch full of smaller marbles into the circle.

Jake knuckled down and flicked his shooter with his

thumb. His marble ricocheted off one of the smaller targets, knocking it from the circle.

"That's perfect," Peter said. "That's exactly what you want to do. Jake is good at this. You have to get all the smaller marbles out of the circle without letting your shooter roll out. When you shoot a target outside the ring, you pick it up, then you try again from the spot where the shooter landed. We're not playing for keepsies or anything."

Lily glanced up from the game. "What's *keepsies*?"

"It's when you get to keep the marbles you win in the game."

"That hardly seems fair."

"Sam lost a whole bag of marbles once." Peter chuckled. "I still can't believe you've never played before."

"I've never been one for games."

"Not even when you were a kid? In school."

"I stuck to myself a lot." Lily rolled her marbles together in her palm. "I've never found games to be practical. What purpose do they serve?"

"They're fun," Peter said. "You get to know people better when you play games with them. You can learn a lot about someone by how well they take a loss."

"Who loses better? You or Sam?"

"Sam." Peter shrugged. "It's good to learn about people when you have to make new friends all the time. Everyone shares the same stories with you when you're the new person. You have to be interesting."

"I was never very interesting." Lily spun the shooter in her hand. "Benjamin, my brother, never had trouble making friends."

"That's why you have to stick together," Sam chimed in. "Like Peter and me. If one of you isn't interesting, the other one can be. Didn't your brother ever look out for you?"

"There were three years between us. I don't think he ever took much notice of me." Benjamin had always been the brightest star in the class. He was smart and adventurous. Adults and children alike were drawn to his boundless energy. "He was looking out for himself."

"My mom said we had to look out for each other."

"Your mom was right."

"Who did you live with after your father died?"

"No one," Lily replied. Given their current circumstances, Peter's curiosity was understandable. "I was older than you. I didn't need looking out for."

"How old were you?"

"I was seventeen. We lived at a boardinghouse. After my father died, I had no place else to go. So I stayed. I went to work and earned my keep. Mrs. Hollingsworth, the current owner and landlady, is going to retire soon. I'll take over for her."

"How does that work?"

"I gave Mrs. Hollingsworth part of a down payment to buy the boardinghouse. I'll continue to make payments to her until the house is paid off in full."

"Wow. Houses are really expensive. Won't that take a long time?"

"Yes." Lily's calculation of the numbers had been daunting. "A very long time."

"Can we come visit you?"

"Absolutely," she said easily, though a sudden melancholy permeated her.

She snuck a glance at Jake, but he was concentrating on his next shot. He didn't appear at all interested in their conversation. She was certain her mixed feelings were readily apparent.

She sincerely hoped Emil moved away from Frozen Oaks once he came out of hiding, but she didn't know where he'd take the children. The thought of never seeing them again left her empty and cold.

Before, she'd always thought there was something wrong with her. She'd never felt things as deeply as the other members of her family, especially her father and Benjamin. They'd thrown themselves headfirst into all their endeavors, while she'd quietly watched from the sidelines.

She'd seen people come and go from the boardinghouse without a flicker of yearning. While other girls had fallen in and out of love on a weekly basis, she'd never been tempted by passion.

Her time on this trip had changed her. Sam and Peter had opened a place in her heart that she hadn't known existed. She'd never considered herself lonely. She was always busy. Yet the closer she came to returning home, the less enthusiasm she felt.

Her inertia must have been contagious. None of them showed much enthusiasm for catching the next train. As much as they'd been focused on returning to St. Joseph, the end of the trip meant the end of their partnership. They lingered in the parlor. Peter taught her the best way to knuckle down on a marble. In an effort to find a distraction, they formed teams and played chess. The girls handily beat the boys.

All the while the clock ticked. And as the clock hands turned, her discontent with her current dreams intensified. She'd never dreamed past the basics of survival. Growing up, she'd always been the practical member of the family. Practical, sensible people had practical, sensible dreams.

She'd assumed the role and never considered another

alternative. The world was limitless, and limitlessly frightening. There were too many possibilities to calculate. She'd never been very passionate about anything but surviving.

Perhaps that was why this past week had been invigorating. She'd called on the one skill she'd honed all these years. Surviving from day to day was the one thing she did best.

Despite a last raucous game of marbles, lunch was a somber and quiet affair. Sam pushed her food around her plate and Peter was unusually subdued.

As they packed for the final leg of their journey, the doctor visited and checked on Lily's leg. He declared her wound free of infection, and advised her to continue changing the bandages each day. He also brought a paper bag full of gingersnap cookies his wife had baked.

"These are for you, miss," the doctor said. "They'll help with the sickness on the train. My wife and son won't travel without a dozen or so."

The kind gesture brought unexpected tears to her eyes. Though she had little faith in the remedy, she gratefully accepted the thoughtful gift. For the first time in days, the sun broke through the clouds. Even though the temperature had dropped, the light was cheerfully welcome.

The last leg of their journey proved singularly uneventful. Much to Lily's surprise, the cookies actually helped. When they reached St. Joseph, she waited for the comfort of familiar sights and sounds. The underlying realization that she'd probably never see Jake again tugged at her. She shouldn't mind, and yet somehow she did. She minded very much.

The fate of Sam and Peter weighed on her, as well. As Jake arranged for a ride to the boardinghouse, she found herself dreading the homecoming instead of anticipating her return.

They had agreed to stop at the boardinghouse first, giving Lily a much-needed opportunity to change and clean up before visiting the courthouse. None of them had broached the subject of the future beyond the next step of the journey. With the end of their adventure nearing, the four of them were unusually somber. As they neared the final turn, Jake clasped his hands before him.

"How's your leg?" he asked.

"Fine."

"Good."

They lapsed into uncomfortable silence once more. The boarders always had stories to tell, and Lily finally had one of her own. She'd escaped cross-country with an outlaw, she'd even kissed him. The carriage rounded the corner and Lily gasped.

"What happened?"

Jake looked at the burned-out building and back at Lily once more. "Is this the correct address?"

"Yes." She cupped her cheek with one hand. "That's my home. That's the boardinghouse."

Fire had ravaged the building. The top floor was almost completely decimated, charred and ragged with only three brick fireplaces rising through the wreckage. The windows on the first floor had been boarded over, and ash and debris darkened the snow surrounding the structure.

Furniture and personal belongings had been haphazardly scattered across the lawn. Jake gazed at the devastated building and back at Lily, gauging her reaction. She appeared numb and disbelieving.

Sam blew out a low whistle. "Wow. That must have been some fire. There's hardly anything left."

The scent of burning wood lingered. Footprints smeared the ash into the snow, transforming the once pristine front lawn into a sloppy gray mess.

Keeping a close eye on her, Jake helped Lily from her seat, and she took a few halting steps toward the house. "I don't understand."

He returned to the wagon and met Peter's and Sam's questioning gaze. "Lily has had a shock. Will you two be all right if we take a look around?"

"Yes, we're fine," Sam replied. "We'll wait."

"Are you certain? Are you warm enough?"

"We're all right," Peter said. "You'd best take care of Lily. She doesn't look so good. She looks as pale as that day she fainted in Frozen Oaks."

"Don't worry, I'll take care of Lily," he said. "Holler if you need anything. We'll be in sight. We just need enough time for Lily to take stock of the damage, and see what's left of her things."

Peter leaned to one side and shook his head. "That should go fast. Doesn't look like there's much left."

Jake caught sight of a movement around the side of the building. Someone was sorting through the wreckage. While the furniture littering the front lawn was haphazardly placed, attempts were being made to make order of the chaos. Some pieces of the salvaged furniture were stacked in a neat row. The broken and charred fragments had been tossed in an ever-growing pile.

Lily wandered through the wreckage, her expression dazed. He read the emotions flitting across her expressive face. She was confused and disbelieving. A part of him understood her confusion. Her mind was struggling to catch up with the devastation.

She knelt and retrieved a shard of broken glass from the snow.

"This is the lamp from the fourth bedroom," she said. "It's the only lamp with a green shade."

He knelt beside her and gently took the shard from her grip. "Be careful where you walk. There's glass everywhere."

She tipped back her head and studied the charred remains of the building. "It's gone. It's all gone."

His heart ached for her. He felt her pain as though it was his own. Beneath his concern was a nagging sense of suspicion. He didn't believe in coincidences. What were the chances of a fire destroying Lily's home while she'd been away? How had Vic discovered where she lived?

She met his gaze, her eyes twin pools of anguish. "Everything I own was in that house. Everything."

"Maybe they were able to save some of your belongings." He took her hand and helped her up. "Someone is here. We can ask."

He led her around the side of the house where he'd noticed the movement before.

A robust woman with wispy gray hair pulled severely off her head bustled amongst the scattered furniture. She wore a faded blue calico gown with a stained apron tied around her waist. Her cheeks were mottled red with the exertion. She rested a chipped enamel ewer on a wooden crate.

The woman caught sight of them and recognition spread across her face. "Lily! Land's sake, child. I was starting to think you were never coming home."

"Are you all right?" Lily rushed to meet her and the two shared a quick embrace. "What happened? Was anyone hurt?"

The other woman sniffed and swiped at her nose. "Everyone was able to escape in time, thank the Lord. I'm afraid the building is a complete loss. Your room was destroyed beyond anything. There's nothing left. The man from the city said we can't even go up the steps. Too dangerous. There's nothing beyond the second floor anyway. Nothing but ashes."

"Everything is gone?" Lily whispered.

"I'm afraid so, my dear." The woman plopped down on a chair stuck in the snow. "I was ready to retire anyway. These old bones were getting too old for climbing up and down those stairs. I'll have that cottage nearer my boy now."

"What will happen to this house?"

"There's no repairing the damage. They'll tear it down."

Lily swayed on her feet. Jake took her hand, guiding her to another chair perched on the snow-covered lawn. He discovered a stack of blankets on a trunk and wrapped one around her shoulders. Though the wool smelled of smoke, the blankets appeared clean enough.

She hardly seemed to notice. "But I don't understand. What happened?"

"Came home from church and the place was ablaze. The neighbors had already sent up the alarm, but it was too late. Nobody saw nothing. The man from the city thought maybe one of the boarders left a candle burning on the second floor. Of course everyone denied everything. Don't suppose it matters much now. Nothing is bringing the place back."

"But...but... I have nothing."

The woman—Mrs. Hollingsworth, he presumed—reached in her pocket and fished out a wad of bills. "Here's half of the money you gave me for the down payment. Good thing I kept the extra cash in a metal box. I'm afraid I don't have the rest."

With Lily too dazed to respond, Jake accepted the money.

"But what will I do now?" Lily directed her question toward the landlady. "I haven't anyplace else to go."

"You'll have to figure that out yourself." Mrs. Hollingsworth folded her hands over the dome of her rounded stomach. "Time for you to move on. I've got my own problems, missy."

Her sharp tone incited his anger, though Lily didn't even blink.

Lily wasn't acting like herself.

In an instant Jake sized up the relationship. Lily had been living here since she was a teenager, and Mrs. Hollingsworth had grown accustomed to ordering her around. Lily probably didn't even realize what was happening. She'd been living the same routine for too long, and she'd grown subservient under the landlady's orders. She'd gone from losing her father to living under Mrs. Hollingsworth's roof as a dependent.

On her own, Lily was perfectly capable of standing up for herself. Around Mrs. Hollingsworth, she'd reverted to old habits. She needed to take back her authority.

Jake stood before the landlady and displayed the bills she'd given him. "You owe Lily more than this."

"There ain't no more money. Lily here is fortunate to be getting what she's getting. Other people might not be as Christian as me."

Jake figured there were a few hundred dollars there, which meant Lily had been shorted a few hundred more. She'd bought them all clothing and supplies in Steele City with money he doubted she could afford to spend.

This wasn't the time for questions about her finances. She was still in shock, her face a white mask.

"What about my coffee grinder?" Lily asked. "I kept a coffee grinder in my room."

Mrs. Hollingsworth shook her head and muttered. "Whatever do you mean, girl?" She chortled. "Everything is gone and you're worrying about a coffee grinder. I ain't never heard of anything so foolish. You ought to be wondering where you're going to live from now on. Not everyone will be as kind as me."

"I had a coffee grinder." At once Lily appeared small and forlorn. "With a crank and a drawer. There was a brass plate on the front."

"I told you, nothing on the second floor survived." Mrs. Hollingsworth swept her arm in an encompassing gesture. "Everything that's left is here on the lawn. My boy is coming tomorrow to help me move the rest of my things. Time for you to move on as well, girl. There ain't nothing for you here now. Buy yourself a new coffee grinder. I never heard something so ridiculous. I lost everything and this girl is worried about getting a cup of coffee in the morning."

Lily hung her head.

As though sensing the harshness of her tone, the landlady's expression softened. "You're young. You're a hardworking girl. Don't you worry, you'll land on your feet." She glanced at Jake and back at Lily again. "You should think about settling down and having some children of your own."

Lily was too dazed to understand the implication of Mrs. Hollingsworth's suggestion. He wasn't about to explain their relationship to the woman.

Jake stuffed his hands in his pockets and rocked back

on his heels. "Did anyone see anything suspicious? Any chance the fire was set deliberately?"

"Suspicious? I already told you. No one saw anything. They were all looking out for their own hides once they smelled smoke."

"What about the boarders?" he asked. "Do you have their names?"

"There were two gentlemen and a lady." She rattled off three unfamiliar names. "Business has been slow this past week. Good thing, too, since Lily was gone. Had to do all the washing up by myself."

Served the woman right. Jake had a sneaking suspicion that Lily had taken on the lion's share of the workload in the past.

"Can you describe the two gentlemen?"

"The two fellows were old. I don't know what else I can tell you."

"This gentleman would have stood out," Jake said. "He's extremely fair."

"Doesn't sound familiar." The woman shrugged. "I don't know what you mean. The fellows staying here were just regular folks."

Jake muttered an oath. He doubted the sheriff had been responsible. If someone had deliberately burned down Lily's home, the act had been vindictive. The destruction served no purpose. There was no other reason.

"Would you mind writing down the boarders' names?" He'd check the names against Vic's known associates. Chances were slim he'd find a match, but he didn't have any other choice. "And anything you can remember about them."

"Now, why would I do something like that?"

"In case they were involved in the fire." He couldn't quite disguise his exasperation. How had Lily put up with this woman all these years? Which led him to another thought. "Do you have any enemies? Anyone who'd like to harm you?"

He'd only known her a few minutes and she'd exhausted his patience. He definitely didn't like the way she spoke to Lily. While he mourned the loss of Lily's plans for the future, he was grateful she was out from under Mrs. Hollingsworth thumb. Lily deserved better.

"Are you a reporter or something?" the landlady demanded. "Why are you asking all these questions? I sure don't have any enemies."

"You can trust him," Lily said. "If someone did this on purpose, he can find the person."

"I don't much care why. This fire is the best thing that ever happened to me. There's insurance. I can retire." She caught the look on Lily's face and sighed. "Don't you go looking at me like that. I didn't start the fire. None of this is my fault. I can't go on taking care of you forever. You need to find your own way."

Jake bit off a sharp reply. "I'll take those names."

Mrs. Hollingsworth didn't even recognize the hypocrisy of her words. She'd gone from complaining about having to do all the work, to declaring herself Lily's caretaker.

Beneath his relentless prodding, she reluctantly revealed the identity of the boarders staying in the house when the fire happened, and Jake committed them to memory.

Lily stood. "Do you need any help clearing up the mess?"

"Indeed I do."

The landlady didn't deserve their help, but Lily was too softhearted. He called Peter and Sam from the wagon. With the help of the children, they had most of the furniture and belongings sorted in no time.

"That's everything." Mrs. Hollingsworth planted her hands on her hips. "Everything inside is a complete loss. No use going in there."

Jake had held out a slim hope they might discover the coffee grinder Lily had mentioned, but nothing turned up. If the item was important to Lily, there must be a reason.

He glanced to where she'd opened the rear door and stood peering into the kitchen.

"Be careful." Jake circled his arm around Lily's waist. The fire had left everything in the kitchen black and charred. He was surprised they'd been able to save as much of the furniture as they had. "Come on. There's nothing for you here. You'll catch your death in this cold weather."

Lily paused and glanced over her shoulder. "Regina knew."

"What?"

"Regina knew I lived here. She probably told Vic. Do you think he's responsible for the fire? Do you think he traveled this far for his revenge?"

"I don't know," Jake said. The conclusion seemed logical, but a lingering doubt nagged at him. "I've never known Vic to do his own dirty work, but desperation is a powerful motivator."

Sam and Peter rolled an enormous ball of sooty black snow around the yard in preparation for a snowman.

Lily followed his gaze. "They are remarkably resilient children, aren't they?"

"So are you."

"I'm not resilient, I'm stunned. I feel as though my

life keeps getting whittled away. Pretty soon there'll be nothing left."

"Mrs. Hollingsworth didn't deserve you."

"She's not so bad once you get used to her. I'm happy she'll finally have that cottage near her son. She deserves a rest."

"As do you."

Something about the destruction teased his brain. A sense of the familiar that he couldn't quite put his finger on. While the fire might have been an unhappy coincidence, he had an uneasy sensation Vic had been involved.

They'd been delayed for two days. A lone man on horseback, riding hard, could make the trip in a day. Jake turned in a slow circle, studying his surroundings. What purpose did torching the building serve? If Vic had preceded them to St. Joseph, where was he now? What did he hope to gain?

Jake stared at the ground. Vic would be better served tracking down Emil than chasing after the children. If Vic planned on pressing his petition for guardianship, why not approach the judge? Then again, approaching the judge was risky. If he lost his plea, there'd be no turning back. Either way, something wasn't right about the sequence of events.

Jake shook off the strange feeling. For now, he needed to take care of Lily. There was nothing he could prove with his suspicions. Unless they had a name, or a sighting, everything was conjecture.

Jake stood before Mrs. Hollingsworth. "Are you certain there was nothing of Lily's that was saved?"

"Nothing. I'm sorry. The fire started on the second floor, near her room. Everything is gone. There's nothing left."

"We should go," Lily said. She'd resumed her perch on one of the chairs set in the snow. "Mrs. Hollingsworth is right. There's nothing left for me here."

Dozens of words of comfort balanced on the tip of his tongue, but they were all inadequate. Lily had lost her home. She'd lost her possessions. She'd lost her plans for the future.

He wrapped his arm around Lily's back and urged her upright. As though in a daze, she stumbled beside him.

Jake paused out of earshot of the children. "Is there anyone else?"

"What do you mean?"

"Is there anyplace else you can stay? Do you have any family?"

"Nothing. No one. This was… This house… I have nothing."

He'd taken his family for granted over the years. Though he sometimes went months without speaking to his brothers and sisters, they were always there. He always had the sure knowledge of their assistance if he was ever in trouble.

Losing their mother had shattered them in the beginning, but they had healed together. Those bonds were stronger than he'd ever realized. Lily was alone and adrift. She'd survived in solitude.

He assisted her into the wagon once more. Sam and Peter took their places beside them. Jake gave the driver instructions to the nearest hotel, but Lily interrupted.

"No. First we have to see Judge Ashford. Sam and Peter deserve answers. They deserve to know their future. They are the first priority."

Unwilling to argue, Jake gave the driver the new instructions. He'd contact his superiors as soon as they finished. In St. Joseph, he was beyond the reach of Sheriff Koepke. Though he'd initially been reluctant to give up the character he'd invented for his job, he desperately wanted proof of his real identity for Lily. She trusted him, but he was tired of playing the gunfighter.

He'd created dozens of characters over the years in the name of his job. They were all excuses. Under the guise of enforcing the law, he'd been hiding from his guilt and pain. While the truth was humbling, this was neither the time nor the place for personal revelations.

His own problem could wait.

Lily needed a sense of purpose, and seeing to the children's future gave her that purpose. At least temporarily. He understood her desire well enough. She'd lost control. She'd lost her moorings. She was searching for a problem that had a solution. Lily Winter was nothing if not practical.

The St. Joseph courthouse was a redbrick building that appeared newly built. The color of the bricks had yet to mellow with age and time. Enormous white columns supported a vast overhang, and giant double doors led inside.

Lily directed them through the cavernous foyer and led them down a corridor.

Sam and Peter paused.

Lily turned around. "What's wrong?"

"Will the judge send us to the orphanage?" Sam asked.

"No," she assured them. "I won't let him."

"Then why are we here?" Sam asked.

"We have to do things correctly. We need the paperwork in order. If someone challenges... If someone tries... We have to keep everything legal. The judge may have a clue to your grandfather's location, as well.

If Emil returns to Frozen Oaks and discovers you're gone, he'll contact the judge first."

"You're certain that judge won't send us to the children's home?" Peter asked. "I want to stay with Sam."

She paused and her mouth worked. She wouldn't make promises she couldn't keep, and her despair was evident. How did he tell her that she had an unexpected ally? Jake's influence stretched beyond the US marshals. He'd made powerful friends over the course of his career. He'd been saving up favors, and now was the time to cash in those favors.

"You won't be separated," he said.

Though he wasn't as familiar with St. Joseph, he had contacts in Kansas City that owed him. He'd tap into the web of backroom deals and secret alliances. Whatever happened, he'd keep them together.

Men in suits carrying batches of paper scurried to and fro. The whole building smelled of ink and paper and tobacco smoke. For the first time since leaving Frozen Oaks, Jake breathed easier, though Lily kept darting him worried glances, unaware that he was in no danger from the law here.

They waited only a few minutes before Lily spotted the judge returning to his chambers between sessions. Though clearly surprised to see Lily, he motioned them toward a door with a placard bearing his name. He hung his dark robes on a wrought-iron coat tree and invited them to sit in his luxuriously appointed office.

The judge pulled two more chairs before his desk and gestured for the children to take a seat, as well. Jake considered the gesture a good sign. The judge clearly had the interests of the children at the forefront of his mind.

Jake took Lily's hand and gave her fingers a squeeze. "Don't worry."

Judge Ashford rested his elbows on the ink blotter protecting his polished oak desk. "I didn't expect to see you three back again."

Lily gave a brief summary of the past several days. She glossed over the jailbreak and Jake's fabricated identity, mentioning only that she was suspicious of Vic's motivation for assuming guardianship of the children.

When she finished, the judge rubbed his chin. "That's highly irregular. I commend your instincts, Miss Winter."

"Then Mr. Skaar hasn't contacted you? And you haven't heard from Emil?" Jake asked.

"No. I've heard nothing from Frozen Oaks. I haven't heard from Emil since the last telegram." He opened a drawer at his knee and riffled through the files. He set a folder on his desk. "This is the last correspondence I received from Emil Tyler."

He slid an envelope across the desk and Jake quickly scanned the contents. Lily accepted the letter and read through the pages, as well. Nothing in the letter gave any indication as to why he'd disappeared or where he might have gone.

"I'm sorry, folks," Judge Ashford said. "I can't tell you anything more. That's all I know."

Lily cleared her throat. "What will happen to the Tyler children?"

The judge shuffled the papers on his desk, a frown knitting his dark brows together. "There's no one else to take them in, I'm afraid. Emil Tyler was our best hope at reuniting them with family."

"Surely there's someone else? An uncle or an aunt? A second cousin."

"We looked at all those possibilities before. Sending

the children to an elderly man who lived in the middle of nowhere wasn't exactly my first choice." The judge fanned through more of his paperwork. "We can place them with the Sisters of Mercy. If Emil isn't located within the next six months, they'll be put up for adoption."

Lily half rose from her chair. "No!"

Jake placed a restraining hand on her arm. "I won't let that happen. I promise you." He reached for Sam's and Peter's hands. "I promise all of you. You'll stay together."

The judge gave a sad shake of his head. "I can't guarantee the children will be placed together, but I can add a note in the files. They seem healthy. They shouldn't have too much trouble finding a placement."

"They can stay with me," Lily said.

The judge set down his sheaf of papers. "You live with your family, then? Parents?"

"No. I'm, uh, I'm between living arrangements now."

"You must understand my difficulty." The judge leaned back in his chair. "I was reluctant to let you chaperone the Tyler children in the beginning. You've proved yourself more than capable of the task. Considering everything you've been through the past few days, the children were fortunate for your care. But I can't grant guardianship, even temporary guardianship, to a single woman without a home. Our goal is to place the children in a secure situation with families."

Lily hung her head. "I understand."

Sam and Peter appeared stricken.

"Marry me," Jake blurted.

Chapter Thirteen

Lily gaped. "Did you just propose marriage?"

"If we're married," Jake said, directing his speech toward the judge, "we can be guardians for the children, right?"

"The circumstances are highly unusual." The judge rested his palms on his ink blotter. "But I'm inclined to make an exception given the circumstances. If you went through the proper channels and applied to adopt the children, we'd give your request every consideration. I don't see why we can't accelerate the process. Especially taking into account your previous relationship with each other and the children."

The implications of his words left her temporarily speechless.

"Think about what you're saying." Lily frantically considered the ramifications. "What happens if Emil is never located? What happens if he's unable to return?"

The unsaid words hovered in the air between them. What if Emil hadn't gone into hiding—what if he was dead? Lily glanced between the two men. She was dazed from seeing the boardinghouse in ruins. A gunfighter she'd known for less than a week had just proposed marriage, and she couldn't find anything wrong with the idea. Certainly there was something wrong with this solution.

"What's your situation, mister?" the judge inquired. "I didn't catch your name."

"Jake Elder."

"Any relationship to John Elder?"

"He's my uncle."

"That clears up the rest of my doubts." The judge scratched his temple. "I worked with John on a train robbery case some years back. When you've been around as long as I have, you get to know most of the men breaking the law, and most of the men enforcing the law."

Lily tilted her head. John Elder must be on the right side of the law given the judge's obvious admiration. Was Jake lying about the relationship, or was he simply the black sheep of the family?

"I have loads of family," Jake said. "Sam and Peter will always have a home."

The judge looked between the two of them, folded his sheaf of papers and stuck them beneath one elbow. "Why don't you two step out into the corridor and sort this out?"

He gave a pointed look at the children, who were avidly following the conversation.

Lily glanced at Sam and Peter and nodded. The children's future hung in the balance. They shouldn't be speaking of them as though they were chattel.

"Don't worry." She gently tugged on Sam's braid. "We'll sort this out."

The idea was not without merit. She had no ties to anything or anyone except the children. She had nothing; therefore she had nothing left to lose. The idea was oddly liberating. She simply wasn't certain that Jake understood the entire scope of his proposal. He'd have to leave his old life behind and start over.

"Do you realize what you're saying?" She followed him into the corridor and paced the narrow space. "We have to think about their future. A permanent future."

"I am."

Lily rubbed her forehead. How had such a simple task turned into her entire future? A few weeks ago her life had taken a sudden turn. She didn't regret caring for the children. Though she'd only known them a short time, they were banded together. Someone else might have walked away and left them in Frozen Oaks with Vic Skaar.

"Can you make a home here?" she asked. "With your, you know, reputation?"

"I have an uncle," Jake said. "In Kansas."

"John Elder?"

"A different uncle. Jack Elder."

At least their names lined up. She snorted softly. They all began with the same letter. "Where in Kansas?"

"A place called Cimarron Springs. Just south of here. Near the border. No one will look for us there."

What other options did they have? The judge had made his stance clear. He'd put the children in an orphanage rather than hand them over to her care.

For once Lily sympathized with Sam's complaints about being a girl. As much as she'd like to rail against the judge, she had nothing to offer the children. She had the clothing on her back and a couple hundred dollars. Even if she planned on keeping them only until their grandfather was located, that wasn't much for even a temporary future.

Jake obviously had a past, but if he was willing to change, should she hold that past against him? Nothing in his actions had ever given her any doubt of his character. His actions spoke more eloquently than his history. He deserved a second chance as much as anyone else.

"The marriage would only be provisional," Jake continued. "We'll find a place to stay. My uncle will help. Once Emil is out of hiding, we can have the marriage annulled."

In many ways his solution was ideal. They'd stay together. They'd be well out of range of Vic's influence. If the worst happened, and they never located Emil, what then? She had to consider what was best for the children, not simply what was best for her.

Her mind raced with the possibilities. "You know my circumstances. Can you provide for us? At least until I'm able to find work."

"Yes. The alternative is leaving them in an orphanage. Alone. Or would you rather trust me?"

"Does your family know what you do for a living?"

"They do," Jake said. "Uncle John was my inspiration." He drew himself up to his full, dizzying height. "There's something else. I'm a US marshal."

Lily blinked. "Come again?"

"If we're going to do this, you deserve to know the truth. I'm a United States marshal."

While admission cleared up a multitude of curiosities, she'd developed a healthy skepticism over the past few weeks of people and their motivations.

Why hadn't he trusted her with this information sooner? She sat down hard on a bench set against the wall. "But I don't understand."

"My work requires me to assume other identities."

He rubbed the back of his neck. "I was investigating someone in Frozen Oaks."

"Let me guess. Vic Skaar."

There'd been plenty of opportunities for him to admit the truth. But would she have believed his explanation before now? Probably not. She'd have assumed he was lying for his own gain. Seeing his obvious ease in the courthouse, and the judge's knowledge of his family, the explanation carried more weight.

Besides, at this point, there was nothing to gain in lying anymore.

"I was investigating Vic," Jake replied. "I traced a shipment of faulty guns sold illegally to the Cherokee Nation back to Frozen Oaks. Vic was the obvious suspect. He didn't sell the entire shipment, which meant there was a chance I could lure him into selling the second half. Then I'd have my proof."

"Which meant you had to behave like a man who would buy guns illegally."

"Exactly."

All the odd clues fell into place. He behaved in the manner of a lawman because he *was* a lawman. At the jail in Frozen Oaks he'd referred to them as *civilians*. He'd cared for her during their journey. He'd looked out for the children. He'd chastised her for breaking him out of jail. Taken altogether, there was no reason to doubt his claim. Having gotten to know him, she certainly had a much easier time picturing him as a lawman than a gunfighter.

Despite her belief in him then, she still had questions. "Why were we running? Why didn't you say something in Frozen Oaks? Or Steele City? We dragged those children through the country on horseback for nothing."

His behavior had been much more heroic as an outlaw. As a lawman, his behavior was a deception.

"When I assume other identities, it's imperative that no one else knows. I can't carry any identification in case someone tries to check up on me. Which meant there was no way of proving my identity. I might as well have told them I was the president of the United States."

He was right. She'd made her decision about him from the beginning. Even when the truth was staring her in the face, she was loath to change her first impression. His actions had spoken louder than words, and yet she'd refused to listen. She was letting her personal feelings cloud her judgment. How had she doubted his bravery? Even for an instant.

Lily straightened. "And you think the children will be safe." His confession should have made the decision easier. Yet her courage faltered. Why did marrying a lawman suddenly feel so much more intimidating than marrying an outlaw? She stood and faced away from him, studying a wood-framed oil painting of horses grazing in a field. "In Cimarron Springs."

"No one in Frozen Oaks knows my true identity. There's no way they can trace us. We can buy time while we search for Emil."

She moved to the next picture, a cottage set in a copse of evergreens. "You said you had an uncle who lives there, as well."

"Yes. He's got children of his own. He'll help out."

"Won't he find it odd if you show up with a wife and two children?"

"No odder than anything else I've done. Certainly no odder than the way he met his wife."

"How did he meet his wife?"

"On a cattle drive," Jake replied.

"That's definitely unique."

"I'm fond of Sam and Peter. You're fond of Sam and Peter. Just because we're an unconventional choice, doesn't mean we're a bad choice. They know us. They're comfortable with you."

"I'm afraid I'm growing to love the little beasts." She turned away from the painting. "You knew I believed the worst about you. Why didn't you ever say something? You could have at least hinted."

"Would you have believed me?" A guilty flush spread up from his neck. "You saw me as a gunfighter. I had no proof that I was anything else. If I had simply declared myself a US marshal, what would you have said?"

"I'd have thought you were lying."

She'd already been through this in her head, but she needed to voice the words.

"Exactly. I did what I had to do."

He'd kept them safe. All along she'd seen the signs. She'd known something wasn't quite right in his temperament. She should have been relieved by his confession. Instead she felt an odd sense of betrayal. She'd thought his manner was special…she'd thought *she* was special. She'd concocted a story in her head and made herself the heroine: the incomparable Lily Winter taming the wild gunfighter. What a naive fool she'd been. She didn't doubt his bravery, but she doubted her own judgment.

Lily met his questioning gaze. "Everything you've ever said to me is a lie."

He'd said he admired her, was that a lie as well?

"That's not fair. You never once asked me who I was. You assumed. You assumed who I was, and what I was, just like everyone else."

The truth of the matter didn't make the acceptance of his deception, and her own gullibility, any easier. "We saw what you wanted us to see."

She wanted to lash out, but she wasn't entirely certain of the target.

"I'm the same man I was a minute ago, Lily. You trusted the outlaw. Why can't you trust the lawman?"

She made a sound of frustration in her throat. Why did he have to be so logical? She had counted on him when she'd thought he was a gunfighter. There was no reason she shouldn't continue to do so now. Neither her heart nor her head recognized the difference.

When she'd started falling for the outlaw, she'd known that nothing could ever come of her affection. Falling for a lawman was far riskier. There were far fewer barriers between them, and she had far fewer excuses.

"The judge is right," Lily said. Jake must never know she'd harbored feelings for him, especially if he was proposing a marriage of convenience. She could bear his deception, but she couldn't bear his pity "What happens if we can't locate Emil? What then?"

"That's up to you. Are you willing to care for Sam and Peter indefinitely?"

"Of course I am."

"You've been through an ordeal. Think carefully about your answer. You can find other work in St. Joseph. If you marry me, if you agree to care for the Tyler children, you'll be leaving everything you've ever known behind."

"Everything I've ever known has gone up in a blaze."

She'd counted on a place, not people. She had friends, but no one close. She had people she spoke with, regulars at the boardinghouse and acquaintances she chatted with at the market. Nothing that tied her here. All this time she'd been pinning her hopes on the house for a future, and one candle had destroyed everything. One vengeful act had shattered that future. She'd built her hopes on dry tinder, and not on a solid foundation.

"You saw the boardinghouse," Lily said. "There's nothing left. Everything I had, all my possessions—everything was wrapped up in that house."

"Then there's nothing keeping you here?"

"Nothing."

"This isn't the best solution," Jake said. "I know that. But I don't have any other ideas. You can take care of Sam and Peter. I'll search for their grandfather. If we can't find him, if—if something has happened to him, at least they'll have a home."

"True. And this is just a temporary marriage. Until we find Emil. If we don't find him, what then?"

"We'll find him."

If only she had his optimism. There was no reason she couldn't care for the children if they had the marriage annulled down the road. The judge had other cases. Once he'd assigned the guardianship, she doubted he'd give them a second thought.

She steeled herself for the next question. "Do you have a sweetheart?"

"No." He shrugged. "My work doesn't give me much time for that sort of thing. What about you?"

An unexpected rush of relief surged through her. "No."

"Then we don't have to worry about jealous suitors."

"Nope."

She had plenty of choices. She could walk away now and never look back. She'd taken care of herself before, she could do it again. There was no reason to stay. No reason but a couple of children who were all alone in the world. Two children she'd grown to care for. She couldn't imagine them alone, fending for themselves.

"Yes. Let's do this. Let's get married." She assumed a cheerful smile. "We should speak with Sam and Peter first. We're making decisions about their future. They should be included."

"You're right. Of course you're right." She turned but he held her back. "You have a choice, Lily. Don't feel like you have to do this. I'm not going to pressure you into anything."

Oh, dear. She was definitely falling for the lawman. A cold fear settled in her heart. If loving an outlaw was a poor choice, falling in love with a lawman wasn't much better. For him, this marriage was another case, another identity he assumed. She didn't know how to act. She only knew how to be genuine. All she could think about was him leaving, about never seeing him again. If she hadn't inspired her father to stay, what hope did she have?

"This is the right thing, Lily," Jake said. "I feel it."

His gaze became solemn and piercing, and her objections crumbled.

"I do, too."

They returned to the judge's chambers and he politely excused himself while they spoke with the children.

Lily knelt before them. "You two have been through a lot lately. Too much. You've lost your parents, you've been dragged halfway around the world, you've traveled across America and back. I don't know what happened to your grandfather, but it's apparent he loved you very much. Jake and I are going to do everything we can to find him, but I won't lie to you, we can't guarantee anything."

Sam's eyes shimmered with unshed tears. "You've been through a lot, too. I'm sorry you lost your house and all your stuff."

Lily blinked rapidly. "You're very kind, Sam. Everything I've lost can be replaced. Finding a safe and happy home for the two of you is what's important now. Mr. Elder and I have an idea."

"His name is Jake Elder for real?"

"Yes. And there's something else. He's not really an outlaw. He's a marshal with the United States government."

Sam and Peter gawked at Jake.

"A marshal?" Peter's lips twisted and his voice was tinged with disappointment. "He's not a gunfighter?"

"No."

"Then he was only pretending?"

"Yes."

"Then we weren't really on the run?" Peter demanded. "I thought we were on the run."

"We were," Lily assured him. "Sort of."

She ruffled his hair. Poor Peter might never recover from the disappointment.

"That's kind of neat," Sam said, appearing thoughtful. "He was fooling all those people. He fooled us."

"I certainly believed him." Lily smiled at Jake. "Although not entirely. I thought he was awfully concerned about following the law for a gunfighter."

Peter squinted. "It's not as exciting as being a gunfighter, but I suppose it's all right. I could still write a story about our adventures."

"A very exciting story," Lily said. "And the tale isn't over. Mr. Elder and I have an idea. If we get married, we can become your guardians. Just until we locate your grandfather," she quickly added. "Jake knows a place where we can stay for a while. I'm afraid it's another train ride."

"Ugh." Sam slumped. "I'm sick of riding on trains. Where would we stay?"

"Cimarron Springs, Kansas," Jake said. "It's southwest of here."

"Is it a town like Frozen Oaks? Are there gunfighters there?"

"I'm afraid not."

"I was hoping for gunfighters." Peter braced his hands on his knees and lifted his shoulders in a shrug. "Can I have my own horse?"

"We shouldn't make any permanent decisions until we've located your grandfather."

"All right," Peter said. "I'd rather go with you than stay here. Before Miss Lily became our chaperone, they made us stay in separate houses. One for girls, and one for boys. I'd rather stay together."

"Then that's what we'll do," Lily said. "We'll stay together."

"How will you get married?" Sam asked. "Do you have to find a church or something? Will you buy a dress?"

"Well, uh." Lily blushed. "We're in a bit of a hurry. I suppose the judge will marry us."

"Will you buy a new dress? We attended a wedding in Africa where the bride changed her dress three times."

"There's no time for a new dress. I'll just wear this."

"Jake looks all right." Peter rubbed his chin with a thumb and forefinger. "He looks better since he cut his hair."

Lily smoothed her hands over the coiled braid at the base of her neck. "Well, if that's settled."

At least she'd spent a few extra minutes on her hair this morning, and this dress was prettier than her others.

A mere fifteen minutes later, Lily stood before the judge, her hands shaking. Barely cognizant of her surroundings, she concentrated on taking steady breaths. This wasn't forever. This was simply a temporary solution. They'd find the children's grandfather, and then annul the marriage.

She was homeless and marrying a virtual stranger. A man who, until a few minutes ago, she had assumed was a gun for hire. The majority of her possessions were in cinders. Her lips twitched. Just another ordinary day. If she'd read something like this in one of Peter's books, she'd have scoffed.

Sam and Peter flanked them. Sam took her hand and squeezed, and the last of Lily's doubts faded.

She smiled down at the girl, who returned the gesture.

Lily reached for Jake's hand. His palm was warm, rough and calloused. Her heart filled with unexpected joy. At once her decision came into focus. This was real. This marriage was happening. The judge pronounced them man and wife, and Jake leaned over and kissed her cheek. Peter pressed a hand over his giggle.

After the excitement of the past several days, the train ride to Cimarron Springs was startlingly uneventful. Lily ate her ginger cookies and tolerated the trip with only a mild bout of sickness. Showing remarkable fortitude, Sam and Peter had taken the change of plans in stride. The frantic pace of the past days had caught up with them, and they were more subdued than usual, though not melancholic.

Jake had visited the marshal's office in St. Joseph and discovered that his jailbreak hadn't been pursued beyond the surrounding towns.

The news had left him more confused than relieved. If the sheriff hadn't contacted the law, what were he and Vic planning?

Jake had also wired his uncle in Cimarron Springs. Since Jake's parents had married young, the difference in their ages was less than a decade, and they treated one another more like cousins than uncle and nephew. John had settled in Cimarron Springs eight or nine years back. The youngest of seven brothers, John had left Paris, Texas, to find his own way. Jake couldn't blame him. The Elders were a loving but overpowering bunch.

The train pulled into the station and his stomach churned. For reasons he didn't want to examine, he was nervous about how Lily would view the town. Though he loved Texas and his birthplace, he'd returned to this part of Kansas more than once over the years, and Cimarron Springs was starting to feel more like home than Texas.

Passengers filed past them but the four remained seated. Lily glanced at him expectantly and he offered her a reassuring smile.

They stood and followed the crowd. He exited last, pausing on the stair as he searched the crowd. He caught sight of his Uncle John waving his hat and grinning.

John maneuvered through the crowd and paused before them. "Welcome to Cimarron Springs, Mrs. Elder."

Lily glanced over her shoulder before realizing that she was Mrs. Elder.

"Mr. Elder." She took his hand in greeting. "Thank you for meeting us."

Uncle and nephew resembled each other, though there were more gray strands glinting in John's hair.

His smile was warm. "Jake has helped me out more than once over the years, and I'm happy to return the favor."

Jake and his uncle shared a quick handshake and pat on the shoulder.

"This must be Samantha," John said. "And you must be Peter."

Peter gestured at the wagon John had been leaning against. "Jake says you raise horses. Are those your horses?"

"Those horses were raised by our neighbor, Shane McCoy. They're draft horses, or working horses. I raise riding horses."

"Can I see your horses sometime?"

"Absolutely." John replaced his hat. "I'm sure you folks are famished. I didn't want to overwhelm you by bringing the whole clan. The children can be a handful. The wife says you're invited to dinner as soon as you like."

"Thank you," Lily said. "That's very kind of you. I can certainly tell the two of you are related. You look more like brothers than uncle and nephew."

"We hear that a lot," John said. "Jake's parents married young. How's my brother? I haven't spoken with him since he bought a couple of horses last spring."

"Fine," Jake said.

He hadn't talked with his father in months, but he planned on rectifying the oversight.

"There's a new tearoom in town," John said. "And they serve an excellent meat loaf lunch. At least that's what the wife says. I don't go in for tearooms much my-self. The marshal would like to talk with Jake sooner rather than later."

"He's in town?" Jake raised an eyebrow. "I thought he was traveling this week."

"Garrett is here, for once. He's been traveling nearly every week. JoBeth is not happy about his schedule, I can tell you that. And when JoBeth is annoyed, we're all aware." John faced Lily. "JoBeth is Garrett's wife. She also works part-time at the telegraph office. She's another McCoy. The whole town is full of McCoys. Now that you're here, Jake, the Elders can give them a run for their money."

Though anxious to speak with his fellow marshal, Jake hesitated. "I can meet with Garrett later. I shouldn't leave Lily and the children alone when we've only just arrived."

They hadn't been separated for the past few days, and he'd become accustomed to keeping them in sight. Though he was confident no one had followed them to Cimarron Springs, he was torn between wanting to ensure Lily was settled, and needing to hear the mar-shal's news.

"Don't worry about us," Lily said smoothly. "We're used to taking care of ourselves."

"I can help," John added. "I'll show you around town, introduce you to some people."

"Thank you," Lily said. "I'd enjoy that."

"That settles it, then," John declared. "You head on over to the marshal's office, and I'll finally try this meat loaf and potatoes my wife has been raving about." He faced Sam and Peter. "I have four children, and they know all the best places for ice fishing, the best hills for sledding and the best trails for horseback riding. I can't wait for you to meet them."

Peter had perked up at the mention of horseback riding. "That's a lot of kids."

John rolled his eyes. "You don't have to tell me that."

Jake followed their progress with mixed emotions. He didn't like losing sight of them, even though he knew there was little chance of trouble anytime soon. They were safe enough with John. Though expensive telegrams hadn't allowed him to reveal the full extent of the problem, he'd given Garrett an outline, and he was confident his fellow marshal would fill in the blanks.

His protective feelings for Lily and the children were natural. Plans for the future dominated his thoughts. He'd see that she replaced her ruined wardrobe as soon as they were settled. He enjoyed seeing her dressed in the bright colors she favored. He was looking forward to seeing her in a jaunty hat that showed off her hair instead of the enveloping bonnet.

Perhaps if he bought some land…

Jake shook off the thought. Even Garrett, who was posted permanently to Cimarron Springs, was forced to travel. His absence was obviously causing friction between him and his wife. Besides, there was nothing in this town for Jake. He'd be gone and focused on another case as soon as they found Emil. There was no use thinking about a future that would never be.

Lily glanced over her shoulder and caught him staring at her.

Even from a distance, he admired the striking blue of her expressive eyes. She smiled and his heartbeat quickened. She turned away once more, but he didn't move. He carefully committed the moment to memory. He never wanted to forget the way the sunlight sparkled off the fresh layer of snow, the pink of Lily's cheeks in the chill cold, the way her lips parted in a smile. After a long moment, he made his way to the marshal's office.

Marshal Garrett Cain was much as Jake remembered him. A little grayer around the temples, but tall and commanding. There was an inherent air of authority about the man.

Jake relayed his story with as much detail as he could muster, filling in all the facts he'd neglected in their brief correspondence. When he finished, the marshal steepled his fingers.

"I received this from the authorities in St. Joseph." He pushed a paper across his desk. "They believe the fire at the boardinghouse was arson."

"I had my suspicions." Jake slumped back in his seat. "I don't believe in coincidences."

"Neither do I. There's more. The fire started in a second-floor room."

"Let me guess. Lily's room."

"Yes. The person who started the fire doused the place with kerosene. That part of the building was incinerated. Someone was sending your wife a message."

"That's the part I don't understand. Why force her from her home? What was he hoping to accomplish?"

"Both good questions," Garrett said. "I checked the information the landlady provided against what was reported in the newspaper. All the boarders were questioned. All of them were cleared."

"Somebody is missing something." Jake didn't trust the law in St. Joseph to check all the possibilities. "The blaze was set in broad daylight. I can't believe there's no evidence of the trespasser."

"The house had eight bedrooms including the two Lily and the landlady claimed. Three of the rooms were occupied, and two of the tenants were in residence. Apparently one of the boarders heard noises in the kitchen. Thought it was just the landlady. Lily's room was on the top floor. No one heard anything from up there, but the tenants' rooms were on the north side and Lily's was on the south side. Probably fortunate for those fellows. The fire spread quickly."

"All we can assume is that the target was Lily."

"Which leads us back to your earlier question. Why? The perpetrator knew she wasn't home. What's the point?"

"Maybe he thought she was there already. We were late. The trip took two days longer than it should have. A lone man on horseback, riding hard, could make the distance in a day."

"Or revenge. How well do you know your new wife? Does she have any enemies? What do we know about the landlady?"

"Revenge." Jake mulled over the thought. "No. Lily's not the sort of person who makes enemies. The landlady was taking money from Lily to buy the house. She wouldn't burn down a sure thing."

"Then we have to assume this was a message. What else do we know about Lily? Was she acquainted with Vic Skaar or Emil Tyler before a few weeks ago?"

"No. She answered an advertisement."

"The article you discovered about the Tyler children was printed in the same newspaper. Might be something to that."

Jake stared at his clasped hands. "I don't follow."

"Have you considered that Lily might be involved? There are a lot of coincidences piling up around her. She's permanent guardian to those kids now."

"Along with me."

"She thought you were a gun for a hire when you met."

"Yes. But she knew I was a US marshal when she married me."

Garrett tugged on his ear. "You've known this woman a week, and now you're married to her. She has access to the money left to the Tyler children. I'm telling you to be careful."

A flush of anger heated Jake's face. "And I'm telling you she's not involved."

"All right." The marshal held up his hands in surrender. "I can tell the subject is closed. What have you learned about Emil Tyler?"

"Not much. He's never lived in one place longer than a year. He runs a high-stakes poker game out of the back of his barbershop."

"Emil doesn't stay in one place very long. He won a large sum of money and a hotel from a very powerful man. You think he's a cheat?"

"No. I think it's more a matter of wearing out his welcome. I made a few inquiries around town. My guess is that he sets up shop and starts out small. He runs a few games, loses a little, then starts winning. Once he's acquired a sufficient amount of money, he pulls up stakes and starts over in another town."

"Smart man," Garrett said. "He steers clear of the law, and leaves town before there's trouble."

"That's my guess given his history. From the comments his grandchildren have made, there was no love lost between their father and grandfather. The son didn't approve of his lifestyle."

"Emil doesn't strike me as the best choice for guardian."

"He was the only choice."

"I guess we'll worry about his suitability when we locate him," Garrett said. "What now? We'll keep watch once you're settled. I can have the bank keep watch, as well. Just in case someone attempts to withdraw money from the Tyler children's account. What do you need beyond that?"

"Meet Lily before you make a judgment." Anger tightened in Jake's stomach. Garrett clearly saw Lily as a threat. "Right now she's the best thing for those children. They need some stability in their lives, and Lily cares for them."

"What about you? What's your next move?"

"I won't believe Emil is dead until I gather more proof. Everything leads back to Frozen Oaks."

"You can't get within fifty miles of that town. You're known."

"Do you have a better idea?"

"Let someone else search for Emil. I'll watch out for your family as best I can, but the Tyler children are vulnerable. Someone set fire to Lily's rooms at the boardinghouse. We can't underestimate the determination of this Vic character. Men like that don't take losing in stride."

Jake shifted in his seat. The air in the room was thick and he tugged on his collar. Lily and the children were his responsibility. They were his family. Leaving them alone was out of the question. Yet doing nothing felt wrong, as well.

"This is my case," Jake said. "I know the details better than anyone. I'm invested in the outcome."

"There are good marshals in the service. If Emil is out there, they'll find him. You're not the only one who can follow a trail, you know."

The pressure in Jake's chest built. He knew Vic

Skaar. He had all the pieces. He was the best person to put them in order and figure out the connections. Letting go of the investigation was wrong. But so was leaving Lily and her charges alone and vulnerable.

"I'll give you everything I have," Jake said. "But we work together on the case."

"Understood. What else do you need? Where are you staying?"

"Don't know yet. I was planning on asking my uncle. Is Agnes still taking on boarders? Is the hotel full up?"

"Agnes has retired. Sarah was helping out, but she's teaching now. There's plenty of room at the hotel, but that's no place to live for any extended period of time. I suggest you think about something more permanent. You have to consider that we might not be able to find Emil, or he might not want to be found. What happens then? You'll be moving the children again."

"We'll find Emil."

Everything about the case bothered him. The timing was all wrong. The events didn't follow a clear line. There were too many variables. The poker game. The children. He'd checked the delivery of the St. Joseph papers to the mercantile in Frozen Oaks. They were two weeks behind the regular schedule. Which meant Vic hadn't seen the story about Emil's grandchildren until after Emil had disappeared. Either Vic had known Emil wasn't coming back, or he'd simply caught a break.

"Do you recall Caleb McCoy?" Garrett asked.

"The veterinarian. He married the suffragist, right?"

"They finished their new house this spring. As far as I know, the old house is empty now. It's a nice-size house—they added on after they were married. Sits on an acre or two of land. The barn is in good repair, as well. You'll be close to town and surrounded by neighbors."

Jake recalled the property. He'd spoken with the vet about a problem he was having with one of his horses the last time he was in town. "Being surrounded by neighbors didn't work out so well for Mrs. McCoy."

A few years before, there'd been a shootout at Caleb's house when someone tried to kidnap his wife.

"The circumstances were different," Garrett said. "Everyone in town was at the Harvest Festival. They repaired the bullet holes."

"Peter will be devastated. The boy would adore living in a house with bullet holes." Jake was arguing just to argue, but that didn't quell his frustration. "All right. I'll talk with Caleb and take a look at his house."

"The sooner those children have a permanent home, the better."

"We left their trunks and the bulk of their belongings in Frozen Oaks."

"We'll sort that later. There's no way of sending for them without tipping off whoever is looking."

Jake stood and crossed the room, then stared out the window overlooking the street. "Fine. You win. Where can I find Caleb McCoy?"

The more time he spent with Lily, the harder it was to leave.

Chapter Fourteen

"We're coming with you," Lily insisted.

If Jake was making decisions about her future, she wasn't being left behind.

"All right," Jake replied. "Everyone grab your coats."

At his easy capitulation, Lily raised her eyebrows. Jake had returned from his meeting with the marshal cranky and uncommunicative. He'd mumbled something about visiting the local veterinarian about a house for rent, and she'd put her foot down. They were a team, and they'd make their decisions together.

"We can walk," he said. "The house isn't far."

Having spent much of the past few days cooped up in a hotel or traveling, Sam and Peter bounded ahead of them. The snow had been well traveled, and the path was lined with leafless trees. Sam stooped and pressed a snowball between her hands. The siblings engaged in a good-natured fight, laughing and chasing each other along the path.

Jake flipped up his collar and stuffed his hands in his pockets.

She caught his gaze. "Did the marshal have bad news?"

"He didn't have any news. We're dead in the water."

"Maybe Vic has given up."

"I doubt it. I think he's bad off. He wants that hotel back. If he can't find Emil, he'll come for the children. I'm certain of it."

Lily shivered. "At least there's no way for him to trace us back here."

"There's always a way," Jake said. "Don't let down your guard. Are you cold?"

"No. Just thinking about what might have happened to us if we hadn't found you."

"You didn't find me. You broke me out of jail."

She bent and grasped a handful of snow. "As you keep reminding me."

He walked ahead of her and she pelted him in the back.

Peter tossed another snowball and caught him in the chest.

"This is war," Sam shouted.

"Boys against girls," Peter called.

For the next ten minute they laughed and fought. Lily skirted around the trees lining the path and waged a fierce battle. Peter took off farther down the road and Sam chased after her brother.

Jake proved surprisingly agile for a man of his size. She hid behind the trunk of an enormous oak tree. Carefully peering around the edge, she squealed. He was poised before her with a handful of the freezing white stuff.

"Stop!" Lily broke down in a fit of laughter. She reached for more snow but she didn't stand a chance against him. "You're too fast."

"We never had much snow in Paris, Texas," he declared. "But my brothers and I made the most of it when we did."

She reached for another handful of ammunition, but he tackled her to the ground, laughing.

"No fair." She pouted. "You're bigger and faster."

He surprised her by dropping a kiss on her forehead. "You've got snow in your hair."

She stilled, trapped between the freezing ground and the warmth of his body. "You didn't kiss me properly during the wedding ceremony."

Shocked by her own audacity, she held her breath for his reaction.

"I better correct the oversight."

He kissed her, a long and lingering embrace that had her clutching the scratchy wool of his coat. Breaking the kiss, he leaned away. She stared at him, dazed. He appeared equally shaken.

Her hair had tumbled free from the knot at the nape of her neck. He ran his hand along the length, reverently pinching a curl between his thumb and forefinger.

"You have the prettiest hair. That day in Frozen Oaks when you stepped off the stagecoach, I noticed your hair first."

"I didn't think you'd even seen me."

"I saw you. I wondered what such a beautiful woman was doing in such a desolate place."

The marvel in his voice moved her. She touched his cheek. "I thought you had the most beautiful eyes I'd ever seen."

"Men don't have beautiful eyes."

"You do."

Someone smashed a wad of snow in his hair. Lily shrieked. Jake rolled away and Sam pelted him again.

"I win!" she shouted.

"You win." Jake stood and reached for Lily. "The ladies take the day."

In an instant the moment was lost. Jake retreated, as though embarrassed by his actions. He yanked his collar up once more, and motioned them forward.

"This is where Caleb lives," he said.

Lily paused before the delightful three-story structure and shielded her eyes from the sun with her hand. The white clapboard house featured gingerbread scrollwork at the eves and a wraparound porch. As she traversed the wide stairs, she admired the porch swing hanging from chains at the far end.

Sam blew out a low whistle. "Veterinarians must do well in this part of the country."

"Caleb does all right." Jake grasped the brass door knocker and rapped sharply. "Doesn't hurt that his wife, Anna, is an heiress."

The door swung open and a stunning brunette stood on the threshold. She wore a satin gown in a brilliant shade of cerise that must have cost a fortune. The square bodice was lined with neat pleats, and her skirts were drawn back to a modest bustle. Instantly aware of her disheveled appearance, Lily brushed a hand over her hair.

The woman smiled at them. "May I help you?"

"I'm Jake Elder, this is Lily, uh, this is my wife, Lily."

"I think we met once before." Anna frowned. "Any relation to John and Moira Elder?"

"I'm John's nephew."

"Come inside." Anna waved them forward. "We can't have you standing out in the cold."

"We should wait outside." Lily stamped the snow from her boots. "We'll track mud into your house."

"Don't fret about a little dirt." Anna lifted her gaze

toward the ceiling. "You wouldn't believe some of the things my husband tracks into the house."

She hustled them into a cozy parlor tastefully decorated in shades of burgundy. Another gentleman joined them. Tall and well-built, his hair was dark and neatly trimmed. His eyes were a distinct shade of green. He wrapped his arm around his wife's waist in an affectionate gesture.

"Jake Elder, if I'm not mistaken," Caleb said. "You came through town last year, if I recall."

"You have a good memory, Mr. McCoy. This is my wife, Lily, and this is Samantha and Peter. We're looking for a house to rent. Marshal Cain thought you might have a suitable property. We need something soon. Immediately, actually."

"Absolutely. I'll get my coat and the keys and we can look right now."

As her husband exited the room, Anna tsked. "You'll find the house neat as a pin, but not dusted or scrubbed. My husband is orderly but he doesn't always see the dust and dirt."

"That's quite all right," Lily said. "I don't mind a little cleaning up."

Caleb returned with his coat and they followed him outside. He rubbed his hands together and squinted at the sky. "This weather is deceptive. I'm expecting a blizzard before long."

Sam skipped up beside him. "Do you really think so?"

"I have a hunch," Caleb said. "You get a feeling about the weather once you've lived in the Midwest long enough. This sort of day fools a body into thinking winter is resting, but she's just biding her time. Mark my words."

He paused before a two-story structure with a white picket fence enclosing the front yard, and a full porch with a porch swing. The house sat on a large tract of land, an acre or perhaps two, with an enormous tree that would shade the front yard in the summer, and a small barn visible out back.

"This is the house," Caleb said. "We added the second story after we were married. Eventually Anna decided she'd rather have my offices separate from the house. There's nothing like having an escaped goat gallop through the parlor."

He opened the door and waited as they filed inside. The entrance led to an open foyer and a cozy parlor with an enormous stone fireplace. Glass-paned double doors opened to a room on their right. A corridor bisected the house, giving a sightline to the back door. Stairs led to the second floor.

Caleb gestured to his right. "That used to be my office." He led them down the center and gestured left and right. "When we added the second story we enlarged the kitchen and added a dining room separated by a pantry. The four bedrooms are upstairs. The house was set up in the Southern fashion, with a center corridor to allow for a cross breeze when it's warm outside. Along with the trees out front, the place stays cool as a root cellar in the summertime."

High ceilings lent an open, airy quality to the home. The kitchen walls were lined with floor-to-ceiling cupboards, and Lily was instantly enamored. She enjoyed cooking, and this kitchen was a cook's dream.

Caleb flicked the curtains aside on the back door. "Do you have any animals?"

"A couple of horses," Jake said. "I'll send for them later."

"You'll have plenty of room for horses," Caleb said.

Peter tugged on her sleeve. "Can we look at the barn?"

"I suppose." The barn didn't seem all that interesting, but the children were probably sick of being cooped up on the train and needed a bit of fresh air. "Stay close and don't go climbing into the hay loft."

"Why not?"

"Because you might fall out."

"You're fussing." Sam rolled her eyes. "We'll be careful."

The two skipped down the path that ran between two garden patches.

Caleb followed Lily's gaze. "I was the gardener in the family. Anna is partial to her rose bushes. You'll have plenty of cuttings come spring."

"Oh, I don't think we'll be here that long."

"However long you need the place," he replied easily. "The house has been sitting empty for months. It'll be nice to have children running around again. Why don't I give you two a moment alone and you can make a decision. I'll keep an eye on Sam and Peter."

He tipped his hat and pushed out the back door.

Jake and Lily stared at each other.

"I think—"

"Whatever you want—"

They both began speaking at once.

Lily chuckled. "I think it's a wonderful property. I admit I'm falling in love with the kitchen."

"Only the kitchen?"

Her heartbeat stuttered. "I like to cook."

"I'm partial to the fireplace in the parlor. I always did like a fire on a cold night."

"Yes. The parlor."

Her breathing returned to normal. She was being ridiculous. Of course he'd merely been talking about the house. The kiss in the snow had her thinking all sorts of crazy things.

"I think the house is perfect," he said. "There are plenty of bedrooms, plenty of space. We won't bother each other."

"No." Bothering each other was the least of her worries. "This is a lovely town."

"Would you, uh, would you consider staying after we find Emil?"

"There's nothing left for me in St. Joseph." Losing the boardinghouse had shaken her more than she'd let on to Jake. She felt as though she'd been set adrift, and she wasn't certain where to steer her ship. "I suppose I'll make arrangements when the time comes."

"If you'd like, I could…" His voice drifted off.

"You could what?"

A shrill scream cut off his next words.

With Lily close on his heels, Jake slammed through the back door and dashed toward the barn. He slid open the double doors and frantically searched the dim interior.

Sam lay flat on her back, giggling. A young goat had two hooves on her chest.

Caleb shook his head and wrestled the goat off. "Sorry for the panic. This is Finnick. He's the son of a very precocious goat named Pipsqueak. I'm afraid Finnick never adjusted to the move. He's quite stubborn, like his father. I've discovered him here on more than one occasion."

Lily assisted Samantha to her feet and brushed at the dirt on her coat. "Are you all right?"

"I'm fine. He surprised me, that's all. I opened up the stall door and he leapt on me."

Caleb rubbed the animal between its ears. "I'll be telling your papa on you."

"Can we keep him?" Sam asked. "I think he likes me."

"I'm not certain anyone can really claim Finnick," Caleb said. "He has a mind of his own."

Jake's heart hammered against his chest. He struggled against the terror that had gripped him when he heard Sam scream. Normally coolheaded, he'd thought of nothing but reaching her. He could have run right into a trap.

Caleb scrounged a rope from a worktable on the far side of the barn. "I'll take him home. Just keep a sharp eye out. He'll be back. Bring him home when he's worn out his welcome."

Jake nodded, not trusting his voice.

"Have you decided?" Caleb asked.

"Yes." Jake found his voice. The look on Lily's face when they'd walked into the kitchen had made his decision. He'd pay any price to see that pure joyfulness again. "But not for renting. I wonder if you'd consider selling the house?"

He caught Lily's shocked look from the corner of his eye. There was a chance they'd never locate Emil, and moving the children again seemed unnecessarily cruel. Even if Emil came out of hiding, there was still the matter of Lily. She'd need someplace to stay. She'd lost everything; there was no reason she couldn't start over in Cimarron Springs.

Caleb hoisted the stubborn goat into his arms. "I'll check with Anna, but I'm certain she won't object.

Come by my offices tomorrow and we can work out the deal."

"Done."

"Isn't that a bit risky?" After Caleb left, Lily turned to him. "What if you can't sell the house later?"

He avoided her questioning gaze. "The house is an investment."

Uncertain of her reaction, he held his tongue. There was no point in worrying about the future until the time came.

Sam hooked her hands on the ladder leading up to the hay loft. "I like the house."

"Me, too."

Together they returned inside, and Sam and Peter dashed up the stairs to pick out their bedrooms.

Lily tugged open a closet door. "At least we have most of the furnishings. There are linens and towels in here. Anna must have a high standard of cleanliness. Despite her warning, everything is pristine."

"We couldn't ask for a better solution."

"Are you certain you want to invest that much money? I can't… I mean, I have a little."

He took her hands. "This is my idea, and my expense."

His gaze dropped to her lips. Only moments before, he'd kissed her. Longing flared in his chest. They were close enough a sigh could close the distance. Did that kiss weigh as heavily on her mind as it did on his? He didn't want to feel anything for her; he didn't want this dangerous draw on his senses. She wasn't a part of his plans.

He'd played the outlaw. Now he was playing a husband. Nothing more, nothing less. More playacting for the case. He'd shed this identity as quickly as he'd shed the last. Except none of this felt like playacting. In fact, everything about Lily was very, very real.

"What do we do now?" she asked, sounding slightly breathless. "What is the next part of the plan?"

"We wait." For the next few days he'd play his part. "The marshal's office has taken the case."

"What do we do while we're waiting?"

"I don't know." She was becoming essential to him, and he feared his growing need. Losing his mother had taught him how deep grief could cut, and he never wanted to feel that pain again. "I guess we do whatever families do."

Jake feared he was already in too deep.

Chapter Fifteen

Two weeks following the move to Cimarron Springs, Lily punched down the bread dough and wiped her forehead with the back of her hand. In order to dissipate the awkwardness of their living situation, she was treating their circumstances as though they were all boarders in the same house.

While the accommodations were slightly smaller, the general idea remained the same. There were meals to be cooked and linens to be cleaned. She and Jake treated each other as though they were fellow boarders, as well. They offered polite greetings and made small talk at dinner.

They didn't kiss.

Though she'd frequently chafed at the monotony of housework before, after the chaos of her trip to Frozen Oaks, she'd embraced the mindless activities with gusto. If anyone had noticed something odd about the arrangement, they were too polite to question her.

They'd blended seamlessly into the town. Samantha and Peter had started school. Though their situation was only temporary, they enjoyed meeting the new children. They'd even made new friends. Their many tales of Africa and other travels had endeared them to the children. Not a day went by that Lily didn't marvel at their resilience.

None of them spoke of the future. Jake met with the marshal in town each day and they continued their search for Emil. In the interim, Jake assisted the marshal with other cases. They'd fallen into a pleasant routine marred only by the nagging fear of being discovered.

Jake's footsteps sounded from the front room and she tucked a stray lock of hair behind one ear.

He stepped into the kitchen and paused. "You're up early."

"I couldn't sleep."

He crossed to the larder and snatched a biscuit from the previous evening's meal. "I don't know if I've thanked you properly for taking over the cooking. You'd be sorely disappointed in my efforts."

"I don't mind. I like having something to keep me occupied."

He propped one hip against the counter. "Do you miss St. Joseph?"

"Sometimes. Not as much as I thought. I was marveling at how resilient the children are."

"They've traveled all their lives. I suppose they're accustomed to being uprooted."

She separated the bread dough into four loaves. "Have you discovered anything more about Vic?"

"Nothing of use. He's gone quiet. According to the man the marshal sent up, he and Regina are running the hotel as though they own the place."

"Without Emil to dispute their claim, they can continue indefinitely."

"Yep."

"Which leaves us exactly where we started. Lots of rumors and suspicions, but no proof of anything."

"Yes."

"I'm sorry."

"For what?"

"This must be very frustrating for you. You're trapped here, with us, when you'd rather be playing the outlaw in Frozen Oaks."

He slathered butter on his roll. "Playing the outlaw isn't nearly as entertaining as it sounds. Besides, I much prefer the company here."

"You're kind to say so."

Truth be told, she was surprised he'd stayed as long as he had. After the first week, she'd expected him to bolt. She knew the signs. She'd seen the anxious tap of his leg at the dinner table when he talked about his work. She'd seen the way he gazed out the window each evening, as though planning his escape. She'd seen those same signs often enough in her father. Jake needed danger, and there wasn't much adventure to be had in a small town with a wife and children.

Jake glanced down the hallway and lowered his voice. "There's been no word about Emil either. I thought for certain he'd surface by now. He must be worried about his grandchildren, but he hasn't contacted the judge in St. Joseph. We've gone through all the mail you brought from Frozen Oaks. He's vanished."

She stepped a little closer in case her voice carried. "Which means he's dead, or he doesn't want to be found."

"Exactly."

"What about the stagecoach and the livery?"

"I haven't heard anything from the stagecoach company, and we can't contact the livery without tipping off Vic and the sheriff."

"And I destroyed any chance of you returning."

"I did that."

The twinge of guilt remained. "In my defense, I didn't realize you were a US marshal. I might have behaved differently."

"Then I'm glad you didn't know. As long as you and the children are safe, then I've done my job."

Peter stumbled into the room, bleary-eyed from sleep, effectively ending their conversation. Lily and Jake exchanged a look over his head. There'd be time enough for talk later. There was no use worrying the children.

Jake rinsed his hands in the basin by the sink. "I'm helping out the marshal this afternoon. I might be late."

"Again?"

"The territory has doubled in size since he was assigned. He can't keep up. As long as I'm here, I thought I'd help out."

"You'll be happier if you keep busy."

"I'm not unhappy."

She raised her eyebrows in question. "You must be bored."

"Excitement is overrated."

Peter asked for milk, interrupting their banter.

Better that Jake assisted the marshal than prowl around here like a caged animal. He'd hidden his discontent well, but it was apparent he wasn't a man who could sit around idly. Though he'd made some minor repairs on the house, there hadn't been much else for him to occupy his time with. If something didn't happen soon, she feared he'd leave them.

She didn't doubt he'd see to their safety, but she'd miss him. She'd miss him desperately.

"By the way," Jake said, "my uncle and his wife have invited us for supper."

"Do you think that's a good idea?" She slanted a glance at Peter. "You know, considering our circumstances."

"Two weeks ago when I asked you how we should behave, you told me that we should behave as a regular family. Regular families have dinners with other families."

"All right, all right. You know them best. If you think it's a good idea, we'll go."

"Friday." He shrugged into his coat. "I thought we might visit with the marshal and his wife, as well."

"You're becoming quite the social butterfly."

"The marshal and I have been working several cases." He took another bite of his breakfast. "As for my uncle, I need another horse."

Her smile faded. She mustn't forget this was all business for him. Meeting with the marshal was a chance to talk work. Meeting with his uncle was a chance to buy horses. She was reading too much into the simple events.

"I'd enjoy seeing your uncle again."

Jake palmed his hat. "Then I'll make the arrangements. Don't wait up. There's a claim dispute with a stack of paperwork."

She glanced behind her and noticed flakes drifting past the window. "We'll be here. Mind the snow. Caleb thinks we might see a blizzard."

"Caleb has been predicting a blizzard for the past two weeks."

"One day he might be right."

"I guess if you throw enough darts at the board, you're bound to hit a bull's-eye eventually." He set his hat on his head and adjusted the brim. "If the weather gets bad, I'll come home early."

He was no more obligated to her than another boarder, but she appreciated that he always kept her apprised of his schedule.

The rest of the morning passed quickly. Samantha and Peter had finished their chores and sat in the parlor playing checkers. Lily stood over the sink and washed their lunch plates. She caught sight of something moving out the back kitchen window.

Crossing to the door, she abandoned her rising bread and wiped her hands on a towel. A very familiar goat scurried across the fresh coating of snow, his hooves leaving a speckled trail over the lawn.

She sighed and fetched the children. "We have a visitor. Finnick has returned."

Their faces lit up. "Has he gone in the barn?"

"I think so. Why don't you fetch him home?"

She glanced outside. The snow fell in a steady sheet. Enormous, beautiful flakes that almost seemed suspended in air.

"Don't dawdle, though. If the snow becomes heavier, it'll be difficult to see your way home."

"Ah, don't worry," Sam said. "Caleb McCoy doesn't live very far. There's no way we can get lost between here and there. We've made the trip a thousand times."

Once the two were bundled from head to toe, Lily ushered them out the back door. Returning Finnick had become almost a daily ritual. The children enjoyed Caleb, and the veterinarian always had some critter or another he was looking after.

Since she had the afternoon to herself, Lily cut the

dough into strips and began forming them into knots. The rolls took a little extra time, but with the snow falling and the stove warming the house, she hadn't much else to do.

Lily was engrossed in the task, and the time passed swiftly. When the clock in the parlor chimed, she started.

She crossed to the back window once more and scratched a bit of frost from the pane. Gone was the cheery scene. Snow sheeted down in a thick blanket. Her chest seized. She swung open the door and sharp flecks of ice peppered her face. The children were nowhere in sight.

As she quickly freed herself from her apron, a myriad of dire consequences swirled through her head. Had Sam and Peter gotten lost? Hurt? Were they simply at Caleb's house waiting out the storm?

She forced a deep breath into her lungs. Probably Caleb had a new animal, and they'd gotten distracted. With that bracing thought, she donned her coat and boots, then fetched her hat and gloves. She'd walk the children home herself.

Once outside, the sharp wind stung her eyes, and she ducked her head. How had the weather changed this rapidly? The few blocks to Caleb's home took an eternity. Though she searched, there was no sign of the children.

Barely visible through the swirling snow, the veterinarian's office was a separate building near the three-story house. By the time she reached the door, her fingers had gone numb in her mittens.

She knocked and Caleb answered, his eyebrows rising in surprise. "Mrs. Elder. Come in, come in. What's gotten you out in this weather?"

"The children. Sam and Peter. Have you seen them? They were bringing Finnick home."

"I've been here all morning." He shook his head. "They haven't been by."

Her heart plummeted. "They haven't come home either."

Caleb guided her to a chair and urged her to sit.

"I'll get my coat," he said. "The marshal's office is only a block from here. We'll fetch your husband and Garrett, then send out a search party."

He spoke with calm, matter-of-fact authority, but she sensed the urgency in his voice. Pressure built behind her eyes. Grateful for his speedy response to the situation, she stood and gazed out the window. Once he'd shrugged into his hat and coat, she followed him outside. The snow nearly blinded her. Without Caleb's back to follow, she doubted she'd have made it to the marshal's office.

The warmth immediately enveloped her. She stomped the snow from her boots and whipped off her chilled mittens.

Jake stood from behind a desk heaped with papers. "What's happened?"

A surge of longing rushed through her. She didn't want to be strong anymore—she wanted a shoulder to lean on. He was sturdy, he was capable; he'd know what to do. He'd never let them down. She rushed across the room and threw herself into his arms.

"It's the children. They're lost. I've lost them."

Jake caught her against his chest. "Surely it's not as bad as all that."

"Look outside. You can hardly see your hand before your face. Without Caleb, I'd have gotten lost on my walk here."

He glanced out the window. "I hadn't noticed." He rubbed his eyes. "This paperwork never seems to end."

Caleb rubbed his hands together over the potbellied stove in the corner. "We'd better form a search party. Staying organized is better than flying off in all directions. It's bad out there, Jake. And it's only getting worse."

The edge in his voice sent a chill of anxiety through Jake. Panicking wasn't helpful. He had to treat this like any other missing person. Without emotion. Keeping his head was paramount. Otherwise he was no use to anyone.

"What happened?" Jake asked, softening his voice against Lily's distress. "How long have they been gone? Where were they headed?"

"They left almost an hour ago. I was making rolls for dinner. I didn't realize how much time had passed. Finnick came to visit. They were taking him home."

"That's where we'll start. The path between the houses."

"Yes, except I walked that path already. I didn't see them."

"With this snow, you might have walked right past them. We start with the obvious, then fan out from there."

"I was distracted." She covered her face with her hands and choked off a sob. "I didn't notice the time. I didn't notice how bad the snow had gotten or how long they'd been gone."

"I've been here working. I didn't notice either." He rubbed her shoulders, soothing the tense muscles. "You can't blame yourself."

"I most certainly can, and I will."

"Let's not panic yet." He cupped the back of her head and tucked her against his chest. "There's every chance they're already home and wondering where you've gone."

She hugged him close. "I hope so." She pushed him away and appeared to gather herself. "We're wasting time."

He sincerely hoped he could be the man she thought him to be. He had to find those children, and quickly. In that moment, he'd risk anything for them.

"I'll walk you home and check the house and the surrounding area," he said. "Then we'll retrace their steps."

Garrett and Caleb waited near the door.

"We'll take the opposite direction," Garrett said. "You're not as familiar with that area. Take your gun. One shot means you've found them and you're on your way home. Two shots means you need assistance. Be careful out there. In this weather, we risk losing each other, as well."

They filed outside and Jake took Lily's hand. Her fingers trembled and he offered a reassuring squeeze. Snow swirled around them in dense curtains. The visibility was next to zero. Though he had a good sense of direction, Jake found himself squinting for familiar landmarks.

By the time they reached the house, the empty tree branches overhead were heavy with accumulated snow.

He stepped onto the porch and Lily tugged her hand free.

"No." She shook her head. "I'm coming with you. I'm not waiting inside."

He'd move faster without her, but he knew how powerless she felt. "Search the barn. I'll see if I can find their footsteps."

At least she'd have a modicum of shelter.

"All right."

Together they circled around back. He caught sight of faint depressions between the fences of the garden path and held her arm, then pointed.

"Footprints," he shouted over the howling wind.

She nodded her understanding.

They followed the fading trail. Gathering snow had filled all but the deepest impressions. Upon reaching the barn, Lily grasped the heavy sliding door and tugged. He stepped behind her and reached above her head, easily opening it. They slipped inside and Lily rushed toward the opposite end. Her footsteps echoed through the hollow silence.

"Nothing," she said. "They're not here."

Jake knelt and studied the floor. "They were here today. We can assume they left from here."

Icy flakes swirled through the half-open door and scattered around the dirt floor.

He straightened and motioned her over. "Why don't you wait here? In case they come back."

"I can't."

"I had a feeling you'd say that."

Outside once more, he searched the hazy horizon. With each step his feet sank up to his ankles. They'd accumulated four inches in less than three hours. At this rate, they'd be snowed in by suppertime. There'd be no walking, let alone searching.

Tipping back his head, he studied the sky, and his unease intensified. He'd been certain the children were near the house. He lengthened his stride and picked up speed. There was no way of telling how long the snow might last.

Lily pointed. "This way. This is the path they take to Caleb's."

He followed her a few steps and paused.

She turned around. "What is it?"

Tugging his muffler down, he ducked his head. "This is the way they should have gone." Something nagged at the edges of his consciousness. They'd assumed the children were following a straight line, but what if they'd veered unintentionally? If they'd wandered south, they'd have run into buildings. Which meant they must have wandered north.

"Let's check this way." He indicated the opposite direction. "There's a copse of trees. They might have mistaken them for buildings in the distance."

"Are you certain?"

"No. But this is the only direction without an obvious landmark." He grasped her shoulders. "Don't worry. I won't rest until they're home."

"I know."

She had faith in his abilities. He wouldn't let her down. He wouldn't let Sam and Peter down. They separated and continued the search. He battled his rising worry and focused on the horizon. The dark, spindly shape of the trees appeared in the distance. Spotting them as well, he and Lily broke into an awkward run through the drifts.

When he realized Lily was falling behind, he slowed.

She waved him forward. "I'm fine. I'll catch up."

Keeping her in sight, he trudged through the snow, his thigh muscles burning with exertion. Something in the copse of trees drew him forward. A sound caught his attention and he halted. Wind whistled through the empty branches overhead. The faint noise filtered through the storm. He turned in the direction and frantically fought through the rising piles.

A finger of movement separated from the trunk of one of the trees. His heartbeat rocketed. With Lily close on his heels, he ran the distance. He recognized Peter's familiar red scarf.

The boy waved his arms.

Without stopping to think, Jake grasped Peter and crushed the boy against his chest. "Are you all right?"

"We're fine now that you're here. We got lost."

Sam stood and he caught her in his opposite arm. Lily reached them and the four embraced in a hug. A sense of relief unlike anything he'd ever known filled him. He wanted to shout his thanks and weep at the same time. Something bumped his leg and he caught sight of the goat, Finnick.

"Finnick ran off," Sam explained. "We chased him but then we couldn't find our way back."

"Sam said we should stay put and you'd find us," Peter exclaimed.

"She was right." His eyes burned. "You and Sam did the right thing."

They had become a part of his life, a part of his heart and soul. When he thought he'd lost them, his priorities had shifted. There was nothing more important in his life. Why had he ever thought his work important when compared with these three people?

Nothing else mattered.

"I have to alert the other men who are searching." Jake stepped back and pulled his gun from his holster. "Cover your ears."

He fired the single shot.

"I'll go first," he said. The snow was rapidly building. "Walk in my steps."

He'd forge a trail and make the walking easier. The march home went much faster than the search, with Finnick bouncing through the snow behind them as though it was all some sort of game.

The barn came into sight first. A few more steps and the house appeared in the distance. Light poured from all the windows and smoke puffed from the chimney.

He opened the door and ushered Lily and the children inside first. Anna, Caleb's wife, met them in the kitchen.

"I knew you'd find them. I heard all about the excitement," she said. "I've started a fire and there's milk heating on the stove. Everyone change into dry clothes and come warm up."

Once Samantha and Peter had changed clothes and were bundled by the fire, they cupped their hot milk and regaled Anna with tales of their adventures. Jake glanced around. He hadn't seen Lily in several minutes. Worried, he knocked softly on her door. When he heard the muffled sobbing, his stomach dropped.

He knocked harder, opening the unlatched door with the pressure. "What's wrong? Why are you crying?"

"Don't worry, I'm not sad." She sat with tears streaming down her face. "I'm just so relieved."

He settled on the bed beside her and tucked her against his side. "It's all right."

"I should be out there comforting them and not sitting in here crying."

"They don't know the danger. For them, they've had a great adventure. They're busy telling Anna about their bravery."

She leaned her head against his shoulder. "Thank you."

"For what?"

"For helping. For not arguing when I wanted to go along."

"You're gonna be all right, Lily. We all had a scare, but it's over."

He'd changed inside and he didn't recognize himself anymore. Was he a gunman? A lawman? A husband? Something shifted in his heart, a tight, almost frantic feeling. He couldn't bear to see her unhappy.

He sensed a change coming as surely as the winter wind. Just this morning they'd gotten a lead that might bring them closer to finding Emil. He'd been desperate to solve the case and move on. Not anymore.

He simply wanted another day with Lily, and another, and another, and another. Once he solved the mystery of Emil's disappearance, he'd lose her forever. He'd lose Sam and Peter. How many more days until the children were reunited with their grandfather? How many days did they have left together before their situation changed? A day, a week, a month?

The scent of lilacs drifted over him. Lilies and lilacs would always be intertwined for him. Forever with Lily wasn't nearly long enough.

Chapter Sixteen

Lily was immediately enchanted by the Elder property. Jake had borrowed a wagon and horses from his uncle for the trip, and Samantha and Peter sat on the bench seat behind her and Jake.

There was a charming chaos about the ranch. An army of snowmen in all shapes and sizes lined the winding drive leading to the house. Some of the rounded bodies had sticks for arms, and carrots for noses. There were coal eyes and buttons along with red yarn smiling faces. An array of sleds had been stacked by height along the side of the barn. Only a day out from the fresh blanket of snow, footsteps and hoofprints marked nearly every inch of the property as far as the eye could see.

At least a dozen horses gathered outside a shelter holding bales of hay. Another wagon, almost identical to the one they'd borrowed, was stored near the house. The clatter of wind chimes filled the air. Several of the dangling noise makers lined the porch eves. As she neared the house, Lily noted they were constructed from wires and old silverware.

Jake grinned at her. "The Elders have four children living at home now. There's Hazel, who is fifteen, Preston is five, Liam is four, Rose is two and Moira is expecting another this spring."

"Oh, my. Moira is a busy woman. Your uncle isn't much older than you. I can't believe he has a fifteen-year-old child."

"It's a long story. Moira has a way with children. Hazel is adopted and Preston is staying with them while his mother is away at school. Preston's mother is a widow. She's earning her teaching certificate."

He guided the wagon nearer the front of the house and pulled back on the reins, then set the break.

Samantha and Peter scrambled out, climbing down the enormous spoked wheels. Jake held out his arms for Lily. She leaned forward and he wrapped his hands around her waist. He lowered her gently down, and his fingers lingered.

"Jake," a familiar voice called. Jake's uncle appeared on the porch. "You survived the drive out, Mrs. Elder."

"I thought we agreed you'd call me Lily."

"Of course."

A lovely young girl with blond hair stood beside him. "This is my daughter Hazel. Hazel, this is Lily and I don't need to introduce you to Uncle Jake. Even though Jake is actually my nephew, the girls decided early on that he was their uncle, and the title stuck."

"I think that's charming," Lily said.

"It's so nice to meet you." Hazel took her hand in a warm grip. "I have to warn you before Preston teases you. We have a dog named Lily."

Samantha and Peter giggled.

"My compliments to whoever named the dog," Lily said. "I happen to be partial to the name."

"That would be me," Hazel admitted, abashed. "I was enamored of floral names."

"You're in good company," John added. "She named a dog Rose, as well. That dog went to live with a family in a neighboring town, and they renamed him Buddy. They didn't think Rose was a very good name for a boy dog."

"Preston has never let our Rose forget that she was named after the dog," Hazel said.

John threw up his hands. "She was not named after the dog. You named everything on the ranch. I kept over a hundred horses and when she was younger, she named every one. We were bound to name one of the children after one of your animals, because you used up all the names."

Clearly this was a good-natured argument the two had often.

Hazel turned toward Samantha and Peter. "Lily, the dog, has had puppies. Would you like to see them?"

"Yes!"

"Please!"

"If it's all right with you?" Hazel directed the question toward Lily.

"Of course." She waved her fingers at the siblings. "Be good."

"We will. We promise."

John patted his nephew on the shoulder. "Don't worry. She'll look out for them. There're always children underfoot around here. She's used to watching out for little ones."

"John," a voice called from the porch. "It's freezing out here. Bring them inside."

"That would be my wife, Moira," John said.

Moira was a pretty, petite redhead with laughing eyes. She wore a pale pink gingham dress with an apron knotted over her rounded stomach.

She waved at them from the porch. "Come in. If Liam is unattended for too long, he climbs the bookcases."

The inside of the Elder home was as charmingly cluttered as the outside. Though mostly neat and tidy, clearly the house had been well loved. Rag rugs in all shapes, sizes and patterns had been scattered over the wood floors. There were several mismatched chairs and a settee in the parlor area, each draped with an afghan. Like the area rugs, each of the afghans was unique in color, size and pattern.

Bookcases flanked the fireplace, filled with as many toys and knickknacks as actual books. A table had been set to one side of the enormous kitchen. There was a bench on one side of the table, and chairs lining the other three edges. Each of the chairs and the bench featured a cushion in a different color of calico.

The effect should have been overwhelming and jarring, like the hotel parlor in Frozen Oaks. Instead, Lily was absolutely enchanted. There was a warmth and hominess to the house, a sense of love and peace.

Another bench had been pulled up to the butcherblock table in the center of the kitchen, and three children merrily played with bits of dough.

Moira patted each of their heads in turn. "This is Preston, he's five. This is Liam."

"I'm four and almost five!" Liam announced.

"Yes, you're four," Moira repeated. "And this is Rose. She's our youngest. She's two."

"She's named after the dog," Preston declared.

Rose smiled and nodded. Moira rolled her eyes.

"That's all right," Lily said. "I'm named after the dog, as well. My name is Lily."

Having been denied his outraged reaction, Preston shrugged. "Lily just had puppies."

"So I heard."

"Are you having a baby, Lily?"

"Preston!" Moira admonished. "That's not a question you ask a lady."

"But momma, you're having a baby."

"Yes. I'm having a baby. But you still don't ask ladies that question."

Lily waved off Moira's embarrassment. "Sam and Peter are visiting the puppies. They'll be here soon."

"The puppies will be weaned by Christmas. I don't know what we'll talk about after they've gone to good homes. They consume our days and nights." Moira barely paused for a breath. "I heard you had some excitement over at your place. Anna mentioned the children wandered off the path during the blizzard."

"That was my fault." Lily grappled with her lingering regret. "I was distracted. I lost track of them."

"If I had a nickel for every time I lost one of the children, we'd be dining off golden plates this evening. Even Anna has lost track of her children once or twice, and she's about as perfect of a person as I've met."

Lily recalled Anna's assistance that day. She'd made them dinner and helped with the washing up. "She's quite nice."

"I adore her, but she can be awfully intimidating. Have you seen their home?"

"Only the parlor."

"I've never seen a speck of dust in that house. And everything matches. I don't know how she does it. And her hair is never out of place. Not a strand. I'd hate her if she weren't so nice."

Moira's warm smile and easy chatter had Lily at ease.

The energetic woman bustled around the kitchen, flitting from task to task without ever fully completing one.

Lily plucked a blob of dough from the floor. "Can I help you with something?"

"Absolutely not. John has something he'd like to speak with you about." She leaned closer and whispered. "I'm quite impressed with how you dealt with Preston. He's a bit of scamp. No matter how many times I scold him, he insists on teasing Rose, and anyone else who shares a name with one of the dogs."

"I'm afraid I can't take the credit. Hazel warned me."

"I don't know what we'd do without Hazel."

Moira ushered her away from the stove. John offered Lily and Jake chairs and sat on the bench across from them. "The past two years have been good. Better than I could have asked for. The herd is doing well. I've hired more staff. Tony and her uncle have all but taken over the training of the horses. The two of them are at an auction in Wichita, or I'd introduce you."

"You'd like Tony," Jake said. "She's one of a kind."

The unexpected stab of jealousy surprised Lily. She'd never even met Tony, but Jake's obvious admiration stirred her envy.

"I know you left your horses behind in Steele City," John continued. "I'd like to replace them. As a gift."

"Oh, no." Jake held up his hands. "I couldn't possibly. You know our circumstances."

"Horses have hooves—they'll follow you wherever you need to go. You've been one of my best customers and you've given me some of my best referrals since I started this business. Between you and Garrett, I've sold more horses than I can count to the marshals. They're loyal customers and I appreciate the business."

"You're very generous."

Moira leaned over her husband and rested her hand on his shoulder. "I lost my parents when I was young. I know what that's like. What it's like to feel adrift. Those children are truly blessed to have the two of you looking out for them. I know your circumstances are ambiguous, but Samantha and Peter are welcome here anytime."

The truth of her words sank in, and Lily bit the inside of her lip, holding back an unexpected tide of emotion. "I'm certain their grandfather is fine. He'll come back for them."

"I'm sure you're right," Moira said easily. "If you ever need anything, you know where to find us."

"At least hang on to the wagon and the draft horses," John insisted. "You need transportation."

Jake chuckled. "Deal."

The rest of the evening passed in companionable talk. Moira put on an excellent meal, and John regaled them with stories of Jake's childhood antics. Samantha and Peter could talk of nothing but the puppies.

The evening passed quickly, and soon they were bundled and calling goodbye to their hosts.

On the wagon ride home, Sam asked, "Can we have a puppy?"

Lily's heart broke a little. If she knew their future, she'd agree immediately. "I don't know what will happen when your grandfather returns."

"But what if he doesn't?" Peter asked. "What if he never returns?"

Lily caught Peter's hand. "Then we'll stay together as long as you'd like."

"Until I grow up?"

"Until you're grown and beyond."

"Can we stay in the same house?"

Jake caught her questioning gaze.

"Absolutely," he said. "The house belongs to all of us."

She didn't doubt his words. He'd purchased the house, and he'd let them stay as long as they needed.

Jake adjusted the reins. "Garrett's wife is coming by the marshal's office tomorrow. She's a telegraph operator. We're going over all the mail and correspondence we have that belonged to Emil. Why don't you come along, as well? A fresh pair of eyes is always helpful."

"I'd like that."

She'd sensed a change in Jake recently. He was pulling away. Pulling back from them. They were all balanced on a precipice. A heavy sense of the inevitable hung over all four of them. They were living in a heightened sense of anticipation, waiting for the dam to break. Something had to give, something had to change. Though she couldn't explain her certainty, she sensed that Emil was alive. They couldn't go on this way indefinitely.

In the weeks since she'd known Jake and Sam and Peter, she'd grown and changed. She wasn't the same person she'd been all those weeks ago. She'd found her courage. Sam and Peter had shown her unconditional love, and she'd learned that same love in return. Even if Jake was gone, she'd stay and fight for them.

He'd tapped into a strength that had been within her all along. He'd given her her independence, and she'd always be grateful. She wasn't bound to Mrs. Hollingsworth or a useless clapboard house.

She owed Jake for showing her a different future, a brighter future that hadn't been chosen for her. Whatever the future brought for them, she planned on making the most of what little time she had left with him.

* * *

The following day, Jake took Lily's hand over a rough patch of packed, slick snow. After she'd traversed the spot, he kept hold.

The marshal's territory had outgrown his office over the years, and rows of storage cabinets lined the walls with stacks of boxes piled on top. Since Garrett hadn't needed both the jail cells at the same time in over a decade, they'd reclaimed the space for paperwork and storage. Keeping the files behind lock and key added an extra layer of security, as well. The marshal had cleared hundreds of cases over the years: missing persons, land disputes, cattle rustlers, land and water easements.

During the past two weeks of working with the man, Jake had come to admire the marshal's steady, methodical approach. While the slower pace had initially frustrated him, he'd gradually recognized the benefit of being meticulous.

They swung open the door and discovered the marshal and his wife, JoBeth, leaning over a desk.

Garrett glanced up. "Excellent. Good to see you, Lily. We need a different perspective."

"I don't believe we've met." JoBeth stuck out her hand. "I'm JoBeth Cain. My brother serves as sheriff." She rolled her eyes. "Part-time sheriff. Thankfully there isn't much crime in these parts. He's got too many children to count these days."

"It's a pleasure to meet you," Lily replied. "Any relation to Caleb McCoy?"

"He's a younger brother, as well. There are five of us altogether. I'm the oldest and the only girl."

"I thought those green eyes looked familiar."

JoBeth was striking in an unconventional sort of way. Her dark hair had been looped into braids, and her vivid McCoy-green eyes were honest and forthright. Her dress was simple and purposeful, a shirtwaist in a burgundy plaid shot through with lines of yellow. From her unadorned appearance to her quick, firm handshake, she struck Lily as a resolute woman without a lot of fuss. Though they'd only just met, Lily sensed that JoBeth was not a person who'd skirt around the truth.

As with Moira from the previous evening, Lily liked her immediately.

"We're putting together the connections." JoBeth indicated a handwritten sheet with two rows of lists. "We have our group of people. Vic Skaar, Sheriff Koepke, Emil Tyler and the Tyler children."

"Don't forget Regina."

JoBeth's hand stilled on the paper. "Regina?"

"Regina is Vic's friend, uh, sweetheart, of a sort," Lily said. "The sheriff let slip that Regina considered the hotel as her special project. If Vic lost that property in a poker game, she's angry."

"A woman scorned." JoBeth drummed her fingers on the desk. "I'll add her name."

The four of them pored over all the pieces of paper they'd gathered from Emil's possessions. After forty-five minutes, the ladies gradually elbowed the two men from the process.

Garrett disappeared into the apartment upstairs and returned with a pot of coffee he set on the burner of the potbellied stove. Jake poured two cups and Lily accepted the steaming mug with only a flick of thanks in his direction.

"They're engrossed." Garrett grinned. "I say the two of us step out of their way and let them work."

"Agreed."

He and Garrett set their chairs around the desk on the opposite side of the room and studied the paperwork from a land-dispute complaint Garrett had received that week. Jake found his attention drifting toward Lily. She was bent over the desk, and that familiar, rebellious lock of her blond hair curled over her ear. He knew the silky feel of the strands, the delicate scent of lilacs.

Garrett cleared his throat.

Jake glanced around. "What?"

"I was saying that I've applied to have another field marshal assigned."

"You'll need an addition on the office, as well." Jake glanced through the open door to the cell full of cabinets. "Appears as though you've got plenty of work for him."

"Or her." Garrett jerked his thumb in the direction of the ladies. "These days, I don't discount anything."

"You need the help, that's for certain."

"David, the deputy sheriff, helps out some." The marshal kicked back in his chair and threaded his fingers behind his head. "JoBeth is right, though. He's busy at home more often than not. Until his children are a little older, I can't trust his focus. JoBeth and I are fortunate. My niece, Cora, lives with us. When I'm called out, she's able to help around the house. David's wife is alone. She's not as, well, let's just say she's not as self-sufficient as JoBeth."

"I can't imagine many women who are."

"Lily seems to be adjusting well."

At the sound of her name, she turned. The sight of her vivid blue eyes left his heart hammering and his mouth dry.

"She's one of a kind," Jake replied. "I've never met anyone quite like her."

"Indeed."

The speculative look in the marshal's gaze had heat creeping up Jake's neck. "She's amazing."

JoBeth turned toward them and rested her hip on the edge of the desk, then crossed her arms. "Have you folks gotten a Christmas tree yet?"

Jake blinked at the unexpected change in subject. "Haven't thought about it."

He glanced at Lily's bent head. They'd both assumed they'd be parting ways by now. After Vic had burned down the boardinghouse, he'd expected a higher level of motivation from the man. The move to Cimarron Springs had bought them some time, but he'd counted on Vic appearing, or at least challenging his guardianship with the judge.

Jake had also figured on hearing something from Emil. Surely if Emil cared for his grandchildren even a little, he'd have reached out by now. Nearly three weeks had passed, and neither thing had happened.

"You'll need a tree," JoBeth continued. "There's a grove on the edge of town. You take the road past your house to the twin oaks, then turn east. We've been planting trees there for years. It's unofficial, of course. No one really keeps track. You're welcome to cut one if you'd like."

"I think we should," Lily said. "Samantha and Peter deserve a regular Christmas. As regular as we can give them. They found presents from their grandfather in Frozen Oaks, and they've been waiting to open them."

Garrett stood and crossed the room, then cupped his wife's cheek in a carelessly affectionate gesture. "There's a candlelight service at the church on Christmas Eve. David's son is playing Jesus in the manger scene."

JoBeth snorted. "How many of his boys have played Jesus over the years?"

"Five at last count," Garrett replied. "This is the sixth. Every year like clockwork."

Lily smiled. "He does have his hands full."

"I adore his wife," JoBeth said. "Don't get me wrong, but she always has a wild-eyed look like she's about to be hit by a tidal wave and she can't swim. Which leaves Garrett working extra hours whenever David is called home for some crisis or another."

"I don't mind," Garrett interjected. "He's a good worker."

"I know that poor woman does her best. I only wish God had gifted her with some girls early on, something to counterbalance all those boys." JoBeth shook her head. "We got off the subject. The offer stands. There are trees for the taking, and the finest Christmas Eve service this side of the Missouri."

Jake's stomach clenched. He tried. He'd desperately tried to treat this as simply another clandestine mission. He was playing a role, just as he'd played the role of gunfighter in Frozen Oaks. Yet in Frozen Oaks, he'd kept a distance between his work and his feelings.

With Lily and the children, that distance had shrunk. Who was he kidding? That distance no longer existed. The four of them were completely intertwined. They were forging together into a unit, and he feared the day when the partnership must end.

Lily raised a piece of paper and squinted. "I've seen this name before."

She riffled through the papers and chose three more pieces of correspondence from the pile. "Beatrice. There've been at least three different references to Beatrice over the past six months. There's a receipt from a grocer, there's a stub from the livery, and there's a room number and a hotel jotted on the corner of the envelope. 'Argo in Bea.' Who do you think she is?"

"Beatrice is a place, not a person." Garrett flipped the envelope around. "The Argo Hotel in Beatrice, Nebraska."

Jake rubbed the back of his neck. "I saw that. I thought Beatrice was a person, as well. I checked in and around Frozen Oaks, but didn't find anyone by that name."

How had he missed such an obvious clue? Except the name had been dispersed in obscure pieces of the information. The women had spotted the repeated reference.

Garrett lifted the envelope before the light streaming through the window. "If Emil has spent time in Beatrice, he's comfortable with the town."

"Exactly." Lily studied the receipt from the grocer's store. "If he's gone into hiding, it stands to reason he's chosen someplace familiar."

JoBeth snapped her fingers. "Mildred is the telegraph operator in Beatrice." She flipped up the watch pinned to her collar. "Mildred is on duty for another hour. I'll wire her and see if she's seen or heard anything."

"Alert the sheriff in Beatrice, as well," Garrett said. "In case Vic has discovered the same information."

"Will do. Mildred has an ear on every piece of gossip that goes through that town. If he's there, we'll know before lunch."

After JoBeth's exit, the three of them continued searching through Emil's papers, looking for anything more that might reveal his whereabouts. Each time the wind rattled the windowpanes, they jumped and looked for JoBeth's return. Garrett made another pot of coffee, and Jake's stomach rumbled.

The door flew open in a flurry of snowflakes. "We've found him!" JoBeth declared.

"He's been in Beatrice the whole time?" Jake demanded.

"He sure has. Broke his leg three and a half weeks ago. He's been laid up at the hotel ever since."

"Why didn't he send word?"

"According to Mildred, he's been sending telegrams to Frozen Oaks for the past three and a half weeks."

Jake muttered an oath. "Then someone has been intercepting them?"

"Worse. Emil didn't know he was missing. According to Mildred, he's been sending updates to a certain Miss Lily Winter in Frozen Oaks, and she's been replying. Last week, Sheriff Koepke informed him that Miss Winter had disappeared with the children. Apparently Emil is hopping mad. He's got the sheriff looking for Lily."

Lily paled and Jake led her to a chair. "Everyone knows the sheriff is lying."

"Vic is still planning on using the children as blackmail." Pressing her palms against her eyes, Lily groaned. "He figured he could buy me off and claim the bigger prize. But Vic wasn't counting on Jake's interference. He followed us back to St. Joseph. Regina knew where the boardinghouse was located."

"But why torch the place? Why not wait and set a trap there?"

"We've all been assuming that Vic set the blaze, but maybe the fire was simply bad timing. Which meant he lost track of us after St. Joseph."

Understanding finally dawned on Jake. "He needed the children for blackmail, but he'd lost track of them."

"He had to change his plans," Lily said. "Instead of stalling Emil, he needed Emil's help."

Jake huffed a breath. "Because once Emil sent up the alarm, he'd have the law after Lily. As long as Vic got to you and the children first, he'd have his blackmail."

Panic skittered across her face. "What now? If we contact Emil, he'll lead Vic here. Emil thinks we're the villains."

"Then we let Emil bait the trap," Garrett said. "We catch Vic in the act. We have to let Vic follow Emil to Cimarron Springs. Otherwise you'll spend the rest of your lives looking over your shoulder."

"No." Lily shook her head. "We can't put the children in danger."

Chapter Seventeen

Jake knelt before her and clasped her chilled fingers. "I won't let anyone put them in danger, but we have to do something. There's no other choice. If we don't catch Vic in the act, we'll always be waiting and wondering. Those children will never feel safe."

"Make Emil return the deed to the hotel," Lily begged. "Who cares about the property?"

"This is about more than the hotel now. Vic isn't giving up. You know that as well as I do. He's after the bigger prize. Emil is an elderly man. Once he and the children are back in Frozen Oaks, how long before Emil meets with an accident? Those children will be back under the sheriff's jurisdiction."

"Then Emil can move here."

"How do we guarantee that Vic won't simply follow him? We have to force his hand. That's our only choice. That's the only way we'll know that Emil and those children are safe. We'll take the children far away." Jake cradled her face in his hands. "I'll go there myself and escort Emil back. We'll control the situation."

She rested her fingers over his. "I trust you."

"You can't go to Beatrice," Garrett said. "You'll be

recognized. We might gain some time if I go. Besides, you should be here. Close to your family."

Lily backed away and snatched her coat from the peg. "The children will be home from school soon. I should go home."

"I'll walk with you." JoBeth reached for her coat. "You're on my way."

Lily would have preferred being alone, but she couldn't refuse the offer without appearing rude. She was happy they'd found Emil. Happy he was safe and sound. Why, then, did she feel as though a sinkhole had opened up beneath her feet?

JoBeth walked beside her in silence for a few minutes. Their feet crunched over the snow and their breath formed clouds in the chill winter air.

"Don't forget about the trees," JoBeth said at last. "There's a fine selection."

"I won't forget."

What was the point of a tree? Christmas was two weeks away. Samantha and Peter would most likely spend the holiday with their grandfather.

JoBeth scooted before her and halted. "Garrett is good at his job. He won't let anything happen to those children. If he thought they were in danger, he'd never agree to the plan. I can promise you that."

"I'm sure you're right."

"Jake adores Samantha and Peter," JoBeth continued. "He'd give his life for them."

"I know."

"Then why do you look as though you dropped your toast butter-side down?"

JoBeth offered a smile to soften her words.

"This is right," Lily said firmly. "This is what the children need. This is what I wanted to happen. They'll be reunited with their family. I'm happy for them. I'm truly happy for them."

"There's always a place for you here," JoBeth said. "You know that, don't you?"

"I'm only here because of the children."

"There's no reason you can't stay."

They'd reached the front gate, and Lily tugged the latch free. "I suppose we'd best make sure the children are settled before I make any plans."

"If you need anything, I'm just down the road. I'm sure the men are putting together all sorts of overly complicated plans. We should let them have their fun."

Lily sketched a wave and made her way into the house. After doffing her coat and winter boots, she stood in the kitchen and gazed out the back window. She'd grown more than fond of the children. Truth be told, she loved them. Staying near them was a good thing. And yet a part of her held back. She'd be the outsider again.

She couldn't go back to how things were when she was young. She'd always felt as though she had her nose pressed to the window of the candy store.

Was she being selfish for wanting to leave, or selfish for wanting to stay?

The door opened and she didn't turn around.

Jake cleared his throat. "We have to do something."

Her pulse thrummed. "I know."

"This is the best way."

"I'm not a part of this, remember? I'm just the hired help."

"Don't say that." He stood behind her and rested his hands on her shoulders. "You saved those kids. Who knows what might have happened if someone different had been there? They need you. I need you."

But for how long?

"What happens next?"

"Garrett will fetch Emil. Once he's here, we'll send a telegram to the sheriff in Frozen Oaks that the children have been found. Sheriff Koepke will tell Vic straight away. If he's going to make a move, he'll move then."

"Are you certain the children will be safe?"

"Emil and the children will be long gone from here by the time Vic arrives. We won't drop the bait until we're certain they're out of sight. Cimarron Springs is the best place. We know all the local law. We know every way in and every way out of town."

Everything was working out exactly the way it was supposed to. "Can we keep the wagon another day? Will your uncle mind?"

"The wagon and the horses are ours as long as we need them."

"Good. I think we should cut down a Christmas tree. Tonight."

They needed to keep everything normal. Sam and Peter mattered most. They'd be united with their grandfather, and they'd move on. For now, they needed a sense of security, a sense that they were safe and everything was fine.

Decorating for Christmas would both cheer them up and distract them.

Time was slipping away quickly. There was no time to lose.

Lily glanced up when Jake entered through the back door. He brushed the snow from his shoulders and knocked more flakes from the brim of his hat. "Are you ready?"

"Almost."

He peered over her shoulder. "What do you have there?"

"Hot cocoa." She'd filled two jars full of the steaming liquid and wrapped them in towels to insulate them. She tucked the containers into the basket she'd set on the counter. "To keep us warm."

Samantha and Peter were already sitting in the second row of the buckboard when they stepped outside.

"We haven't had a Christmas tree in two years," Peter said. "They celebrate Christmas differently in Africa."

Jake squeezed Lily's hand. "You were right. About getting the Christmas tree. Peter talked of nothing else while we were hitching the horses."

She squinted at the sky. "What about the weather. Are you worried about more snow?"

"We aren't going far. If the weather worsens, we'll come home early."

He yanked the ax from the chopping block and rested the tool in the bed of the wagon.

Lily waited until he paused before her. He reached out and gently flicked her nose. "You've got snow on your lashes already."

"Hurry up, then. I haven't had a Christmas tree in years either."

He grasped her waist and swung her into the seat. He took his place beside her, gathered the reins, and released the brakes.

"You strike me as the sort of person who loves Christmas."

"I do," she replied. "I simply haven't had much to celebrate the past few years. Trees always seemed like more work, and I was usually overloaded anyway. With people traveling to visit family, winter was a busy time at the boardinghouse. There was never anyone to share in the decorating either. Mrs. Hollingsworth considered Christmas trees an unnecessary mess. Decorating a tree alone isn't any fun."

"Then this year will be three times the fun."

The road required his attention and they drove in silence. Lily spotted the twin oaks. Wagon wheels marked the trail and they turned off. Sure enough, not far down the lane, a copse of evergreen trees had been planted. Someone had divvied them off in neat rows, with the older trees farther back.

Jake set the brake and helped her down.

Samantha and Peter scrambled from the wagon.

"Can we pick out the tree?" Samantha asked.

"I want to pick out the tree alone," Peter grumbled.

"Each of you pick out a tree," Jake said. "And we'll let Lily decide which one she likes best."

The two shouted their agreement and set off in opposite directions. Lily meandered toward a row of small trees, their tips not reaching her waist.

Jake paused beside her. "When I was young, I found a bird's nest behind the barn. My mom saved the nest and we put it in the tree every year. She said the nest brought happiness to the coming year."

"I'm sorry. About what happened to your mom. You must miss her very much."

"When I was younger, I used to dream about her. I'd dream about resting my head on her knee while she stroked my hair. I stopped having the dreams years ago. I miss them. Sometimes I miss those dreams as much as I miss her. They seemed so real. I felt as though she was visiting me in my sleep."

"My mother died two weeks before Christmas. My brother had died the week before. We didn't tell her.

She was sick. Weak. We worried she might give up if she knew. I used to have dreams, too. I'd dream they couldn't find each other in heaven."

"That must have been difficult."

He lifted his hand and she moved away. "I didn't say that to make you feel sorry for me. I guess maybe that's the true reason why I never put up a tree. I didn't feel I deserved to celebrate."

"Children carry guilt they shouldn't. For a long time I felt as though my mom died because of me. When the outlaws entered the bank, there was chaos. I couldn't move. I couldn't do anything. I was just frozen in place. If she'd dropped to the ground immediately, she'd be alive. She hesitated. At the trial the outlaw said he didn't mean to shoot her. He was turning toward the movement, and his gun fired."

"If that outlaw had gotten a job instead of robbing, she'd be alive. That had nothing to do with you."

"I became a US marshal to prevent those kinds of tragedies. The gang had robbed other banks. If someone had taken them seriously sooner, if someone had put them in jail, they wouldn't have been there that day. I can't go back and change the past, but I can change the future for others."

"I envy you," she said. "I thought owning the boardinghouse would fulfill me, but I recognize that I was wrong. I was clinging to the idea because I didn't have any other dreams."

"Then pick a new dream. No one is stopping you. Life only moves in one direction. Forward. What happens to you shapes you. You're in control. You decide."

Peter called and they followed the sound of his voice. His tree was perfectly shaped, nearly six feet tall, with full branches and thick needles. Lily made a point of circling around the tree and inspecting all the angles.

"This is a beautiful tree."

Samantha shouted for their attention. They trudged through the snow and discovered her tree, as well. Shorter than the one Peter had claimed, this tree was fatter and more squat.

Jake rubbed his chin and stepped back a few paces. "Let's test the needles."

He leaned forward and shook the tree. A bird flew out, startling them all. Lily shrieked and held her hands over her face. Jake stumbled back and they fell into the snow. Peter made his way over to them.

"I found mistletoe," he said. "Now you have to kiss."

"That can't be mistletoe," Lily scoffed. "I've never seen mistletoe grow around here."

Jake didn't know what possessed him, but he said, "Let them have their fun."

He pressed his lips against hers and a shuddering thrill rippled through him. With the children as their audience, the kiss was over all too soon.

Jake stood and reached for her hand. He pulled her up and she braced her fingers against his chest. Rather than disturb the bird's nest, Jake retrieved his ax and cut down the tree Peter had chosen.

With much laughter and stumbling, the four of them dragged the evergreen back to the wagon.

Lily retrieved her jars of hot cocoa and they huddled together in the shelter of the wagon. Once home, they decorated the tree with ropes of popcorn and berries.

As dusk fell over the horizon, they sat in the parlor, admiring their handiwork.

"I never want this day to end," Sam said.

"Neither do I," Jake replied.

The words were authentic. Playing husband was the only part he ever wanted to play again. The marshal needed extra help, and Jake enjoyed working with Garrett. He'd discovered an aptitude for settling disputes. He loved the town and adored the house.

If Sam and Peter weren't there to tie them together, would Lily stay? Did he even have a right to ask her? He'd made a vow. He'd promised to annul the marriage once Emil and his grandchildren were reunited.

He was a man who honored his promises. Or was he?

Lily finished her order at the mercantile and stepped outside once more. The evening train had arrived at the depot twenty minutes earlier. Porters hustled the bags and trunks into waiting wagons. Passengers scurried from the cold.

The children had already left for school, and the house was unnaturally quiet. Garrett was leaving for Beatrice to fetch Emil that evening, which meant the children would be reunited with their grandfather in less than a week. Everything was going according to plan.

Her feet dragging, Lily carried her groceries into the kitchen and unpacked them on the counter.

The click of a gun hammer being pulled back sounded, and Lily froze.

"Turn around," a feminine voice ordered.

Lily obeyed and discovered Regina, a pistol in her outstretched hand. "Where are they?"

"Who?"

"Don't play stupid. I want those children."

"Vic isn't worth this."

"Vic?" Regina scoffed. "Vic is an idiot."

Lily scooted away. "I don't understand."

"It's very simple." Regina leveled her gun at Lily.

"Men think they run this world, but they don't. I manage my own business out of the hotel right under Vic's nose. No one paid any mind to the women coming through town. Even after Vic lost the railroad depot, I managed to overcome. All he had to do was maintain ownership of the hotel, but he couldn't even do that. He couldn't even beat a pair of eights. What kind of idiot folds for a pair of eights?"

"It was you." Understanding finally dawned on Lily. "It was you all along."

"I had a good thing going. No one notices a bunch of women. They think we're stupid. I've been running all sorts of scams out of Frozen Oaks, and no one is the wiser. Not Vic, not the sheriff, not anyone. Then Vic had to go and ruin everything by losing the hotel. I needed the cover of the business. I can hide trunks full of contraband in a hotel. I can hide my customers as hotel guests."

"Then you were the person selling the guns."

"A man came to Vic last year wanting to sell a shipment of stolen guns. Vic refused the offer because the guns were junk. Relics from the War Between the States. That's the problem with Vic—he lacks imagination. I bought them for a considerable discount and sold them to the Indians for a tidy profit. They didn't know the guns were worthless, and I made a lot of money. That's imagination."

"The US marshals were looking for those guns. How did you smuggle them out of town?"

"A layer of petticoats. I told you. No one pays any attention to ladies. If your trunk is heavy, they don't even blink an eye. One of the railroad detectives even offered to help the porter carry the extra weight. I tipped him. He was such a wonderful help."

"You're very clever. Vic was the perfect cover. He makes a convincing villain." Lily frantically searched the countertop for some kind of weapon. "Why did you intercept the messages from Emil?"

"I needed to buy some time. After Emil sent the telegram saying that he'd broken his leg, I searched the barbershop. He was too smart, though. He'd taken the deed with him. I guess he figured Vic couldn't be trusted." Regina's lips curled up at the edges. "He was right."

"Is that when you decided the children were a more lucrative scam?"

"After I read the newspaper story I figured I'd use the children to get the hotel back, and make some money in the process. You certainly weren't a threat. I hadn't planned on Jake, though. I hadn't planned on a gunfighter turned nanny. Locking the sheriff in his own jail cell was inspired. Wish I'd have thought of that. Koepke was hopping mad."

All along they'd been chasing the wrong villain. "Then Vic and the sheriff were in the dark about all your dealings?"

As long as Regina liked to brag, Lily was willing to stall her. Maybe she'd set down the gun or drop her guard.

"Vic makes a very nice smoke screen. As long as everyone was paying attention to him, no one was paying me any mind."

"But why did you burn down the boardinghouse if I wasn't a threat to you? What purpose did that serve?"

"Because you deserved some punishment after forcing me to chase you across the countryside. I don't like being inconvenienced. You didn't even have the decency to show up on time for the grand inferno. I snuck in the same window I used all those years ago when Mrs.

Hollingsworth locked me out." Regina tapped her chin with the barrel of the pistol. "When you think about it, I had my revenge on both of you. You should be thanking me instead of glowering and plotting a way to turn this gun on me. Losing the boardinghouse was for your own good. Mrs. Hollingsworth was never going to sell that place."

"You'll forgive me if I don't send a note," Lily said. "You enjoyed setting that fire, didn't you?"

"I won't lie. I enjoyed giving the old biddy a little payback for all the times she looked down her nose at me."

"Someone might have died."

"Lots of things might have happened, but they didn't." Regina waved the gun. "Everyone got out all right. All's well that ends well."

"You took your sweet time in coming to Cimarron Springs. What took you so long?"

"I lost track of you again after I burned down the boardinghouse. The inferno was beautiful, and very distracting. I never expected you'd marry the gunfighter. I thought I knew you. I remembered you from when I stayed in St. Joseph. You were always making lists and harping on routine. That sort of person is easy to predict. I had a watch on the nearest hotel. I figured you wouldn't drift far from home. Strays never do. Except you're full of surprises."

"It's over, Regina." Lily reached behind her, groping for the knife she'd left on the counter. "They'll catch you."

"Don't be silly. I've worked too hard. I'm not giving up now. I'm not giving up when I'm this close to having everything I want on a silver platter. That would just be foolish, wouldn't it? But please, as long as we're divulging all our deep, dark secrets, you must confess. I still don't understand why that gunfighter helped you. He didn't seem the rescuing type."

"He's a good man."

"Oh dear. I certainly didn't see that coming." Regina tsked. "That's the problem with this world, there are far too many do-gooders mucking up the works. Do-gooders are bad for business."

Regina poked a loaf of bread. "Enough chatting. Let's get on with this. I don't want to miss lunch."

Lily's knees grew weak. She was rapidly losing ground.

"You're certainly cleverer than all the men. How did you arrive here before Emil?" Lily tucked the knife against her back. Regina responded to flattery, her one constant. "How were you smart enough to find us before anyone else?"

"The telegraph lines. Funny thing about Western Union, they tend to hire women. There's been quite a bit of chatter back and forth from Cimarron Springs to Beatrice." She nudged her gun in the direction of the door. "Tell me where I can find the children. I'm growing weary of your voice."

"This is ridiculous." Lily turned, keeping the weapon hidden in the folds of her skirts. "How can you ransom the children without their grandfather?"

"Emil is on his way. I'm not stupid, Lily. I sent for him first. Your little trap won't work. Ah, I see by your expression that you assumed help was coming. I thought you were more loquacious than usual. Tut tut. Let's put a lid on that optimism and get this over with."

"All right, all right." Dread settled in Lily's stomach. "The children are out back. They're playing in the barn."

There was no way she was leading Regina to the children, which left her with no other option.

She tightened her grip around the knife. She'd have to take her chances with Regina alone. She had to think of a plan quickly. If something happened to her, Jake would never forgive himself. She wouldn't let him wallow in guilt.

With nothing left to lose, she'd finally accepted that she loved him, and she sensed there was a part of him that cared for her, too. A part that went deeper than playacting. She desperately wanted to survive long enough to discover if her instincts were correct.

Regina waved the gun barrel. "Come along. Your destiny awaits, Miss Winter."

"Mrs. Elder," Lily corrected. "If you're going to kill me, at least get my name right."

The door to the marshal's office slammed open and an extremely agitated elderly man stood on the threshold. "Where are my grandchildren?"

The man was tall and fit with graying hair. He carried a cane in one hand and his leg had been splinted. He was of average height and build, with neatly trimmed sideburns that touched his chin.

Jake stood. "Emil Tyler?"

"Yes." Emil brandished a telegram. "Apparently someone named Lily Winter has kidnapped my grandchildren. She's asking for a ransom. I'm supposed to stay at the hotel in town and wait for the next instructions."

"You've been misinformed." Jake's chest seized. They'd been double-crossed. Someone had beaten them to setting a trap. "Lily is not the kidnapper."

Grasping the implications as well, Garrett came out

from behind his desk. "We'd best have the whole town on alert for Vic Skaar."

"Vic is in Frozen Oaks," Emil said. "He's not responsible."

"How do you know?" Jake asked.

"I ain't stupid. I won money off the man. Ida works over at the hotel and keeps tabs on him for me. He hasn't left town."

"Then who? The sheriff?"

Garrett shook his head. "From what you've said, Vic would never send him for this kind of job."

"Regina," Jake exclaimed. "We've been blind to everything. This is about Regina."

He reached for his gun belt and hat.

Emil held out his arm. "How can you be certain it isn't this Miss Winter person?"

"I know." They'd all been duped, even Vic. The irony was impressive. "This was about Regina all along. Get everyone you can. If she's in town already, she'll go for the children. Which means Lily is in danger, as well."

David burst through the door. "Someone has Lily."

"A woman?"

"Ycp," David replied. "I was watching the house like you asked. I saw a woman go inside. I didn't think too much about it since we weren't looking for a woman. I heard them arguing and snuck closer. The woman pulled a gun on Lily."

"And you left her there?" Jake snatched the man's lapels and shook him. "Alone?"

"Hold on." Garrett blocked his exit. "You can't go storming in there without a plan."

"The woman wants Lily to lead her to the Tyler children," David said. "There was nothing I could do."

Garrett pried Jake's hands free from David's coat. "Did you hear anything else?"

"Lily said the children were doing chores. She said they'd be in the barn."

Emil's face suffused with angry color. "She's leading them to my grandchildren? What kind of town are you running here, marshal?"

Jake forced air into his lungs. He wasn't doing anybody any good by panicking. "Your grandchildren aren't in the barn, they're at school."

"Stay here, Mr. Tyler." Garrett ordered. "We'll explain everything later."

Jake and Garrett ran full out to the house, David close behind them.

Jake held his finger for silence and they crept around the back of the barn. Voices sounded from inside. Fearful of spooking Regina, Jake kicked over a crate and climbed up to peer in the window.

The two women were locked together, grappling over something. Jake caught a glimpse of steel. His stomach folded. They were fighting for possession of the gun.

Without hesitating he broke the glass with his elbow.

At the commotion, Lily turned.

A gunshot sounded.

Jake dove forward. Both Lily and Regina collapsed to the ground. Bile rose in the back of his throat. He dragged Lily away, cradling her in his arms. Blood spattered the front of her apron.

He frantically ran his hand along her stomach, searching for the wound.

"Not me." Lily gasped. "I wasn't hit."

He glanced around as Garrett entered the barn. The marshal kicked the abandoned gun from Regina's grasp and knelt at her side. Blood oozed from a wound in her abdomen.

"I've shot myself." Regina moaned. "I didn't think she'd fight back."

"You thought wrong," the marshal replied.

Regina grimaced. "Never underestimate a woman."

Alerted by the gunfire, Caleb arrived a moment later. He took in the scene and approached Lily and Jake.

"She's not hurt," Jake assured the other man. "Regina has been hit."

Caleb lowered himself to one knee and grimaced. "I've seen this sort of wound before. You'll live."

"Are you a doctor?" Regina moaned. "I need a surgeon. A good surgeon. Not some country bumpkin with a rusty scalpel."

"I'm a veterinarian, ma'am."

Her head lolled to one side. "If I die in this backwater town, promise you'll bury my body in New York. I refuse to spend eternity in Kansas."

"You're not going to die."

"I don't find your assurance the least bit comforting."

Lily clutched Jake's lapels. "Take me back to the house."

He hoisted her in arms. Garrett and Caleb were well equipped to deal with Regina. He carried Lily through the back door and up the stairs, then laid her on the bed.

He moved away but she pulled him closer.

"What?"

"Don't let go of me." She shivered. "Not even for a minute."

He climbed onto the bed beside her and crushed her in his embrace. "Do you want to talk about what happened?"

"It was Regina all along. She was using Vic as a cover."

"I guessed as much." He pressed his cheek against her hair. "Coming here alone was risky, even for Regina."

"I think she simply became desperate. All her plans and schemes were falling apart one by one, and we always managed to be a step ahead of her."

"She can't hurt us now."

"Will she live?"

"Caleb thinks so," Jake replied. "Her fate is out of her hands."

Lily absently toyed with the buttons on his coat. "How did you know to come for me?"

"Emil arrived. He'd received the telegram."

Violent shivers tormented her body. He rubbed her back and whispered soothing words.

"You didn't hesitate," she said. "That's what you were always worried about. When you saw I was in danger, you didn't hesitate."

"I've never been more focused in my life."

She pressed their lips together in a desperate kiss. She kissed him as though she could never get enough of him, and hope soared in his heart. She must feel something for him, as well.

Lily broke away from the kiss first. "I love you, Jake Elder. I started falling in love with you when you were an outlaw, then when you were a lawman, but I finished falling in love with you as a husband. I know your job is difficult and dangerous, and I know that craving for excitement is part of who you are. I won't try and change you, I promise."

He pressed a finger against her lips. "Stop. I've already changed. I love you, too, Lily Winter. I can't picture a future without you. Will you consider staying with me, even if Sam and Peter leave with their grandfather?"

Though he loathed shattering the moment, he had to ask. He had to know.

Her smile faded. "I love them. They will always be part of my heart, but you're a part of my soul. We'll face the future together, whatever future that may be."

He kissed her then, long and deep.

"As long as you're in my future," he said a long while later, "I have everything I need."

Epilogue

Lily awoke to the patter of footsteps down the stairs. She touched Jake's shoulder. "Wake up."

"Already?" came the groggy reply.

Whispers and giggles sounded from outside their door.

"It's time." She pressed a kiss against his shoulder. "I'll start the coffee brewing."

Ten minutes later, they joined Sam and Peter in the parlor. Lily stifled a yawn behind one hand. The children, clad in their pajamas, rifled through the presents beneath the tree. Emil emerged from the office they'd transformed into his bedroom. He tugged his suspenders over his union suit, and wiped the sleep from his eyes.

The adults mumbled their good-mornings, still half-asleep. Lily and Jake slumped on the couch, and Emil took the chair set before the fireplace.

"Can we open our presents now?" Sam pleaded.

"Please," Peter chimed in. "We've been waiting for months to see what grandpa gave us."

"Yes," Lily said. She rolled her eyes. "Please open your presents."

The next ten minutes passed in a flurry of paper. Gifts were opened and exclaimed over, then tossed aside in their excitement. Emil's gifts were finally unwrapped. Sam received a lovely doll, and Peter exclaimed over a set of carved wooden soldiers.

The children presented their grandfather with handmade pictures, which he dutifully exclaimed over.

Jake reached beneath the tree and plucked a package from the chaos. He set the colorfully wrapped gift on Lily's lap.

With a smile she carefully peeled back the paper and unwrapped the box. A shiny new coffee grinder met her delighted gaze.

Her throat tightened. "It's beautiful."

"I knew you were sad about the one you lost in the fire. I couldn't replace that one, I know. I hope you like the gift."

"That was the past, you're my future. This is perfect. I love my gift." She kissed him and hugged him close. "I love you."

Lily stood and retrieved a box from the tree, and resumed her seat next to Jake. "For you."

She held her breath, awaiting his reaction. He opened the box and stared at the watch nestled inside.

"Thank you," he said. "This is beautiful."

"Look inside."

He flipped open the watch. "My penny."

Sam and Peter crowded around him.

"I saved your penny all this time," Peter said. "I had the watchman fix the penny into the side. You gave that to me the first day we met. It brings me happy memories, and now it can bring you happy memories."

Lily anxiously searched his face. Tears shimmered in his eyes.

"Thank you," he said, his voice thick. "For all the happy memories. I love my gift, and I love you both."

After Sam and Peter returned to their own presents, Lily rested her head on Jake's shoulder. "He was so excited, I didn't have the heart to tell him why you kept the penny all these years. We can store the watch in my drawer if the memories are too painful."

"The memories are good now. The sad ones have been replaced." Jake draped his arm over his shoulder. "The gift is perfect. I will treasure this watch always."

Emil slapped his knees and stood. "Who wants breakfast?"

The children shouted their approval and followed him into the kitchen.

Lily sighed, feeling blissfully content. "He's adjusting well."

Jake tugged on a lock of his hair. "And all my haircuts are free."

She playfully elbowed him in the stomach. After the incident with Regina, the three of them had decided to raise the children as an extended family. Emil wasn't certain his age and health made him suitable to raise them alone, and Lily and Jake were happy to include them in their family.

Given Jake's history, she'd been determined not to fuss when a case forced him out of town. To her astonishment, he'd taken to serving as the local marshal like a duck to water. He never tapped his knee beneath the table or stared out the window. He and Marshal Garrett worked well together, and the partnership suited both families. Lily was used to living with other folks underfoot, and adding Emil to their family hadn't changed a thing.

Having already grown accustomed to living with

Jake and Lily, the children adjusted smoothly to the additional changes. There were the occasional bumps along the way, but everything always managed to sort itself out.

She'd never been happier.

A knock sounded on the door.

"Who can that be?"

Lily started to rise, but Jake stopped her.

"Wait here," he said. "I'll be right back."

She rested her head against the back of the settee. A moment later he returned holding a large wooden crate.

The crate barked.

Lily bolted upright.

Two furry paws appeared over the lip of the box.

Sam and Peter came rushing from the kitchen.

Jake set the box on the ground. An adorable white-and-black ball of fluffy puppy leapt out.

Jake clapped his hands. "Merry Christmas. He's one of Lily's puppies. John and Moira were so anxious to be rid of him, they offered free delivery on Christmas morning."

Lily crossed her arms over her chest and shook her head. "Jake Elder. I don't recall agreeing to a dog."

"You said the idea had merit."

"That's not an agreement."

As the puppy barked and danced around them, the children rolled around in delight.

Emil watched their antics with an indulgent grin.

Lily managed a half grin. "Having a puppy around the house is not very practical."

"Neither is breaking an outlaw out of jail and falling in love with him, but that didn't stop you."

"You're right." Lily let her arms drop to her sides. "He's adorable."

Jake grasped her around the waist and spun her. "I love you, Lily."

She laughed. "I love you, too. My outlaw, my lawman, my husband."

* * * * *

Don't miss these other PRAIRIE COURTSHIP
stories from Sherri Shackelford:

THE ENGAGEMENT BARGAIN
THE RANCHER'S CHRISTMAS PROPOSAL

Find more great reads at www.LoveInspired.com.

Dear Reader,

Thank you for taking the time to read *A Family for the Holidays*. Nine years ago I had a crazy idea to write a novel. While I had always been an avid reader, I knew nothing about the actual mechanics of writing a book. In an effort to learn all I could, I joined online writing chapters and I read instruction books. Early in my fledgling endeavors, I joined a critique group. For nine years, Barb, Cheryl, Deb, Donna, *lizzie and I have spent most of our Friday evenings laughing, talking, learning and teaching each other craft. We've become a family.

There's something extraordinary about the families we choose in life. The ladies in my critique group don't just help with my writing; I am a better person for having known them. This past September we lost a member of our family, Barb, and we're all grieving together and healing together, because that's what families do.

I hope you enjoyed Jake and Lily's story, and the family they create with their love. I enjoy hearing from readers! If you're interested in learning more about the Prairie Courtship series or other books in the Cowboy Creek series, visit my website, www.sherrishackelford.com. You can also find me on Facebook at www.Facebook.com/SherriShackelfordAuthor and on Twitter @smshackelford. Email me at sherrishackelford@gmail.com, or send a letter to PO Box 116, Elkhorn, NE 68022.

Thanks for reading!
Sherri Shackelford

"There's the land office," Simon said, nodding to a whitewashed building ahead. He strode to it, shifted Nora's case under one arm and held the door open for her, then followed her inside with his brothers in his wake.

The long, narrow office was bisected by a counter. Chairs against the white-paneled walls told of lengthy waits, but today the only person in the room was a slender man behind the counter. He was shrugging into a coat as if getting ready to close up for the day.

Handing Nora's case to his brother John, Simon hurried forward. "I need to file a claim."

The fellow paused, eyed him and then glanced at Nora, who came to stand beside Simon. The clerk smoothed down his lank brown hair and stepped up to the counter. "Do you have the necessary application and fee?"

Simon drew out the ten-dollar fee, then pulled the papers from his coat and laid them on the counter. The clerk took his time reading them, glancing now and then at Nora, who bowed her head as if looking at the shoes peeping out from under her scalloped hem.

"And this is your wife?" he asked at last.

Simon nodded. "I brought witnesses to the fact, as required."

John and Levi stepped closer. The clerk's gaze returned to Nora. "Are you Mrs. Wallin?"

She glanced at Simon as if wondering the same thing, and for a moment he thought they were all doomed. Had she decided he wasn't the man she'd thought him? Had he married for nothing?

Nora turned and held out her hand to the clerk. "Yes, I'm Mrs. Simon Wallin. No need to wish me happy, for I find I have happiness to spare."

The clerk's smile appeared, brightening his lean face. "Mr. Wallin is one fortunate fellow." He turned to pull a heavy leather-bound book from his desk, thumped it down on the counter and opened it to a page to begin recording the claim.

Simon knew he ought to feel blessed indeed as he accepted the receipt from the clerk. He had just earned his family the farmland they so badly needed. The acreage would serve the Wallins for years to come and support the town that had been his father's dream. Yet something nagged at him, warned him that he had miscalculated.

He never miscalculated.

Don't miss
CONVENIENT CHRISTMAS WEDDING
by Regina Scott, available November 2016 wherever
Love Inspired® Historical books and ebooks are sold.

www.LoveInspired.com